I0639622

Fight Like A Girl

Vol. 2

Fight Like A Girl

Volume 2

Roz Clarke & Joanne Hall

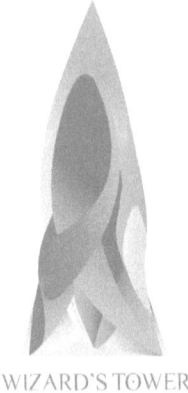

WIZARD'S TOWER

Wizard's Tower Press

Rhydaman, Cymru

Fight Like A Girl

Volume 2

Text © 2024 by Danie Ware, Gaie Sebold, Dolly Garland, Cheryl Morgan, Juliet E McKenna, Anna Smith Spark, K R Green, Julia Hawkes Reed, K T Davies, S Naomi Scott, Lou Morgan, Charlotte Bond, Roz Clarke & Joanne Hall

Cover art by Oisín McGann
Book design by Cheryl Morgan
Labrys image by Feòrag NicBhrìde

First published by Wizard's Tower Press,
November 2024

ISBN: 978-1-913892-84-5

http://wizardstowerpress.com/

Contents

Foreword   8
Roz Clarke & Joanne Hall

Introduction   11
Charlotte Bond

The God of Lost Things Or Ethel, Dragonslayer   14
Danie Ware

Ambition's Engine   38
Gaie Sebold

A Human Response   75
Dolly Garland

More Trouble Than She's Worth?   94
Cheryl Morgan

Civil War   118
Juliet E. McKenna

Lady Cona   142
Anna Smith Spark

Ready for Combat   172
K R Green

We have Always Been Here   202
Julia Hawkes-Reed

The Seamstress, the Hound, the Cook, and her Brother   233
    K T Davies

A Way Out   262
    S. Naomi Scott

Amplify   283
    Lou Morgan

About the Authors and Editors   309

Praise for
Fight Like A Girl, Vol. 1

"Any of these stories could be a novel and you appreciate how many variations on a lead woman in the story there can be and how many worlds there could be to explore. As someone who strongly pushes for a bit more open mindedness in genre I really think this is an excellent way to start exploring outside of the stereotypes plus some more great authors to find!" - Runalong Womble, *Runalong the Shelves*

"If you like action, adventure, violence, and kick ass female characters, this is for you!" - Joel Cornah, *Goodreads*

"... the quality of the writing is excellent and there's enough variety that you're bound to find something you like" - A.F.E. Smith, *Fantasy Faction*

FOREWORD

By
Roz Clarke & Joanne Hall

It started, back when it was useful, on social media. Way back in 2013 acclaimed SF author Kameron Hurley wrote an essay titled 'We Have Always Fought; Challenging the "Women, Cattle and Slaves" Narrative'. The essay, which first appeared in *A Dribble of Ink*, was republished several times and went on to win the 2014 Hugo Award for Best Related Work.

The essay was written in response to discussion (:furious row) online at the time about whether contemporary SF and Fantasy was accurate in its portrayals of female fighters, or whether it was an outspilling of what they now, eleven years later, refer to as 'wokeness'. And it went viral. *Fight Like a Girl* was born in the fiery pits of Twitter, sparked by a suggestion from Danie Ware that we produce an anthology of stories about women who not only fought, but were true warriors. Danie went on to create the Sister Augusta series for Warhammer 40k, and her haunting story 'The God Of Lost Things, or Ethel, Dragonslayer' opens this anthology.

Years later, people were still approaching us at cons and asking us if we were going to do another one. When writers you *hugely* admire are coming up to you and saying 'I really wish I'd been in that', you know you've done something special. Following the closure of Kristell Ink, Wizard's Tower took the project on, for which we are forever grateful.

The world has shifted in the decade-and-a-bit since FLAG 1, and we wanted to reflect that by increasing in scope the definitions of both 'fight' and 'girl'. Not all fights, after all, are undertaken with fists or blades and not all fighting 'girls' are girlbosses in the line of Joan of Arc, or Buffy. Nor do fighting women have to be dropped into roles written for men, like Emma Peel or Ripley, though our love for those characters still knows no fuckin' bounds fr. Representation has definitely improved, and perhaps now we can look beyond a direct kick back against the idea that women can't fight, and start to reintegrate more traditionally acceptable forms of feminine power with that warrior archetype.

Women have always fought by whatever means were available. Danie's heroine, for example, shows persistence and courage. We have women here exercising cunning, as in Gaie Sebold's delightful 'Ambition's Engine', and diplomacy, and teamwork—particularly prevalent here in Juliet McKenna's 'A Civil War', and KT Davies' 'The Seamstress, The Hound, The Cook and her Brother.' Cheryl Morgan's military midwives combine hard and soft power.

We have older heroines and disabled heroines, and Dolly Garland's 'A Human Response' brings us a non-Western perspective.

Of course we still enjoy a good bloodthirsty battle, for example Anna Smith Spark and Lou Morgan bring us compelling but very different fighting generals in 'Lady Cona' and 'Amplify'.

The definition of a girl/woman has become a matter of increasing contention lately, especially in the UK. In speculative fiction, a field in which the definition of a *human being* has been up for discussion from its inception and explorations of all other aspects of human identity likewise, we have never shied away from pushing and poking at assumptions and challenging dominant social narratives.

Being a woman is vastly more than a matter of physical biology. Here we have trans women in both Julia

Hawkes-Reed's 'We Have Always Been Here' and KR Green's 'Ready for Combat'. Trans women are women, and AI's, or ship-minds who have been stripped of their human bodies (as in Naomi Scott's 'A Way Out') but identify as women are also women.

The calls for both anthologies have been open to women and anyone identifying as a woman. We're absolutely delighted to be able to showcase three stories by trans women. We wish we could have done this quietly and without fanfare as we did in 2014, but right now we both feel a strong need to be seen standing proudly beside our trans sisters. After all, they fight like girls too... because they *are*.

Perhaps in another ten years, we will be able to stand down from that particular fight. Perhaps society will have moved on from both of the arguments to the extent that a third volume won't be needed, although it seems slightly more likely that the world will catch fire and we'll all be too busy surviving to worry about it. Watch our comms channels for anthologies on saving the world.

Fight the good fight, sisters, whatever shape or form that takes for you.

With love, Jo and Roz

INTRODUCTION

By
Charlotte Bond

You look like a girl
You run like a girl
You dress like a girl
You fight like a girl

Comments such as these were standard in my grandparents' and parents' time. Even when I was at school in the
Eighties, they were spoken by boys and girls with definite
conviction. They're less prevalent now, but my daughter still
comes home from school with comments about how girls
are excluded from the rougher games or told they can't mix
with the boys (mostly by the kids, but she also came home
complaining about how the boys got to do sport for their
free time and the girls had to do craft).

Opinions and perceptions are changing, but it's a slow if
steady process. What contributes to permanently embed-
ding these new ideas and roles into society? Why, fiction, of
course – whether that's books, films, or TV series. And right
now, female audiences are being offered more and more
options where they can enjoy women fighting – in proper
battle clothes, on an equal footing with men, and without any
misogyny getting in the way.

For just a few examples of this we can include *She-Ra*
making a welcome return, and Millie Bobbie Brown not only
playing the superhero in *Stranger Things*, surrounded by a
group of four boys, but also outwitting the famous Sherlock

Holmes in *Enola Holmes* and fighting dragons in *Damsel*. And that's just on Netflix.

I read Anne Lyle's introduction to book one of *Fight Like a Girl*, and I was intrigued to see that we shared quite a few of the same influences growing up. I, too, found Doctor Who's female companion to be inspiring, but when I watched it, the companion was Ace. I very much wanted her leather jacket. Not only was she a fighter, she was fun and witty too. It struck me at an early age that women could easily be both but weren't always presented that way.

I also have to acknowledge the influence of Diana Rigg's portrayal of Mrs Emma Peel. Despite her name reeking of the male gaze (it literally means "M-appeal" as in: appeals to the men), she was frequently shown as the equal to John Steed in fights. Sure, she got into scrapes and was rescued by John more than she rescued him, but the fact that she did any fighting or rescuing at all was just marvellous to my young eyes.

Of course, there was also *Buffy the Vampire Slayer* (the series rather than the movie). Here was a girl who didn't have her power handed to her on a plate but had to train regularly and didn't always win. She was powerful but flawed, and it was made clear as the series went on that her friends kept her safe and alive as much as her own skill.

So, a book like *Fight Like a Girl* is absolutely essential not just for entertainment but for changing perceptions. In a way, an anthology can be more powerful than a novel because, in a novel, you've got maybe a handful of characters and one setting or world for them to inhabit and change. But in an anthology, the reader is presented with a wealth of characters in a variety of settings, and each of them has a powerful message. In book one, you encounter women in a traditional fantasy setting, like a camp for sell-swords, as well as female characters inhabiting the real world (albeit a dystopian one where cults hold sway). Then there are the stories of the distant future and far-flung planets where humans fight aliens not just for survival but for money and fame.

In the second volume of *Fight Like a Girl*, there are even more women ready to show you how to fight like a girl. Perhaps you'd like to read about how a crown is stolen by three women in a high fantasy drama, or a steampunk story about hairdressers and dragons' eggs. Or perhaps a space opera with a sentient ship is more your thing.

Whatever your taste, whatever you're looking for, in these pages, you will learn one thing: how to fight like a girl.

THE GOD OF LOST THINGS
OR
ETHEL, DRAGONSLAYER

By
Danie Ware

On the coast, the spirits feel strange.

I've lived my long life in London, where they wreathe like the smoke of old pollution, or like haze, fine and grey, hanging in the air like dreams. Most are tied to one place—the ghosts of old memories. Some are new, created by flash-moments of great intensity; some have existed for centuries, their recollections gaining depth and layer. Yet all of them like to share tales, and they mutter, whispering undetected across the heads of the bustle below.

But I can hear them quite well.

Let me introduce myself. I'm Ethel, and I like finding things. Call it a hobby, if you like, something I started after

I lost my husband. Were I a younger woman, I might term myself a 'private investigator', but such conjures images of smoky offices and femmes fatales, of frosted glass door panels with my name seen in reverse, and I'm too old for any of that. Mostly, I sit in the window of my little flat, looking out across the long, slow roll of the Thames.

I sketch, too.

Below me, the river's great spirit pays me little mind. He remembers aeons, but he's sleepy these days, like a soft grey fog across the water. I can spend hours watching him, shifting like some huge and dreaming cat, while I listen to the murmurs about him. The spirits react to emotions—passions of feeling—and they linger, learning images and sounds, and then passing them on.

This time, the image was recent. A girl, small and pale and furtive, maybe fourteen. She was depressive and struggling, sickened with anxiety and a strange determination. Needing to be unseen, and yet needing people to care...

Running away.

Moments like these, I offer things. Memories of my own—and I have many—or gifts of incenses or burning oils. This time, I gave the lingering spirits light, the facets of a crystal shining out across the winter dusk. It caught their notice, and they told me of the girl. They offered me her story, like a tail of grey shadow, following her to Victoria Station, and to the yellow-eyed smoke-dragon who curls about the old clock. He likes the people, I think; they keep him curious and awake. Occasionally, he even unwraps himself, out along the railway lines, watching those that have caught his interest.

It's his tale of the girl that has brought me here.

And like I said, the spirits don't feel the same.

#

G reywater.

A small seaside town, and well named, it seems.

It's more than an hour on the train, and now I walk its winter streets, feeling the chill, and listening to the hiss and wash of the waves on the shingle. The beaches are deserted, carved by groynes and scattered with flotsam. They offer ranks of tiny, brightly coloured huts, but no-one needs them, not in November, and their paint is thin and peeling.

There's a pier, classic and Victorian, falling down, judging by the wire-mesh fences. Red signs tell me to keep my distance. I leave it be and keep walking, the collar of my hiker's coat up and my hands deep in my pockets. With my bag across my shoulder, I head for the lone hotel, creatively called the 'Sea View'. It's wonderfully dilapidated, standing like a sentinel on the cliff-top. The wind whines round it, rattling at the old windows.

Here, the spirits dance oblivious. Unlike the ones in London, they're free and alive, enjoying the openness, the sky and the water. They don't know me enough to speak to me, but once I'm settled in my room, I can address them and see what they remember.

Seabirds caw, rising in spirals. It's an uncannily summer sound, set against the low-bellied clouds. I pass a handful of storefronts—cafes and souvenir shops, places to buy postcards and surfboards and buckets-and-spades. A beaded wristband with your name on it, assuming your name isn't unusual.

A few of these are even open, and their windows glow warm in the chill.

On impulse, I walk to the closest for a cup of tea. It's called the 'Rosie Lea', though its rosebush has seen better days.

'Hello?'

The door jingles as I open it, and there's a wash of warmth. The place is almost deserted, only a woman behind the counter who glances up as I come in. She's younger than me, probably in her forties, and she has the lined, faintly sun-beaten look of a long-time local. As I approach the counter, she grunts what might be a greeting.

'I'm closing in ten.'

'I'm Ethel, dear,' I tell her, smiling. 'Can I please have a tea to take away?'

I feel her looking at me, examining my lined face and my solidly utilitarian clothes, but my own attention has been caught by the shop's inside. The walls, the tops of the windows, the back of the counter, are all absolutely covered in junk. Shrimp nets and fishing floats, pieces of water-worn glass or wood, a child's toy boat, the torn remains of brightly-striped windbreak.

They make my smile deepen, and I try to catch her eyes. 'Collector, are you? My husband and I used to mudlark, along the shores of the Thames. It's amazing what you can find.'

The woman fits a white plastic lid to a steaming, polystyrene cup, and glares. 'Not too many here, out of season,' she says, like she's doing me a favour. 'Writers, sometimes. Photographers.' The glare doesn't fade. 'Which are you?'

'Neither,' I tell her, not losing the smile. She may be rude, but there's no reason I have too be impolite in my turn. 'I'm looking for someone.'

It's an opening, the hook that should catch the conversation, but it only makes her sniff, flaring her nostrils and shying backwards like a startled horse. 'Well, you won't find them here.' With aggressive dismissal, she turns her back on me. 'I close in two.'

I pick up the tea, and try one last time, 'How's the hotel?' I ask her. 'Quiet, I expect?'

'Same as everywhere else,' she says, not turning round. Her broad back shakes as she cleans the rear counter. 'You'll probably be the only one there.'

#

Outside the shop, I walk and think and sip scalding hot tea, looking in through the other stores' windows. They're all closed now, their frontages salt-rimed and fading, their glass reflecting the sky. Some have grilles, pulled down to protect displays of wind-chimes and dream-catchers, but all of them have layers of *stuff*.

Forgotten stuff, lost stuff. Books and boxes, hats and scarves and umbrellas, tote bags with broken handles. Cameras, their lenses smashed. One has a music-box; another a doll's head, eyes open and hair tangled. Still more have old comics, their pages sun-faded, or porcelain cats, the sort my grandmother would have brought me as child. One is a genuine 'vintage' store, laden with chairs and tables and lamps and clocks, all of them wreathed in cobwebs. In its window is an old, brass barometer, the needle stuck on 'fair'.

I'm fascinated, and honestly a little creeped out. The local spirits swirl about my ears, like the scents of wind and wet stone. They're still not speaking to me, and the sea hisses cold on the shore. I pass a bus-stop, all filled with blowing trash, and finally climb to the hotel, huge above me at the very top of the cliff.

It's colder up here; chill enough to make me shiver. The moon is ghostly behind the clouds, and the hotel is more of the classic Victoriana, grand and decaying. Its spirit weaves gently about its single tower and stares out across the huge, dark sea. I hope I can speak to it. For the moment, though, I bang in through the double front doors and ping the little bell on the desk.

18

Ping it again, a polite time later, when no-one seems to have heard.

'Hello? Can I book a room, please?'

There's junk in here, too, though not as much of it. It smells faintly of mildew, faintly of rusting metal. The wind rattles at the windows, trying to get in.

'Coming, coming.' The words precede a stooped, middle-aged man. He eyes me, exactly like the woman in the café had done. 'Just you?'

A grandfather clock tick-ticks in a corner, the sound ponderous. As I listen, it grates and rattles, then chimes the quarter-hour.

'Just me. Two nights, if you don't mind?' I take my card out of my purse.

'Single room, that'll be seventy-six sixty. Breakfast's eight 'til nine. If you miss it, Tabitha's on the seafront is open all year.' He waves at the card machine and I obediently tap. It beeps approval, weirdly chirpy in the surround.

'Thank you,' I tell him.

'Room four,' the man says, placing a metal key on the counter, complete with label. 'Down on your right. We've a bar, if you're wanting dinner. Seven 'til eight, though we're on the winter menu. You'll even have company—you're the second person I've seen today.' He grins, ghoulish, and shuffles off.

I pick up the key and follow his instructions.

This place feels very strange.

#

The room is on the corner, two massive windows at right-angles. It's both cold and draughty. One of the windows, the one facing the sea, has a metal-framed door that leads out onto what might be a sun-terrace, in season, but is currently a flat expanse of puddles, the paint peeling on its black metal railings.

I try the key, and to my faint surprise, the door opens. I put my bag on the bed, and head out.

The wind hits me instantly, fierce and somehow electric. It makes me smile—it's why I do this, why I learned to speak to the spirits in the first place. My husband used to joke about it, when we were down by the Thames, 'What if he could tell you where stuff was? You'd always find the treasure!'

I guess I taught myself, after that.

Holding that recollection, I stand on the terrace. I open my arms and mind and I beckon to them, *Come.*

Let me share my thoughts with you.

Let me share my memories with you.

Let me listen!

I half-expect surprise—that happens sometimes when they're not used to you—but they pay me absolutely no heed. The smaller ones dance in the wild, seaside air, zephyrs like laughter, elated and uncaring. They have less substance, somehow, than the old smoke-spirits of London; they're more like waveforms, twisting and turning, peaking and embracing one another. The bigger spirits, of hotel and promenade, are completely uninterested, lost in their own contemplations.

From somewhere, I see a single, yellow beam. It shines out and then vanishes again. A lighthouse, perhaps, another fragment of the past.

I find myself shivering, and wrap my coat about me. Beneath the sky-spirits' coiling dance there lurks something I can't quite detect, something much more aware, something about which the spirits cavort, all but concealing it from view.

What is that?

For a moment, they seem to part and I can feel it looking back at me.

It knows what I am; it knows that I'm here—

But then it's gone again, and I have no idea what I've just seen.

#

Downstairs, the bar is almost empty, but the concierge was right. There's another person here. He's my age, weathered and balding and comfortably fleshed, his garments like mine, a sensible shirt and waterproof. There's a camera on the table at his side and something in his face makes me like him immediately. I head over.

'Hello,' he says, smiling. He's got a menu in his hand that's had most of the choices crossed out. 'I heard there was someone else here, but wouldn't believe it until I saw it for myself.' His gaze twinkles. 'I'm Aubrey.' It's delightfully antiquated and it suits him.

'Ethel,' I tell him. 'May I?' I indicate the other chair. 'Though I don't want to intrude...'

'Please, please,' he gestures, moving the camera. 'The Nikon's a lovely thing, but it's no good for conversation.'

'Photographer?' I ask him, taking the cue.

'Student of life, inevitably. What else, at our age?' Winking, he places the thing on the bench beside him, patting it like an old friend. The window at his back is scattered with rain. 'I come out here to think, and to take pictures of the birds. I write, too, but I'm not really very good at it.'

His tone makes me chuckle, and I find myself warming to him further. 'Surely that doesn't matter?' I say.

'Of course not. And you, Ethel, may I ask why you're here? Are you also a writer?'

'Actually,' I tell him. 'I'm looking for someone. A missing girl.'

He frowns. The concierge appears at our side, pad and pencil in hand, hovers for a moment then mutters and drifts away again. He looks like he's the only staff member here. The grandfather clock chimes the three-quarter hour. The rain is growing stronger.

Aubrey looks at me, frowning. Leaning over the table, he says, 'Family?'

Something in his tone makes my skin prickle. I say only, 'Just a friend.'

He pauses, as if waiting for me to explain, and when I don't, he goes on. 'This is a funny place, Greywater. I lost my wedding ring, about two years ago. Had it on a chain around my neck, and the chain must've broken. My wife—my ex-wife—had it inscribed with the date.'

He's talking very softly, his eyes all over the room. There's junk in here, too, a single high shelf almost more like a picture rail, offering brassware, and old photographs. I glance around at it, but Aubrey's still pulling at my attention.

'There's a plain gold band in the souvenir shop, engraved with the same date, in exactly the same format.'

I blink at him, startled. 'Surely that's a coincidence? Hundreds of couples must have got married on that date?'

'I don't know,' Aubrey said. 'I...'

He tails off as the concierge returns, now quite pointedly brandishing his pen.

'I'll have the fish and chips,' I tell him.

'Make that two,' Aubrey says, beaming. 'And a gin and tonic, please. Will you join me, Ethel?'

'Oh, yes. Another of those, I think.'

The concierge scribbles, grunts, and shuffles off. I wonder if he's doing the cooking as well.

Aubrey waits until he's gone, then leans back over the table. 'My son brought his family on holiday here, last summer. He's the one that told me about it. He just thought it was funny. But what are the odds? Really?'

I sit back, trying to digest what he's told me. One part of my mind argues rationality, but another part of me, that part that cavorts with the spirits outside, is twisting round some truly uncomfortable thoughts. Why is there all this junk in Greywater? Where has it all come from? It can't all be flotsam? Why was the woman in the Rosie Lea so curt?

And what about little Eva?

The thought of the missing teen makes me worry, reaching for a conclusion that's still not there. I want to go back to the terrace, to the spirits, but I'm caught by Aubrey's story.

'It doesn't make sense,' I tell him. 'How would a lost ring find its way down here?'

How would a lost child?

He shrugs, then sits back as the concierge appears with two tumblers of gin and tonic, neither with ice or lemon.

When he's gone, I say, 'Would you mind if I came with you? I'm...curious.' He eyes me, half-delighted and half-questioning. 'Of course,' he says. 'We could meet for breakfast? At half-eight?'

'I'd like that,' I tell him, and the matter is closed.

#

In the morning, I wake sandy-eyed and groggy. I've slept badly, tossing and turning, disturbed by the wind rattling at the glass, by the constant, pattering rain. There had been ominous thundery rumbles, but they've not yet manifest into a full-on storm. As I look at myself in the bathroom mirror, splashing water on my face, I wonder what I've been dreaming about.

Spirits, capering. Laughing at me. Picking things up—lost things, shiny things—and carrying them away. Facets of light in the dusk; memories tossed aside like trash.

And something about the pier?

The thought is a sudden compulsion, strong as a tug. It brings me to a stop, wondering where it had come from, so abrupt and so powerful.

I'll mention it to Aubrey over breakfast.

The room's shower is dribbly and not very warm, but it wakes me up well enough. Pulling on my clothing and my hiking boots, I head down.

He's not there.

I order tea, and wait. Order another. I don't want to order food, as it would be rude not to wait for him, but the grand-father clock chimes the quarter-to, then the hour, and the long, slow bongs of nine.

Nothing.

At last, I ask for a croissant and the concierge comments, slightly sniffily, that breakfast has closed, and that Aubrey had checked out that morning.

'Family emergency,' he tells me. 'He asked me to apologise.'

Checking irritation—now you bloody tell me!—I gulp down the tea and go back to my room. I'm going to look at that wedding ring myself.

Going to look at the *pier*.

Outside, the air is thick and still. It's warm, for November, and still raining, fat drops like harbingers.

I get to the shop, and pause.

The ring is obvious. There's a jewellery display board with all sorts of necklaces and bracelets pinned to it, odd earrings and lost pendants. The wedding ring, a man's plain gold band, hangs from a pin at the top.

Beside the board sits a Nikon camera, almost brand new.

What?

I stare at it, my heart thumping. It's identical to Aubrey's.

One coincidence is possible. But two?

Spirits tickle my ears, laughing on the breeze. They're no help whatsoever. They seem to be mocking me, chuckling as they head outwards, to cavort over the open sea.

What do they know? Like the locals, they're not telling.

Making a decision, I push into the shop.

'Morning.'

There's a young woman behind the counter, thin faced and pale. Her hair is almost black, and pulled back in an unflattering knot. She eyes me, then goes back to her book.

'The camera in the window,' I say to her. 'How long has that been there?'

She looks up again, with an edge of resentment. 'No idea.'

'Is it for sale?' I reach for my phone, take out my card.

Watch her gaze follow it.

'S'pose.'

'How much would you like?'

That makes her look at me fully, her eyes a washed-out, pale blue. 'Why d'you want it?'

'I want to take some pictures, and I forgot to bring mine with me.'

For a moment, we measure each other, and I smile, all affability though my heart is still pounding.

'Two hundred.'

'All right.'

I don't know why I did it, why I gave up that much money on a hunch. Perhaps because I'd warmed to Aubrey, perhaps because I was worried about both him and little Eva. Perhaps because I don't like mysteries. I find things; it's what I do. Perhaps because the spirits were still not talking to me, yet the call to the pier was strong as ever. I put the card in the machine and paid her without question.

And then I took the camera down the seafront and sat on the bench in the bus-stop, in the lee of the wind, and flicked back through the pictures.

It was Aubrey's all right.

Pets and garden parties. Smiling children, running in the sun. But I wasn't there to stalk the poor man and I flicked forwards until I found his studies of Greywater—the cold sea, the cliffs, the birds, the faded colours of the beachside huts.

And...

The pier itself. Rickety and tumbledown, its access closed. The images strike me hard, making my heart pound louder, thumping in my ears and chest. He'd taken a lot of pictures of the rusting, barnacle-covered metal supports, and the newer concrete that had reinforced them. There was junk under it, too, piles of it, buried in the stones. He'd not disturbed it, but treated it as a project, macro shots of green sea glass and worn-smooth pennies. Of pieces of plastic fishing weight, all garishly orange, and rotting fabric still caught on the struts.

But it didn't stop there. The place had fascinated him, it seemed. There were night-shots, taken of the old arcades, the shops, the collapsing funfair. And they held heaps and heaps and *heaps* of lost things. Forgotten things, abandoned things. Things that waited there, almost like offerings, like the treasure hoard of some unseen dragon...

Dragon.

The thoughts catch at me, making me look up from the camera. The pier had not had a spirit of its own, not that I saw, last night.

So why...?

My pulse still drumming, I put the camera away carefully, back its case. Out over the water, the morning sky is sinking even lower, and slants of sunlight angle down through the cloud. The floor of the bus-stop is all cigarette butts and empty bottles of pop.

Something about the pier, and its invasion of my dreams. Its invasion of Aubrey's camera...

Why is it calling me so?

I am going to find out.

Heading along the seafront, I ease between two of the rattling metal fences. Whatever is out here, I will find it.

#

The pier's planks are rotting, but they hold.

Trying not to look between them at the seethe of grey below, I walk carefully, staying tight to the once-white buildings so I can't be seen from the shore. There are old stalls here, faded signs that offer churros or tarot readings, something else that might once have been a shooting gallery. But I bypass all of that, stopping only to peer though the grimy window of the main arcade.

Here, the junk is piled—Aubrey's pictures hadn't quite captured the *scale* of this apparent dragon's hoard. The light is poor, but I can see that the stuff at the bottom is older, crumbling almost to nothing. It's rust and verdigris, and...

...and it's bones, some yellow with age.

I stop dead, caught like a fish on a hook, staring to double-check. Those are bones, all right. A spread hand, tarsals and meta-tarsals; the unmistakable curve of a skull, its eye-socket empty.

Was this what had happened to Eva? To Aubrey? Are they here, somewhere?

And who—or what—has brought them here? Like so much *junk?*

And was that same something now calling me?

Invading my dreams?

It seems highly likely. A flare of adrenaline brings focus, tight and strong. Corrupted spirits do happen, damaged by trauma and cruelty, by sick memories—you might call them 'ghosts'—and I have seen them before. I am no hero, but a long and full life has given me weapons of my own.

And now, I think I'll need them. I raise the little crystal, the same one I'd shone from my window, and I let it glitter in the cloud-slants of sunlight. I remember my husband, the most magical times of our long, long marriage and I call to them once more.

Come.

This time, though, it's not casual. This time, I offer them wonders, fragments of sparkling light. My wedding day, the home we built together. Laughing as we stood in the garden.

And I say, *Come to me.*

I think of little Eva, of the sheer ferocity of her need to run away. Of Aubrey, and his wedding ring, and his camera. Of all the times when I have been the happiest, or the most broken-hearted. Not only the day of my wedding, but the night I finally lost my dear Stanley.

The recollections are strong. The spirits are noticing me, now, stirring and turning and drifting past my shoulders. They're curious, touching me with unseen fingers, with thoughts that drift and whisper. They can feel me, and it's making them responsive.

What is it? I ask them. *What's here?*

But that brings sparkles of fear, and they shy away. Despite my offerings, they are suddenly smaller, almost like a seaside's children, playing at the penny arcades. They part, and for a moment I see, just as I had done the previous evening, that there *is* something else behind them, something darker and older, and far, far bigger.

Something *twisted*.

Gooseflesh flashes down my arms, my back.

This was what I had been dreaming about, and now, I *remember*. Past the derelict funfair, at the pier's very end, there's an observation point. There's a telescope there, the kind you could once pay a pound to use.

And there's something else, something that says to me, as I have said to its underlings:

Come.

#

The pier ends in a spiral tower, a tall and twisting stairwell that leads up to a viewing platform. It looks like some forgotten helter-skelter, and the whole thing is studded with a pebbledash of junk. Pieces of shells and broken ceramic. A vertebra that might have come from a seal. Newer things, plastics and a still-gleaming metal key.

Pulled by my own curiosity, by some on-going magnetic fascination, I climb the rickety steps and put a coin in the telescope slot.

The thing works. And there he is, out over the water, his eyes a burning yellow against the roiling sky:

The spirit of the pier.

I shiver, cold to the bone. He's huge, far, far bigger than the one at Victoria station. He's the colour of sky and water, his grey form washing like the currents of the deep, cold sea.

Thunder grumbles, like his herald.

But I do not fear him.

Where is Eva? I throw the thought upwards, defying his might. *Where is Aubrey? You will give them back to me!*

My communications are not words, they're concepts, images. Feelings and memories. The dragon blinks its great yellow eyes and its form shifts and billows. It seems surprised, yet its power is absolute. I find my mind filling, as if it searches me: Stanley, thin and pale and fading. My parents, long gone. I've never had children, but I've lost many things in my life, things that I've loved and that did not return, and now the spirit drags them forth and throws them at me, like weapons of despair.

You, too, are lost, it says. *You, too, seek the final answer.*

I face it, throwing aside the memories and bringing others—joy and sunshine, friends in the pub, a black cat, sleeping in my lap.

I picture Eva and Aubrey again. *Where?*

With a yellow flash of ire, the dragon replies. *Mine.*

The response is silent but it echoes across the clouds, bigger than the pier, bigger than the crumbling funfairs and arcades, bigger than the town, tumbledown as it is. Bigger even than the cliffs, and the beach.

This is no local pier-spirit, bound to some tiny, Victorian comfort...whatever he is, he's older. Ancient even, vast and ponderous and powerful. Encrusted with time like barnacles.

In the back of my head, a sudden thought: is there something else here, some old site, or memory, under the water...?

But the grasp for comprehension is brief, and I do not yet understand. His eyes burning, he says, *Tiny thing, yet so defiant. You have lost so much more than all the others.*

A slew of memories assail me, all of them painful. That same black cat, his body cold and stiff. Things and places that I had done or seen for the last time, and to which I never returned. The unstoppable trickle of sand that is losing one's youth and health. Aches of nostalgia and regret—all those times when I had wished that my life had gone another way...

But it's *my* life. Not his.

I tell him, in the same tone, *Eva. Aubrey. Mine.*

That makes him stare at me, his gaze as yellow as fire. He blinks. There is rage in in him now, but it is buried and slow to rise.

I am the God, he says to me. *All the lost things come to me, all belong to me. And all stay.* He is still watching me and the fire in his gaze is growing—I wonder if that was the light I'd seen the previous evening, the thing I'd thought was the lighthouse.

I am not lost, I tell him.

Rippling, he hisses, like waves on the shore. The air is still thick with thunder, and too warm, but still I do not release the scope. I face him without fear. I repeat, with images of both Eva and Aubrey, *Mine.*

His hiss deepens, rattles like laughter. He's colossal now, towering against the clouds like some primeval, temple statue. He's been here...

...been here for *such* a long time.

As I understand, his memories flash past me with the speed of train windows. This area was forest, then small farms and fishing boats, then roads and houses and people. Horses, then cars. I see the seaside as new and bright and interesting, dandily-clothed gentlemen, and ladies with parasols. And then I see it fade again, its colours smearing to grey.

And I was right: there *is* something under the water, some seaweed covered ruin, some shrine now all but lost...

His home. His memories. The things he's trying to keep alive.

A brief flash of sympathy, but it does not last. The dragon's great age has brought with it fear, insecurity, and a terrible hunger. It has corrupted him as surely as the spirit of some misused sanatorium. His anger is making him swell, as vast as the sky, the smaller ones now retreating from him. They know him and they're terrified of him; he is a God to them, too.

But I say to them, once more:

Come.

Gently, I offer them treasures—my black cat and his thunderous purr, my Stanley, tending the roses on a Sunday afternoon. The thoughts are peaceful ones, good ones, and in return, they offer me stories—the crashing rage of wind and water, the collapse of the ancient shrine as it fell below the waves. The people, generations of them, forgetting that it had ever existed. The God-thing getting angry as it loses what it loves, and the damage that its anger always brings. They show the local people appeasing it, offering it pieces of their own lives, their own memories.

But soon, those gifts are not enough.

It hungers.

And it *calls*.

And the lost things always come.

#

Noises start me from the telescope.

Crackling radio sounds. A flare of siren from the road.

Police.

My first thought is of Eva, but they've not found the child. I don't think they will. No, they're coming down the pier now, and they're coming after me. Whether the dragon has somehow called them or whether I'm just trespassing, I don't know and it doesn't matter.

I am out of time.

Looking back though the eyepiece, I see the thing's teeth are bared. They're sharp, pointed—very unlike the spirits of London, who have little anger left. All the wildness of Greywater is in this thing and it's coming for me.

It will kill me, one way or another.

Boots rattle on the planking.

I ignore them; saying for the third time, *Mine.*

The dragon laughs, a snort of smoke through its fangs. I see a brief image of Eva running down the pier, climbing the steps to the top of the little tower. She looks out over the water like it was the answer she'd been seeking, the anchor her soul had so badly needed.

Then she throws herself from the platform.

And as its Eva, it's also Aubrey. It's a hundred, a thousand, a million, faces and names, people down through years without number. I see the shrine's watery ruin, all covered in a mossed growth of sea-rotten bones. I see the pier's construction, and the workers that died; I see the farmers and fishers who waded out into the water, compelled to offer themselves.

It calls them, and they feed it.

It needs their memories to live.

I have no more sympathy for this thing. Now, I raise my arms and the wind spirits come back to me, they swirl around me like a cloak. I feel them lift me, a dozen of them, more. I find myself—

Come, it says to me, thunderous with power. *Are you not lost also? Are you not alone, bereft of your life's love? Come. Find your answer!*

It's hard to resist, so strong. It's partner and lover, it's mother and father, it's youth and fulfilment and the children I never had. It's creative release, it's the ultimate in self-expression discovered and satisfied. It's my Stanley. It's all of my cats, each one loved and missed. It takes my every good memory, and it makes of them ashes—because I am old, and I have the all good things behind.

Are you not lost?

Are you not alone?

Your answer awaits!

Yes, I think, I am alone. Alone in my window, drawing my pictures, looking out over the Thames. Alone in my strange obsession, finding others' forgotten treasures. Alone on this cold grey pier, staring down at the churn of the water...

Oh, so tempting.

Come, it says. *Let me take away the pain.*

Boots come closer, and there's shouting. Somewhere behind me, the planking creaks, snaps and gives way.

There are splashes, cries.

The dragon coils in sudden glee, its eyes all firelight. It's hungry, it wants fulfilment.

But the noises have reminded me of myself. I no longer have hold of the telescope; I'm swathed in spirits. There, upon the platform where Eva had died, where Aubrey had died, I say:

No.

I feel it hiss, surprised.

I say:

No.

It tries to touch me, lift me, throw me. It shows me every tragedy of my life, every thing that I've missed, every opportunity that has passed me by or that I could not or would not or did not take. Every regret, every wrong turning.

But I say:

No.

And I understand now. I understand how to beat it. No longer do I throw those memories back, or deny them. I keep them, embrace them. I find them and hold onto them. Radiate them forth and use them as offerings of my own. The smaller spirits gather to me thickly, called by those same recollections. I am not lost. I am the sum of everything in my life, good and terrible, light and dark, hope and grief. I am fused, I am resolution and courage, and they can *feel* it. They lift me from the tower until I'm floating in the air above the end of the pier, until I can see the coiling God-thing clearly.

It tries to strike at me and they stop it, flaring outwards in flurry, flocking at it to drive it back.

I cannot save Eva, I cannot save Aubrey, but I can save myself. I can save Greywater. And I can save the lost souls of the future.

With a gesture, I send them at it and they mob it, their numbers to its lone strength. I lend them my own steel, my age and experience, my wisdom, and my refusal to submit. I have lost much, of course I have—we all do—but those losses are not what define me. For every loss I have known, there is gratitude that it happened. For every cat that passed away, there is its warmth and its purr. And my dear Stanley...

I have known so much joy.

The spirits revel in this, bright and strong. I have lived a rich life; I have no fears of the things I've lost. I am the sum of everything, all of my experiences. And this becomes my strength, my call, my offering, my summoning. A swirl of wind, of spirits, of power, driving the God-thing back.

And I say again:

No.

Over me, the storm breaks like fury. A clap of thunder, echoing from horizon to horizon. A jag of yellow lighting strikes the sea. I hear a motorboat, it must be coming for the frantically splashing police, but I do not listen.

For it is *my* storm, *my* defiance, *my* life. It is *everything* I am.

I am not lost!

And as the rain reaches its crescendo and hammers out of the sky, ripples in gusty waves across the trashing water, my wind spirits overwhelm the God and take it down.

Until nothing remains but bubbles.

#

Back at the hotel, the concierge is wide-eyed with gossip—trespassers on the pier, the coastguard out to rescue the drowning cops. I say nothing. I'm drenched, and I feel drained. Like I have poured myself out upon the whipping grey water and come back empty.

But I just need rest, and I will be fine. Patting my camera, I go to head back to my room.

Behind me, the grandfather clock creaks and chimes the hour, then ponderously bongs eleven.

At the noise, the concierge eyes the picture rail, his hands on his hips.

'You know,' he says absently. 'I really should have a clear out, it's getting ridiculous in here.'

And, tutting at the hoardings of his past, he walks away.

Smiling, I turn back to the stairs.

THE END

AMBITION'S ENGINE

By
Gaie Sebold

Caliest Deapa—a man with hair strenuously pasted over a balding crown and the meaty complexion of a little too much good living—snatched the letter from the tray. 'Opener, opener!'

'Lord.' The slave passed him the slender pearl-handled blade. Caliest ripped open the envelope, flung it away, and sent the opener after it. It clattered to the floor, but he barely noticed the sound, or the slave bending to pick it up.

The letter unfolded before him, the Imperial stamp with its deep blue dragon curled protectively around a scarlet diadem. He scanned the niceties without bothering to read them; the important part was near the end.

...by order of the Emperor of the Divine Dominion, Lord Caliest Deapa, son of Lord Greno Deapa, is hereby appointed to the post of Chief Defender of the Dominion's Transport.

As part of your duties, you will accompany the engine, the Dominion's Envoy, *on its maiden run, carrying essential supplies* *to the garrison at Endaklion...*He did not recognise the name. A garrison. Hardly an appropriate destination for an important official such as himself! Some ghastly outpost where it would be impossible to get a decent meal. Still, accompanying the latest example of the superiority of Dominion technology would be prestigious, if dull. Duller would be the meeting he apparently must have tomorrow with the Governor of the Railways. Bureaucrats. So tedious.

In the Hand of the Fabricator we lie.

An illegible signature, and the seal of the Governor General, faint and askew. After wielding the seal he had probably needed a little rest, since he was at least a hundred years old. More than time someone else took over, but *that* post would no doubt go to one of the Emperor's many relatives when the Governor General finally decided to stop merely *looking* dead.

No matter! Caliest had the post of Chief Defender of the Dominion's Transport. And he had earned it. The endless, tedious, wildly lavish suppers for utterly dull but influential people! The tickets to the most fashionable theatrical performances, which he sometimes had to actually sit through! Not to mention the commission itself, which had been ball-crushingly expensive. He had worked for this, he swore, harder than any slave.

But the post would pay him back a thousandfold. Soon *he* would be the one being invited to dinner, offered theatre tickets (his wife could go, women liked that sort of thing). And money. Not bribes, merely gifts to help ensure the smooth passage of this package or that group of slaves across the Dominion's vast territories.

Nowadays, with many of the conquered territories irritatingly restless, people would be even *more* anxious about things getting safely to their destinations. Might as well make the best of it until the wretched barbarians accepted their fate as Dominion colonies and settled down.

He clapped his hands for the steward. 'A celebration, tonight. I want the best of everything.'

'May I ask for how many persons, Lord?'

Caliest considered. He wanted, of course, to boast to his friends. And how *green* some of them would look! Especially Metifo, who despite being distantly related to the Emperor had been unsuccessfully angling for a high court post for at least a decade. He would have to swallow his jealousy with his meat, and what fun that would be!

But on the other hand, even the steward, efficient as he was (if his wife knew little else she knew how to choose slaves) could not produce a meal appropriate to such an occasion in less than a day. Also, such short notice would give too many people the excuse to cry off. 'Just us tonight,' he said. 'But in, oh, about twenty days, we shall have a proper feast. Ilian ruby wine, and those little roasting lizards from Calmatia, and...well, well, get to it, man!'

\#

The meeting with the Governor of the Railways took place in an obscure corner of the Dominion Palace. The Governor was clearly one of the Emperor's bastards, the Imperial profile stamped on his face as though he were a coin. Caliest, already irritated by the necessity of this meeting, was further irritated by the Governor's fussing about with papers and dismissing the slaves before so much as offering him a cup of wine.

'Can't be too careful,' the Governor said. He picked up a pair of spectacles and jammed them onto his high-beaked nose. 'Hmm, hmm—now where—ah. Yes.' He jabbed his finger at a sheet bearing the seal of the State Treasury. 'Here we are. The *Dominion's Envoy*, maiden trip. Very important. *Very*. Discretion, you see?'

Not in the slightest. 'That goes without saying.'

'Wages,' the Governor said. 'Back pay, for the troops in the North. So. There'll be a company of soldiers on the train, for security. Their Commander is in charge if there's trouble, but of course, you are the senior official. The Company's officially going to support the garrison at Endaklion. No mention to be made of the cargo. Rely on your discretion, Lord Chief Defender.'

'Of course, of course.' As though he'd gab about something as dull as soldier's wages. A few hints to his acquaintance as to the importance of this mission, that would be something else altogether.

The Governor finally summoned a slave to bring wine (not the best wine, either, considering this was the Imperial palace) and shuffled the papers, including the manifest, into a heap to make room. The slave, one of those stolid, pale-haired northerners, poured and then went off to do whatever they did when not serving their masters. Thievery and lazing about, no doubt.

#

A few days later, over a dinner that Caliest barely noticed for thinking of the exotic dishes he would soon offer his friends, his wife Idikraine said, 'Lord Husband, I need a new hairdresser. If you will give your permission, I have heard of a good one on the market. A little expensive, but very well trained.'

'Really? What's wrong with the one you have?'

'She's heard of some trouble back wherever it was she came from, and she's utterly distracted. She simply can't do the latest styles. I went to the theatre with Falini Benideth two days ago, and *she* told me how *charmingly old-fashioned* I looked! I could have sunk!'

'Spiteful bitch. Really I don't know why you should trouble yourself about such nonsense.'

'But Falini *patted* me and told me not to worry. She said if we were struggling, she would lend me *her* hairdresser. 'I had heard perhaps your Lord Husband had overextended himself,' she said. 'But your friends will rally around, my dear.' Borrow *her* hairdresser? What if *your* friends were to hear of it?'

Caliest, his buttocks poised above the chair, thumped back down. '*Overextended?* Where did she get *that* idea?'

Idikraine shrugged. 'I'm sure I don't know, Lord Husband. I told her that you were doing very well, and about the new house you were looking at in the Discovia district, but she just smiled in this *knowing* way, and told me to pay her a visit next time I wanted my hair done, and she wouldn't say a word to a soul! As though I'd believe for a moment she wouldn't be whispering to everyone about how generous she was to poor, suffering Idikraine! Next she'll be offering me her old gowns!'

'Intolerable,' Caliest said. 'Buy the hairdresser. Tell the steward I've given you permission to spend as much as you wish. And get some new gowns too, I won't have my wife looking as though she needs other people's cast-offs.' He would have told her not to see Falini Benideth again, but her husband, Lord Benideth, was too influential to risk insulting.

\#

The celebratory feast eventually rolled around. Caliest admired his newest robe—nothing too flashy, he was not a barbarian, after all—and went to check on his wife.

Idikraine sat at her dresser, a cotton wrap draped over her new and undoubtedly extremely expensive gown of pale blue watered silk. The new hairdresser was putting the finishing touches to a crown of tiny plaits, with curls cascading below.

'Lord husband,' Idikraine said. 'Look, the *Imperial Diadem* style! Just the latest thing!'

'Very fashionable,' Caliest said. He thought the style overly elaborate himself, but if it was what the high-ranking ladies were wearing, well, what was a man to do?

He glanced at the hairdresser, who stood with her eyes downcast. She was stocky and pale, her own light hair tightly wound and plaited close to her head. She had a look of the northern barbarian tribes—they seemed to be everywhere these days—and the arms she lowered from above his wife's head were notably muscular. Thoroughly unappealing, but she seemed to know her business.

'Is all well, Lord Husband? I directed the slaves to set out the rose garland dishes for the men's dinner.'

'For once, they seem to have managed to take orders,' Caliest said. 'Well, carry on. You don't want to be late for your friends and all that lovely gossip.'

'Enjoy your dinner, Lord Husband.'

'Oh, I will.'

He did. Lord Metifo congratulated him with the face of a man suffering severe indigestion. The others jabbed or fawned, according to nature and their own current standing. The lizards (each one worth at least a stable-boy) were delicious, the pears glazed with powdered butterfly wings, the songbirds stuffed with their own eggs, all perfection.

The wine, alas, was not Ilian ruby. A shipment had been raided, and there was none to be had. There had been silk on that train too, and wool, and various other goods. Lord Benideth, whose family's money came from his silk plantations, but had gained sufficient sheen by judicious application in the right places to raise him to the ranks of the nobility, raised his glass in Caliest's direction. 'We look to you, now, to deal with this nonsense, Lord Deapa. More troops on the ships and trains, that's what we need.'

'The majority of our troops are engaged in expanding our borders,' Metifo said. 'Some might consider the advancement of the Dominion of slightly greater importance than a shipment of ladies' scarves, hmm?'

'My dear Benideth, the safety of *your* goods will always be of the greatest concern to me,' Caliest said. 'Metifo, my good fellow, if our ladies do not get the frivolities all women desire, our lives will be made miserable, and we will all be forced to flee to the borders and fight alongside the troops, simply in order to get some peace!'

Everyone laughed, except Metifo, who managed to squeeze out a smile so sour a lemon could have improved on it. Satisfied, Caliest excused himself. On his way back he almost ran into the hairdresser, hurrying to the ladies' dinner. Slightly drunk and feeling genial, he favoured her with a smile. 'Your mistress keeping you busy?'

'It is my pleasure to serve, Lord.'

He noticed she was fidgeting, rubbing her hands together nervously.

'What is it, are they bullying you?' Women, so catty. They were probably jealous of Idikraine's hairstyle.

'Oh, no, Lord. It's only...forgive me, I couldn't help overhearing. Is it true, that there have been more raids?'

'I thought you slaves heard all the news before the Dominion spies did, the way you all chatter! Don't worry, we'll soon have everything under control.'

'The Imperial Dragon will arise,' the hairdresser said.

'Quite right,' Caliest said. 'Now off you go.'

He shook his head as he rejoined his guests. *The Imperial Dragon will arise*, indeed. It was the founding story of the Dominion, that the Fabricator Himself had gifted tame dragons to Adimak the First to fight for him and help him establish the Dominion. But if anyone other than the Fabricator had ever managed to tame a dragon, Caliest had never heard of it.

#

'Are you well, Lord Husband?' Idikraine settled herself next to Caliest on the terrace, and gestured for another glass. 'I hope your new responsibilities are not weighing too heavy.'

'Well, preparing for this journey to the north, you know—a very important trip, very—it's fatiguing, but a man must do his duty to the Emperor.'

'Have you seen the engine? I should like to see it.'

'Pah, why? They're noisy, filthy things. You'd get smuts on your gown.'

'Aikash says her people call them Iron Dragons.'

'Who?'

'My new hairdresser.'

'That's just like barbarians. Do they think they're magical too?'

'She was telling me many of the barbarian tribes consider the dragon to be the mark of a true ruler, and only a true ruler could tame one.'

'Really, wife, why do you listen to slave chatter?'

'Well, I thought it was interesting, so I asked her. I said if that's the case, why do they not recognise the Emperor? After all, the Imperial dragon is on everything, the standard, everything. And she said an image of a dragon isn't the same as an actual dragon, like the ones that obeyed Adimak the first.'

'*They* were a gift of the Fabricator. No mortal can *tame* a dragon.'

'So I told her. And she said many tribes believe the true ruler could do it. She's seen real dragons, she told me, where she lived before.'

Caliest let her chatter wash over him, the sun flickering through the vine over the courtyard and his closed eyelids, red and black shadows, dancing.

#

While gifts certainly came in, they were not as lavish as might have been expected. The new house in the Discovia district *was* lavish, but also draughty, and the kitchen so inconveniently placed that despite having the servers beaten, food constantly arrived cold to the table.

Though the district was a fine one, all the best shops were now further away, and Idikraine, the steward, and who knows who else sent an endless stream of messenger boys running back and forth. Caliest almost ran into one—yet another of those pallid northerners, they seemed to be everywhere these days. A squirmy little fellow who squealed when Caliest grabbed his ear and went even paler than before. 'Lord?'

'Watch where you're going, you clumsy little wretch!'

'Yes, Lord, I'm sorry, Lord.'

'If you're going by the market, tell the butcher on Aflio Way that last week's beef was a disgrace.'

'Yes, Lord, sorry, Lord.'

'Go on then, and don't idle!'

Caliest released him and wiped his fingers on his robe. His life was full of vexations. At least he had received an invitation from one of his new neighbours, a famous former general. The man was known as a bloviating old bore, forever reliving his campaigns, but he still had the Emperor's ear.

#

The dinner was as unrelentingly tedious as might have been expected, to the point where Caliest, hearing laughter from the room where the ladies were dining, almost considered joining them to see if their gossip was more entertaining than hearing about the Stand at Moreth Bridge, the Dovingian Triumph and the Brisilli Seige in agonising detail. Twice. The food, geared to the General's aged and touchy stomach, was also less than appealing. But Caliest nodded and smiled and exclaimed in the right places until the General finally rambled himself to a pause.

After some pleasant discussion about a delicious scandal (a High Court lady of ancient lineage was rumoured to have run off with an *actress)* and her family's futile efforts to squash the story, talk turned inevitably to the borders, and the barbarians. 'Lost *another* railway line in the western reaches last month,' announced Lord Pelifen, a cadaverous fellow who insisted on dressing with an almost insulting plainness, despite being one of the Court's most influential financiers. 'Bad business.'

'What is *wrong* with these people?' Caliest said. 'We're bringing them civilisation and all they can do is blow it up!'

'I heard the Emperor, Fabricator protect him, is considering withdrawing from the western reaches altogether.' The speaker was younger than the other guests by some two decades, and had, until this moment, been very quiet.

'A tactical withdrawal only, surely,' someone said.

The young man shrugged. 'I state only what I have heard. Some troops have not been paid in months. Entire battalions are deserting. The Emperor plans to cut his losses and concentrate on the north.'

'I myself am being sent North,' Caliest said. 'A diplomatic mission...'

He was interrupted by the rattle of crockery as the General pounded his fist on the table. 'Nonsense. None of my troops ever deserted! The dragon standard is destined to fly over all the nations of the world!'

'Had we an actual dragon to fly over them, that destiny might come sooner, grandfather,' the young man said.

'So I've heard,' Caliest said. 'It's a belief among the northern tribes.'

The General's grandson cast him an interested look. 'What exactly *have* you heard?'

'That they believe the true ruler will have a real dragon at his beck and call.'

'Ah! Intriguing how dragon lore seems to cross tribal boundaries.'

'This grandson of mine, always in a library instead of on the drill ground.' The General glared.

'Now, Grandfather, you have at least a dozen grandsons following the family's proud military tradition,' the young man said. '*One* of us was destined to be a mere intellectual.' He turned back to Caliest. 'Dragons as the right hand of conquest are not confined to the Empire. It's not surprising, really—no beast is more magnificent. I visited a nest, off the coast of Antiver. You could see them basking on the rocks. The leader—a great glossy blue creature with black flashes on his wings, I swear he was the length of a train carriage. And all the little females crawling about, I say *little* but only compared to him! All competing for his notice, of course. They stand up and stretch out their wings to catch his eye. They're a deal more colourful, like a mosaic floor—their skins would make marvellous leather, if one could get it.'

'I'm amazed you found a ship to take you,' Lord Pelifen said. 'Don't they attack anything that approaches?'

'Oh, we stayed far enough out not to trouble them—the sailors on that coast know their business! They wouldn't go even that close when there are eggs in the nest, though. A shame. I'd pay a lot for an egg.'

'Has anyone ever got hold of an egg?' someone said.

'I had a trader try and sell me what he claimed was a dragon egg once.' The General's grandson smiled. 'It was made of stiffened paper and painted, and filled with the Fabricator knows what to make it weigh heavy. He gave me quite the tale about how he'd risked his life to obtain it. I said it was a shame he'd taken such risks for a piece of painted paper, at which he became even more inventive, though insulting.' He laughed. 'No, no-one's ever got that close. They seem impervious to most weapons and are extremely aggressive if you threaten their eggs—even the females.'

'It is the nature of females to protect their young, after all,' Caliest said, absentmindedly. That was Idikraine's main failure—she had never succeeded in giving him a son. Or even a daughter, for that matter. One of these days—when he had settled into his new post—he would have to think about replacing her.

It was at that moment that the General's steward—a man worn thin and polished in the service of the household, like an antique spoon—announced a late-arriving guest.

'It is my honour,' the Steward said, 'to announce Admiral Lord Metifo.'

For all the blandness of the meal, Caliest found himself suddenly nauseous. All the guests crowded around Metifo, admiring his new brilliant blue sash, embroidered with Admiral's insignia.

Caliest pasted on a delighted smile, and pounded him on the shoulder. 'My dear fellow, I'm delighted to see that all your efforts have finally been rewarded!'

'Mind the sash, Deapa!' Metifo carefully smoothed the glossy silk. 'The Emperor put it on me with his own hands,' he said. 'He spoke of my late father, may he rest in the Fabricator's embrace. I was moved almost to tears.'

You loathed your father, Metifo, Caliest thought. *I remember at least one drunken conversation on how much you looked forward to arranging the old fart's funeral with singing boys and flower garlands, and every trimming he most despised.*

How like Metifo! What had he done, or offered, to finally get the post he'd been angling for so long? A post that not only came with a handsome stipend, and a great deal of influence, but put him above Caliest in rank?

'I hear you've a trip coming up,' Metifo said. 'To the garrison at Endaklion.' He gave a theatrical shudder. 'Rather you than me.'

'Well, it will probably be a smoother ride than a ship in a storm.' Caliest stretched a smile over his teeth. 'I'm sure I shall manage.'

'I hope that shiny new engine is fast enough to outrun bandits.' Lord Benideth appeared at Caliest's shoulder like an unpleasant memory. 'Have you managed to get more cover for the latest transports to the Therian coast?'

'My dear fellow, do have a little patience! Have you any idea what it's like dealing with the military?' Truth to tell, Caliest was already finding the post required more effort than he had expected. The sheer amount of bribery required to reach the right ear was both expensive and frustrating. And even once that ear was reached, responses of, 'I can't send what I don't have,' and mentions of overdue back-pay and missing supplies were all too frequent. Really, if the military couldn't manage its own affairs, why was *he* supposed to do it?

'Deal with the navy instead.' Metifo smirked. 'I'm sure you'll find things go more smoothly.'

With churning belly and sour mouth, Caliest somehow made it through the rest of the evening, and arrived home in a vile temper. The ladies' dinner had finished earlier, and Idikraine was long abed. Not that she would dare object if he woke her and ranted, but she would have little to offer but platitudes.

#

Caliest slammed into the house, breaking the low-lit hush, and found the only slave still awake was his wife's hairdresser. Aikash was sitting quietly in the foyer, a lamp at her elbow, working on some sort of frivol—a thing of beads and feathers and lace.

'What are you doing here?' He snapped.

She got up, and bowed. 'My apologies, Lord, but your body slave is sick, so I said I would wait up for your Lordship's return. I have a soothing drink ready, if you should wish it.'

'If it's a posset, you can throw it out. I've eaten enough pap for one evening.'

'It is *dinkait*, Lord. A drink of the far northern peoples, taken after meals, to aid the digestion.' She glanced at him, then immediately lowered her eyes. 'It is also taken after disputes, to calm the mind, and give clarity of thought.'

'Hmph. Well, I suppose I could try some. Bring it into the salon.'

He settled himself in his favourite chair, and Aikash appeared with a small glass. The liquid within was a rich purplish red, the aroma spicy-sweet. Cautiously, he sipped. The flavour was unusual—a little like plum wine, with a darker undercurrent—but not unpleasant, and after a few sips his stomach definitely felt better. 'Where did you discover this stuff?'

'When I was with the Beliori, Lord; a tribe to the north. That town is part of the Dominion now—Binasa, a few miles south of Endaklion.'

'Endaklion eh? I'm going there soon.'

'I had heard so, Lord. A great responsibility, and most prestigious.'

'Hah. See? Yet do I get any respect? No. Everyone fawns over Metifo. Admiral, indeed! The man can't even *sail*. When we went boating as boys he was forever getting tangled in the ropes or falling in. Men like him will be the ruin of the Dominion. How, after all this time, he managed to get the Emperor's attention, I don't know!'

'Perhaps he gave the Emperor something,' she said. 'Some gift that he has been wanting.'

'Unless it was a hundred thousand soldiers or the money to pay them, I can't imagine what.'

'Indeed, the Emperor has had much to trouble him. I wonder what might make him feel better after such recent setbacks? But truly it is said, the Imperial Dragon will arise.'

'Yes, yes quite. Dragons, eh? Some fellow talking about dragons, tonight. Said he's seen a nest. And your mistress mentioned you'd seen dragons, is that right?'

'Yes, Lord, when I was with the Beliori. There was a nest quite close to the town.'

'Indeed?'

'Yes. There was supposed to be a passageway through the cliffs, from a point near the town, leading right into the heart of the nest. The boys would search for it, wanting to creep in, and steal an egg. I heard one of them even managed it, some years before, but a dreadful curse fell on the town as a result, and he was made to return it. Of course, it is only a legend. But they believe it.'

'A curse! Ah, these native superstitions.'

'Indeed, my Lord. But dragons are terrible enough without any curse being needed. I once...but my Lord does not want to hear my silly tales.'

'No, no, tell me.' He found her low voice surprisingly soothing. Anything to take his mind off the evening.

'I had been left in charge of my master's son, because there was no-one else, his tutor having died of a fever and the new one not yet come.' Her voice took on a new timbre, rhythmic and soothing, almost like that of a marketplace storyteller. 'He was a bold boy, who would not listen to me—I was only a slave, and his mother's hairdresser. There was a great storm, with rain like hammers and winds that threw great waves at the cliffs, and he had not been able to go out for many days. As soon as the weather cleared, he went climbing, and found a place where some rock had fallen, leaving a gap. He crept in, saying he was going to get an egg. I was so very frightened that he would injure himself, and I would be blamed. Of course I went after him, but when I got there he was already disappearing into the darkness. I hurried after him as best I could, calling and calling, but he would not stop. It grew darker and darker until I could only feel my way, hearing the sound of him scrabbling ahead of me, and narrower and narrower, until I feared it would narrow so much that he would be able to pass, but I would not, and how then would I fetch him back? Then I saw there was a little light, a low thick fiery light, and I could see the shape of his head against it, and he had stopped quite still. There was a scraping, slithering sound, and the smell of meat and sulphur and hot stone. I came up behind him, and glimpsed a great clawed foot, and a vast shining tail that slid past us like a huge snake. He had found the passage to the dragon's nest! We could see an egg, quite close to us, though of course it rested within the circle of the dragon's tail.'

'What happened?'

'He froze,' the hairdresser said. 'Very fortunately for me. There is a difference between saying you will face a dragon, and steal its egg, and seeing a beast that is near as big as your town's feasting hall, with claws like longswords and fire in its throat, and taking an egg from its embrace. I pulled him back, and he came, silent. He made me pile rocks in front of the place, and swear to tell no-one. But I think he did not trust me, because he told his mother I had let him climb somewhere dangerous, and he had nearly fallen, and so soon after I was sold away.'

Caliest yawned.

'I have wearied you, my Lord. Forgive me. Lean on me, let me help you to your room.' She continued to speak quietly, as she guided him to bed, and turned out the lamp, but what she said sank away into the soft shadows.

#

Caliest woke to sunlight leaking through the shutters, tracing the intricacies of the courtyard vine on the wall. While his head ached a little, it felt clear, and alight with possibility.

He knew exactly what he had to do, to bring himself to the Emperor's notice, in a way that would establish him at the heart of the court, put Metifo's nose *thoroughly* out of joint, and also serve the Dominion! What could be better?

As soon as he had taken his morning's glass of watered wine, he summoned the hairdresser to his room. Idikraine, inevitably, sent one of her slave girls to hover about outside—really, did she believe he was going to bed this stolid barbarian? She must think very poorly of his taste. Aikash looked even less appealing in the chill morning light, with her stocky build and thick arms and oh, dear, she even had a scar, running from her brow into that tightly woven hair, how very unpleasant. But she was his key, so he could not help smiling at her.

'You will be coming with me on an important trip I am taking,' he said. 'I require your knowledge.'

'My lord?'

'We will be passing very close to Binasa. I will have the train stopped, and you will go through the passage you spoke of, and get me a dragon's egg as a gift for the Emperor.' He wagged his finger at her. 'But you are not to mention this, not to anyone, you understand?'

'An egg?' She dropped to her knees. 'But my Lord, the dragons...they would kill anyone they found in the nest! We only escaped because they did not know we were there!'

'If some barbarian boy managed it I'm sure it can be done.'

'I beg you, my Lord, don't ask this of me! I am only a hairdresser!'

Caliest began to feel irritated. 'You are a slave of my household, and I may ask of you anything I wish. I tell you what. If you succeed, I will consider giving you your freedom, and even some money. Perhaps you can set up a little business, hmm? Dress the ladies' hair, but get paid, eh? Won't that be nice? Now, the train leaves in three days. Make whatever preparations you need. And you, girl, listening at the door, send your mistress to me, and keep your mouth shut about this, or you'll be beaten until your spine shows, you understand?'

The girl gasped out an incoherent apology, and ran away.

Caliest dismissed the hairdresser, who stumbled to her feet and out of the room as though she had been hit on the head. He worried for a moment that she would attempt to run away, but with that scar she would be easy enough to track down if she did anything so disloyal and foolish. Nevertheless, he would tell the steward not to let her leave the house.

Moments later, Idikraine appeared.

'You sent for me, Lord Husband?' She kept her eyes cast down.

'What did that silly girl tell you?'

'Only that you had sent for me. She was shaking, and seemed quite frightened. I hope she will not break something.'

'If she does, sell her. I am going to take your hairdresser with me on the *Dominion's Envoy.*'

'May I ask why, Lord Husband?' She kept her eyes down, but he could *feel* her thoughts sliding towards his bald patch.

'No, you may not,' he snapped. Then he relented. If it wasn't for her vanity, he would never have had this great opportunity, after all! 'I have a plan,' he said. 'It will be of great advantage to us, and soon you will have such splendid gowns and so many slaves that you may lord it over Falini

Benideth to your heart's content. Perhaps she will be begging to borrow *your* hairdresser, hmm? Rest assured, my dear, your Lord Husband knows what he is about.'

'Of course!' Idikraine said. 'How could I doubt it?'

He patted her shoulder as he left the room. He felt too full of pleasure and excitement to stay in the house, and decided to head to his favourite wine-shop. On his way out he saw the pallid little messenger-boy again, the one whose ear he had grabbed, but at least this time the boy stayed out of Caliest's way as he raced off. No doubt to waste time throwing dice or chattering to girls instead of doing whatever errand he was supposed to be about.

#

Caliest scowled down at the map on the table. The black train track, the blue line of the coast, the garrison town of Endaklion clearly marked. Binasa was a tiny smudge in comparison, it had taken him a long time, running his finger along the track, to even spot the wretched place. It was tucked close under the cliffs. There was nothing nearby. How was he to get the train to stop, without arousing interest or suspicion?

He clapped his hands, and told the slave who appeared, 'Fetch my wife's hairdresser to me. She has some native drink I like, Inkat or some such. Tell her to bring me some.' After all, it had helped him think the last time.

Aikash arrived shortly after, with a flask, poured him a glass, and turned to go.

'Stay, I need you. When you lived at Binasa, did you see the trains?'

'Yes, Lord. My master's son liked to watch them.'

'Is there a station?'

'No, my Lord. There is a place with a platform, not far from the town where the train takes on water, but no station.'

'How long does it stop for water?'

'Perhaps half an hour, no more. Longer, once, but that was because the train was not working.'

'I suppose that will not be sufficient, if you must clamber about looking for the egg.'

'Lord...I beg...'

'Don't.' He shook his finger at her. 'My mind is quite made up. How long will it take you?'

'My Lord...even if I should succeed...'

'How long?'

She slumped. 'To climb from the station to the caves, perhaps two hours. To fetch the egg...I do not...'

'Come, come, you've been there before.'

'Yes, Lord. If I am very lucky, and very quick, only a little time. Coming back down will be faster. In all, I would say perhaps one should allow five hours?'

'That seems a ridiculously long time.'

'If my Lord were to send someone else, perhaps find someone from the village, a young boy...'

'They would not know the way, since your master's son told you to close it up. Now. Is there any other reason the train might stop?'

'If it broke down. And I did once see someone run up with a parcel, when the train was stopped for water.'

'A parcel.'

'Yes, Lord. It must have been for someone very important, normally they did not do so.'

'Hmm.'

'Perhaps some great lord, or official?'

'Perhaps.' He reached for his glass. All this planning was making his head ache.

'Surely if we took someone else, Lord, perhaps one of the housemen—or someone who would be able to fight? Perhaps your friend Lord Metifo could provide someone from the navy? I could show them the way...'

'No. Absolutely not.' He could not afford to risk anyone of influence getting wind of his magnificent plan, and perhaps forestalling him. *Especially* Metifo.

'Lord, the egg...'

'Yes, yes, the egg.'

'How will it be kept safe? What if it breaks?'

'Well, get a box, and fill it with straw or something.'

'And others, on the train, my Lord? What if they ask questions? What should I say it is?'

Caliest rolled his eyes. Still, she had a point. Soldiers, especially soldiers guarding money, were likely to be suspicious creatures. 'Tell them...tell them...oh, really, must I do *everything* myself? Think, woman.'

'If the train is stopped...could it be something for the train? Some magic to make it go again?'

'Magic! Hah. Magic indeed. Go away now, I need to plan.'

'Yes, Lord.' She bowed and shuffled out of the room, her shoulders slumped. What pitiful creatures these barbarians were.

#

'I need to speak with the driver of the *Dominion's Envoy*,' Caliest said.

'Lord?' The station master frowned. His robes, in the green-gold of the railway, made him look altogether too tall

59

and broad-shouldered, and were surely more elaborate than he should be wearing in his position. 'May I ask...'

'You may not. It is a matter of the Dominion's interests,' Caliest said. 'Have him fetched.'

'He is not here, Lord, he is driving the *Emperor's Pride*. But he will be back within the hour, if your Lordship would care to wait...' The station master gestured at the cracked leather chaise in one corner of his cluttered office.

Caliest regarded it with distaste. 'I will wait at the wine shop across the street. Send him to me the moment he arrives.'

How tired he was of dealing with all these grubby little bureaucrats! The wine-shop, at least, was pleasant and had a tolerable list, though there was still no Ilian Ruby.

The driver, a skinny, weary looking fellow, hovered in the doorway of the wine-shop until Caliest noticed his besmut-ted uniform and waved him in. Irritatingly, he bore the neck-tattoo of a freedman, which meant he would require slightly more careful handling than a slave.

'I apologise for coming in all my dirt, Lord,' the driver said, 'but I was told you wanted to see me immediately.'

'Yes, quite right. Sit, sit. Waiter, get this man a glass of ordinary. And fetch me another of the Lostrian.'

'My Lord is most generous,' the driver said, 'but I may not—I have to drive again in an hour, and it is against the rules to drink.'

'Oh, one glass will not hurt! If anyone gives you trouble about it tell them to speak to me.'

'My Lord.'

'Now,' Caliest said, once the waiter had left. 'Do you know who I am?'

'Of course, Lord. You are the Chief Defender of the Dominion's Transport. The Station Master informed me.' The man toyed with his glass, nervously.

He probably wasn't used to being noticed by such an important person. Caliest smiled. 'And you are the fine fellow who will be driving the *Dominion's Envoy* on her maiden trip. Don't worry, you're not in any trouble! In fact, you can do yourself a great deal of good by simply doing as you are told.'

Caliest hesitated for a moment. The fellows who ran the trains placed a great deal of unnecessary importance on the exact times that things happened. It would not do for the Defender of the Dominion's Transport to seem entirely ignorant of the way things worked. 'I understand this may cause some inconvenience,' he said, 'but if anyone asks, afterward, you are to tell them it was a direct order from the highest authority, you understand?'

'My Lord?'

'I need you to hold the train at the watering stop near Binasa, while my slave picks up a delivery there. It may take a few hours. No more than five.'

'Five *hours*, my Lord?' The man went pale under his dirt. 'But...my Lord...the timetables will have to be changed...'

'No. This is highly confidential, and no-one must know of it beforehand. Just stop the train.'

'But how will I explain...?'

Yet again, Caliest had to do all the thinking and work for other people. 'It is a maiden trip. Surely, sometimes, a new engine will suffer troubles? You are a smart fellow, or they wouldn't let you drive such an important and expensive engine, would they? Come up with something.'

'My Lord...the soldiers...'

Caliest leaned forward, confidingly. 'You will tell them the parcel is some part you need for the train, to make it go

61

again. There are those...' he tapped his nose, 'who plot against the Dominion. You will be working to uphold the Dominion's interests, and even its safety.' That, after all, was entirely true. If the Emperor had his own dragon, what could be better for the Dominion? 'There may be some sort of medal, or citation, from the Emperor himself, if all goes smoothly.' He leaned back, with some relief. The driver smelled strongly of coal and sweat. 'Oh, and, of course,' he tossed a clinking bag onto the table. 'A compensation, a *generous* compensation, for your troubles.'

The driver looked at the bag but did not touch it.

'I am sure I need not say,' Caliest went on, '*failure* to comply with the order of a high-ranking official such as myself could have...serious consequences. *Very* serious. A manumission can be reversed, under the right circumstances.'

The driver's hand rose, briefly, towards his neck-tattoo. 'Yes, Lord. Of course, Lord. What should I tell the station master?'

'Tell him I was checking that all was well before the engine's first trip, of course. And remember. *Total discretion.* No one must know of this. Serious consequences, you understand? For the Dominion, *and* for you.'

'Yes, my Lord.'

'Good man.' Caliest drank the last of his wine, paid, and left the driver still staring at his untouched glass.

\#

The day of departure came. The station was noisy and full of smelly steam, though quiet around the *Dominion's Envoy*. A pity, cheering crowds and a proper send-off would have been much more suitable.

Caliest strolled up to the engine and nodded at the driver, who ducked his head as though trying to avoid a blow. 'Is all prepared?'

'Yes, my Lord.' The driver glanced around, though in all the noise and fuss of the great iron-bound boxes being loaded onto the cars, the soldiers in their blue and scarlet tramping heavily after them, and the hiss and roar of the engine, it was impossible that anyone could overhear them. 'Just as we discussed.'

'Good, good.'

Caliest moved back to his place. A slave held up a little pot of sacred oil. Caliest dipped the brush carefully into the heavily scented stuff, leaned forward and stroked a streak of oil onto the side of the engine. 'I name this engine the *Dominion's Envoy*. May the gods look favourably on all her voyages!' *Especially this one.* There was not even any applause from the surrounding soldiers. Steam puffed past his face and a smut got in his eye.

At least the car set aside for him was comfortable. The furniture bolted to the floor was of rare, fine-grained woods, the seats and bed fatly cushioned, the windows curtained with silk. It was all in the Dominion colours, of course; Caliest thought he might get tired of blue and scarlet before the journey was over.

He had dispensed with any slaves other than Aikash. He was quite capable of dressing himself, and should he require any assistance, Aikash could provide it. She had turned up in a plain gown, unflatteringly bulky about the hips. She hardly did him much credit, he hoped no-one would think she was his mistress.

He settled himself onto a couch as the train lurched forward. The hairdresser stood hunched in a corner, clutching her hands together. 'Sit down,' Caliest said. 'You're making me nervous looking at you. Wait, where's the box?' Oh, no, he couldn't believe it. That his beautiful plan should be ruined at this late stage!

'I gave it to the driver, Lord.'

'What, why?'

'So he may give it back to me to fetch the magic in, Lord? Was that not right?'

'Oh, I suppose so. Hmph. I hope you did not gossip with him about my business.'

'No, Lord.'

'Good. Now sit.'

She sat on a plain wooden bench, clutching at the seat.

Caliest leaned back and gave himself up to happy contemplation of the future.

#

Looking out at the passing countryside soon palled. One hill or field or scatter of buildings was much like another.

Unpleasant doubts and fears began to sneak into Caliest's mind. He glanced at Aikash, gripping the seat with white-knuckled hands. What if she got too frightened to do her part? If only she had been a man! The story about the boy could be a lie. Perhaps she had dragged him away, in terror.

Maybe the whole thing was a lie, and she planned to use the stop to escape! But she could not possibly have known he would come up with such an excellent idea.

Besides, she was a *hairdresser*. What would she do, run away and live in the woods? Dress the wolves' hair? Caliest snorted to himself. As easy to imagine Idikraine running off and fending for herself. Still, he felt unsettled.

'Lord? You look a little pale. Are you quite well?'

'Fetch me some wine.'

'Perhaps if you are feeling uneasy, *dinkait* would suit you better?'

'Oh, that stuff. Yes, why not?' She still seemed tense herself, he thought, eyeing her. Couldn't have her turning rabbit at the last minute. 'Why don't you take a little yourself. Calm your nerves.'

'My Lord is most generous.'

She poured them each a measure, and after a few sips he felt a great deal better. 'Must order some more of this, when we get back.'

'Yes, Lord.' She glanced out of the window. 'Oh, we are nearly there!'

Then the whistle blew, and a slave in the green-gold uniform of the railway knocked on the door of the carriage. 'I am to inform your Lordship that we will shortly pause at Binasa to take on water. The driver also says that there is a little trouble with the engine, which may cause some slight delay, and hopes that this will not cause too great an inconvenience.'

Caliest waved him off. 'Yes, yes, I'm sure the driver knows his business.'

Moments later, the train jolted to a halt. Caliest ran to the window like a child, but could see only a little platform with no-one upon it, a path leading off it winding up into the rocky hills, and...'Oh! Is that a dragon?' He peered up at the wheeling silhouette.

'I think it is only an eagle, my Lord.'

'Oh. Well, then, get to it!'

'Just a moment,' she said. There was something odd about her tone that made Caliest bristle. She sounded almost... *authoritative.*

'What?'

'Someone is coming,' she said. At that moment one of the railway slaves appeared, bowing, at the compartment door. 'My Lord Deapa, the driver says your slave is a local woman? He asks if he might borrow her to fetch a part for the train, being as she knows the area?'

'Oh,' Caliest said. 'Oh, of course. Right, well, off you go then.'

She stepped out, and the railway slave handed her the box. 'He says you will know where to go?'

'Yes,' Aikash said. 'I...' She glanced over her shoulder at Caliest.

'Go on then,' Caliest said. 'Fetch me...I mean fetch the driver the thing he needs!'

'Yes, Lord.' He watched her move away, disappearing swiftly into the trees at the base of the cliff.

It was very quiet, without the rattle of the train, though the engine kept puffing and steaming. Caliest, after straining his eyes at the cliffs for what felt like at least an hour, opened the door and stepped down onto the tiny, crumbling platform. Up towards the engine he could see a couple of soldiers, brilliant flashes of Dominion blue and scarlet. What were they doing? He hoped they weren't making a nuisance of themselves with the driver. He hurried along the platform.

The two soldiers were grim, tired-looking men, scruffy about the jaws, and close to, those uniforms were on the worn side. Disgraceful. What sort of impression did that give? 'I am Caliest Deapa, Chief Defender of the Dominion's Dragons.' *Gods dammit.* 'I mean, Transport. Where is your Commander?'

'He's speaking with the driver, my Lord. Seems this delay might go on a while.'

Caliest peered around them. He could see the Commander's back, the driver waving his hands and shaking his head. 'I say!' Caliest said. 'I say, Commander!'

The Commander turned. An older man, whose face immediately assumed a kind of shuttered look. 'My Lord?'

Caliest found himself a little tongue-tied. 'Just wanted to say...don't worry about the delay. Not the slightest inconvenience. Sure it will be sorted out soon.'

'Yes, my Lord. Don't you worry yourself.' The Commander himself, however, did not meet Caliest's eye for long, instead scanning the cliffs and frowning.

'I'm not worried. Just saying. Chance for us all to have a break, stretch our legs, yes?'

'Don't get too far from the train, my Lord, if you go to... stretch your legs. Might be some trouble from the locals.'

'Oh, no, no. Anyway, got to wait for my slave. Mustn't go without her, my wife would never forgive me!' Caliest felt his grin stretch unnaturally over teeth that felt suddenly too dry.

The Commander was still scanning the hills. 'I'd have sent some men with her, if this driver had waited a moment instead of sending her off all in a rush. Hope she hurries.'

'My dear fellow, have you *ever* known a woman who could hurry? We'll be lucky if she doesn't stop to try on a new gown!'

The Commander flashed a brief, unwilling grin. One of the soldiers snorted. 'It all seems quiet,' the Commander said. 'How we looking there, driver?'

'We're doing our best, Commander, my Lord,' the driver said, glancing at the other man in the cab, who was even more smut-smeared than himself, and held some sort of tool in his hand as though he didn't know what to do with it. 'Just got to wait for that part.'

'Good, good.'

Caliest wandered back down to his own carriage, and poured himself another shot of *dinkait*. Some of it seemed to have spilled on the floor, there was a purple splotch. Perhaps

Aikash's hands had been shaking. Where *was* the woman? She had had plenty of time, surely? What if it had gone wrong? What if she had fallen down the cliff, or been loud and clumsy and the dragons had caught her? What if...normally the *dinkait* soothed, but now as he sipped his nerves got worse and worse. A bird shrieking in the sky made him jump. A soldier's shout—what was that? Oh, it was a laugh, were they laughing at *him*? They wouldn't dare...where *was* she?

He stared out of the window, considered going up the path after her, but what if she came back a different way, and he missed her? What if they went off without him, leaving him in the wilderness, and her, with his precious egg, to perhaps sell it, or give it to someone else, like Metifo! His eyes hurt from watching. He looked down and realised he had spilled some of the wretched *dinkait* on his good robe. Why had she given him the stuff, it wasn't calming his nerves at all, and now his robe was stained.

He looked up, and...*there.*

She was hurrying down the path. She had the box in her arms.

Caliest opened the door, gesturing wildly.

But instead of bringing it to him she took it to the engine. Of course, the driver. She had to pretend to take some magic nonsense to the driver, but she had better bring it back. Who cared what the soldiery thought at that point, the deed was done. All he had to do was keep it safe until he could give it to the Emperor. His egg, his wonderful egg! He clutched his arms around himself and giggled. Well, who could blame a man for being excited?

Moments later Aikash was at the door, and for the only time in his life, Caliest Deapa opened a door for a slave. She scrambled into the carriage with the box, and he slammed the door behind her as the engine began to huff and churn and the train lurched once more into motion.

'You have it.'

'Yes, Lord.'

'It's in there.'

'Yes, Lord.'

'Let's see it.'

She opened the box and there it was, a pale grey egg about the size of an infant, nestled in straw and faintly shimmering. For the first time another thought snuck up on him. What if...it was just a thought, of course. But if so many of the tribes truly believed that one who tamed a dragon was the gods-determined ruler...well...Emperor Caliest had a certain ring, did it not?

'I should close it, my Lord, or it will get too cold.'

'Yes, yes.'

She closed the box, wedged it under the bench, and sat down. Caliest could not take his eyes off the box, just visible behind the hem of her robe and her solid ankles.

'No one saw it?'

'No, Lord.'

She seemed quite calm, now her part was done, glancing casually out of the window. Caliest found her stolidity remarkable. Of course, barbarian natures were crude and insensitive, even the women, but he felt vaguely disappointed that she did not seem to share in his excitement.

'You look weary, My Lord.'

'Yes, yes I am. Very stressful, all this.'

'Of course. Perhaps you should rest.'

He laid himself on the couch, and closed his eyes. The swaying of the train was remarkably soothing.

#

Caliest woke. Aikash stood in the middle of the carriage, the box at her feet. The egg was cracked! 'What happened? Oh you stupid, careless...'

He hadn't even seen her move, but somehow there was a sword at his throat.

'Wh...' Where had she even *got* a sword?

The crack widened. A claw appeared, then a beaked snout.

'It's hatching!'

'Yes,' Aikash said. 'She is.'

'But...it's my egg! Stop it hatching!'

'Can't.'

'Do as I tell you!'

'Really? Have you noticed the sword?'

'If you're planning to run away the soldiers will catch you!'

Aikash glanced out of the window. 'The soldiers are going to be otherwise occupied. See, that little one there...' the dragonet had now poked its entire head out of the egg. It was a pale silvery blue. 'She's a queen. The next queen. And they'll be coming for her.'

The dragonet opened its jaw and let out a high piercing yawp somewhere between a hawk's cry and a mating cat's yowl.

'But...a queen? What does that mean? Who's coming for her?'

Aikash moved back, still keeping the sword aimed at him, sheltering the box and the dragonet between her feet, and clutching the window frame with one hand.

The train's brakes shrieked. A dreadful lurch jolted Caliest right off the couch and slammed him bruisingly onto the floor. 'Ow!' He scrabbled upright. The train was not moving. 'What's going on? Why has the train stopped?'

'I imagine there must be something on the track. See, if you take an egg from the nest, it starts to cool. If it's old enough, when it cools, it hatches. And if it's a queen, and she's been taken from the nest, well, the nest comes looking for her. And if you've spent months teaching the dragons that Dominion colours mean threat, and damage, and danger, and their new baby queen is surrounded by people wearing Dominion colours...it's all going to get a little *lively.*'

'How do you know all this?'

'I wasn't enslaved by the Beliori. I *am* Beliori. We've lived close quarters with the dragons for generations. We know them quite well.'

'But *why*?' Caliest wailed. 'Why did you have to take my dragon?'

'She's not yours. Gods, you really are thick, aren't you?'

'You're kidnapping me! You're kidnapping me for ransom!' Oh, he should never have taken this post. But surely people would pay, the Emperor...He was an important official...

'You?' She laughed. 'I don't care if you live or die.'

The air darkened, and thundered. There were yells and terrible piercing shrieks, and pounding feet. Aikash opened the door.

'Wait, where are you going?'

He looked back. The baby dragon was staggering across the floor towards him, yawping. For a moment he wondered if he could still somehow retrieve this. Aikash didn't care about him, perhaps he could pick the dragonet up and run into the woods...

A shadow wheeled over the carriage. Caliest looked out of the door. There was a drop below him, a grassy bank, and above him, the air was full of dragons. They were huge, impossibly huge, and *loud,* and clawed and furious, stinking of sulphur and heat, and he was standing between them and their baby queen.

He dropped through the door, landing badly. His ankle twisted under him and spilled him the rest of the way down the bank.

He lay on his back for a moment, winded, then scrambled to his feet. The screaming was dreadful. Further up the train, the soldiers had all tumbled—or been torn—out of their carriages and the dragons were ripping them to shreds, flaming those they didn't catch. He saw a man—perhaps the Commander—caught up into the air and bitten nearly in two.

None of them had come to check on *him.* No-one cared about *his* safety.

Two dragons descended on his carriage, and began ripping the roof off. They had brilliantly patterned underwings, as the young man at the party had described. And apparently these were the *smaller* ones.

What if they smelled him, or something? What if they thought *he* was responsible? None of this was his fault, but you couldn't explain that to a dragon!

He scrabbled to his feet—his ankle hurt—and began to hobble away, towards the trees, glancing back every now and again to see if the dragons had noticed him.

They were gathering around the wreck of his carriage, cooing at the baby queen as she stretched out her still-wet wings, and wobbled up into the air.

They took off, in a great whir and stink, the little queen a pale blue smudge in their midst.

Further up the line, people were descending on the train. Had they come to rescue him? But they seemed to be barbarians, and there was that treacherous wretch, Aikash, in their midst, directing them. He could see figures in the green and gold uniforms of the railway disappearing into the distance—the cowards!

The barbarians were finishing off the few soldiers that remained, and hauling out boxes and crates...oh. The money. The Dominion money that Caliest had been, at least nominally, in charge of seeing safely to its destination.

Caliest backed away towards the forest. He just had to stay out of everyone's way for a little. He was sure, eventually, he would come up with some plan, to get home, and tell everyone how it wasn't his fault, it was that wretched barbarian! She was behind it all! She had wormed her way into his house—and it wasn't even him who had hired her, it was Idikraine, his wife. How had she let herself be so deceived? He would never let her hire another slave, that was certain.

He would come up with a plan that would put him back in the Emperor's favour. Somehow. He would find a way to explain it all.

#

Meanwhile, in the garrison at Endaklion, the soldiers, hungry and ragged, fingered the hilts of their cheap swords and eyed their commanders.

#

Back in the Discovia district, Idikraine Deapa counted over the money she had squirrelled away from the household accounts over the years, and decided she had enough to, perhaps, take that trip out of the city she had been planning. To her family's old farm, far away from all the unsettling rumours about a barbarian uprising. Besides, it would be a relief not to have to fuss about her hair and her gowns every day. If Caliest wanted her, he could always send for her.

#

In the hills above Binasa, the gold began its journey to a village here, a town there, a group of rebels hiding in the woods elsewhere, and Aikash and her fellow Beliori lifted their cups in a toast to the new Dragon Queen. And in the months that followed, a new tale arose among the children of the tribe, about a ragged madman that haunted the train tracks, claiming to anyone who would listen that he was really a man of great importance, and wailing about the cold, and the wet, and the terrible unfairness of everything.

A HUMAN RESPONSE

By
Dolly Garland

Everyone was rushing to find a hiding place. All our megacities—the ones that the prime minister promised would bring India in line with the first world countries— were being abandoned as people hurried for the wilderness. As if the trees and the mountains could hide them from the spaceships that promised annihilation.

I looked up at the looming grey vessels, casting shadows over the high-rise buildings. There was nowhere to run. We had a day. Just one day.

But that was enough for my mission.

I had to kill my mother.

I kept moving eastward. Abandoned vehicles littered the streets. It looked like an ordinary Ahmedabad traffic jam, except there were no horns beeping, no one shouting. Already the streets were largely devoid of the living. It was only by their absence that I noticed them: no fresh animal excrement, no sweaty humans jostling for space, no exhaust fumes, no street vendors selling roasted peanuts, or chai-wal-lahs serving endless cups of cutting-tea. But there were still looters, fanatics who refused to give up their homes, and several others with their own reasons. Like me.

As had happened for centuries, in the two days since we had learned about our imminent destruction, it was the survival of the fittest.

The weak and the disabled were the first to be abandoned.

Pets were next.

Babies were protected, because we humans are unable to let go of our own genetic validation.

I wondered where the abandoned people and animals were as I walked briskly through the empty streets. There was no point appropriating a vehicle until I got away from the blocked roads.

The years of military training my dad had put me through taught me to stay focused on the mission. That was the first job of a soldier. Stay focused on the now. Assess the threat. There was no time to be overwhelmed about my imminent demise. We all die eventually.

As I entered Navarangpura district, two men coming my way looked at each other. I noticed them eyeing me and my backpack, likely thinking that a lone woman was an easy mark. Their clothes were torn but were once of a decent quality. One of them was short and bulky, with a goatee that was meant to be stylish, but looked out of place on his dirty face. His cheek was swollen from a recent punch. The other was a bit taller, about my height, with thick, curly hair.

Probably robbed recently, now looking to return the favour.

I took the knife out from the inside of my leather jacket, pressed the button on the hilt so the switchblade shot out. I wasn't concerned about my safety, but I really didn't want to harm them.

We were about five feet apart.

They circled me.

Goatee reached out to grab my bag; I ducked and pivoted out of his way.

He stumbled, clutching air.

Curly had quicker reflexes. He shoved me hard. I kicked out as I fell, swiping his ankle with my leg. He landed on his ass with a grunt. Goatee tried to pull the backpack off me, but I was already on my feet, brandishing the knife.

'Just leave,' I said. 'You are not going to win.'

Goatee seemed to consider this, watching the knife in my hand. But Curly had a glint of desperation in his eyes. He didn't yet deem me a threat.

Assess the enemy. Don't waste more energy than you need to. Sometimes that means attacking first.

Dad's words.

I slashed Curly's upper arm. Only a flesh wound, but the blood was enough to shock them both. Before either could react, I grabbed a fistful of Goatee's hair, and pressed my knife against his throat. 'Now, are you going to walk away, or do I need to show you how easily I can kill you?'

'We didn't mean any harm,' Curly said, panic rushing his words, as he backed away slowly with his hands up in the air.

Goatee was literally whimpering. I shoved him towards his friend. 'Sure, you were just chatting me up.'

'Someone stole our things,' Goatee whined.

I adjusted the backpack on my shoulders and sighed. 'Look overhead, you idiots. If any of us survive the next day, then you can worry about getting supplies.'

#

After I was through the worst of the roadblocks, I picked up a Hero Honda motorbike with a full tank. In most other places, a motorbike wouldn't be stuck in traffic. But this was India. Our traffic is different, where even motorbikes jostle for space nose to tail. So many vehicles were abandoned with keys still in them. I had plenty of choices. Not that the lack of a key would have made a difference.

I passed an occasional moped or a bike, a couple of small teams of police and the military, looking like they were going somewhere with a purpose. Though what purpose they could possibly have at this point except for standing around and pointing to the sky, I didn't know. There was an eerie calm on the streets that reminded me of war zones.

Half the roads were blocked with debris from riots mixed with genuine accidents. Here and there, I saw dead bodies. In the normal days, no one would have abandoned their dead, for the fear of bad karmic consequences, of souls not resting at peace...but now, people were only focused on surviving. Good karma was optional.

I made my way to the inner city, which used to be a fortress back in the Mughal Empire days. It had the distinct character of an old city, with narrow roads, older buildings, once grand city gates now looking like they were just plonked in the middle of the road. I used to come here with Dad for the famous Raipur bhajiyas. Dad and I would wait in line for freshly fried bhajiyas, fafda and chutney. It wasn't a regular event because my dad hadn't been a regular dad, but whenever it happened it felt like a special treat.

Now, the Raipur Bhajiya House's shutters were down. Some of the shops hadn't even done that. With others, it was obvious that their shutters had been broken. Looting had started pretty much at the same time as the panic. If we had ever wondered how humanity would fare in the face of impending doom, we had our answer. Same as any other time. Without much grace or honour as far as the collective was concerned, regardless of what Bollywood movies would have us believe.

I was riding slowly through the carnage left behind by the recent riots.

A burned down bus blocked half the road, along with more smashed, half-burned vehicles. Broken bottles, debris from destroyed things that no longer resembled their original form, bits of paper, left behind personal belongings, ripped clothing...all pointing to the obvious; that even against threat from others, humanity still lashed out against their own.

Suddenly, I felt my spidey sense kick in. I didn't see or hear them, but I knew there were people around.

More than one.

I continued as if I hadn't noticed anything. I was already looking for exit routes, playing different scenarios in my head. How would this situation go? There were two main routes to get to Maninagar. I could go a more roundabout way through backroads but that would only take me down more streets which were dodgy at the best of times. So I decided to stick with my plan.

I turned slightly left at the traffic lights which were still working, but just like normal times—almost meaningless. Once I was half-way down the road, with no turns left, a crowd of people, maybe ten or fifteen of them, emerged in front of me, swinging sticks, a skillet even. Most of them were men, but there were a couple of women there too. I looked through the rearview mirror, deciding if I should make a quick turn but there were more coming from behind me.

This was clearly a planned strategy. And it looked too well-rehearsed for me to have been the first target.

I made a split-second decision. I pulled the gun out of the holster and fired a shot towards the gang in front of me.

They weren't expecting a gun. They screamed and scattered a little, but didn't completely back away. It was enough for me. Keeping the gun in one hand, I accelerated towards them at full speed, not stopping even when I hit someone. A man grabbed the back of my bike, but I had momentum and managed to break free. They lobbed things at my back; a stick narrowly missed my head and hit my shoulder, causing the bike to swerve but I regained control and kept going.

I decided to stick with my original plan of going through Kankaria rather than Khokra so I would have wider roads and more options if there were more looters around.

Kankaria Lake—one of the main attractions in the city that was lively each morning with joggers and fitness enthusiasts and laughter clubs, and in the evenings with families visiting various attractions, almost a permanent fair, with a tourist train, balloon sellers, stalls lined with street food and games—was deserted, but signs of destruction were all around it. The lake was built in the 1400s with Nagina Vadi—a little island of green—at its centre. It used to be a place of leisure for the Sultans, and a popular tourist and recreational site in the modern times. I used to come here to feed the fish as a child. Now, I saw fragments of clothes in the lake—I wasn't sure if it was a body.

More burned vehicles. The Hanuman temple that had been there for as long as I remember was defaced.

I was getting closer to my destination.

It took much longer than it should have to get to Maninagar, in the eastern part of Ahmedabad, but at long last I pulled up outside my mother's childhood home.

I dismounted, left the keys in the bike since there was no shortage of vehicles. I remembered this house from my early childhood, but my memory from all the surveillance photos and videos was much sharper. Dad had kept an eye on it over the years. The house hadn't changed: two storeys tall, solid stone, flat roof structure, quite ordinary from the outside. It was detached, with its own courtyard walls that separated it from other similar houses on the street. The other houses, however, didn't have the surveillance equipment that my mother's house had.

I didn't see security cameras, but I knew my approach was already noted. If my mother was here, security wouldn't be shoddy.

I walked up to the front door, slowly measuring my surroundings, looking for exit points. There didn't seem to be any. The solid stone walls didn't make for easy escape routes. The windows, as was normal in the city, were covered with strong iron grills.

I stared at the door. There was no point procrastinating. I made sure my holster was hidden beneath my jacket, knowing it wouldn't get past Mother's security. But you had to make it look like you were trying.

Taking a deep breath, I pressed the doorbell. Through the iron lattice work in the front gate, I could see the veranda, which was mostly taken up by a large white swing. My mother used to sit there with my grandparents on balmy evenings. I remembered her talking about it.

It didn't take long for a servant to arrive. A girl, no more than thirteen or fourteen, dressed in black salwar-kameez that looked like a uniform. She didn't seem scared. She was calm. Too calm, as if it was just any other day.

The girl unlocked the door. No questions. Merely curiosity. That meant she'd already been ordered to let me in.

'Take off your shoes, please.'

'Are you serious?' I blurted, looking at her with wonder. Did she not understand what was happening?

'Yes. Please take off your shoes,' she repeated, locking the gate behind me as I stepped inside.

There were alien ships about to destroy us. The world was in utter shit. And I'd just been ordered to remove my shoes.

I sighed and started loosening the laces of my leather boots. Oh yes, my mother was definitely here.

#

The photos lining the walls were enough of a clue that this was the same home I had spent my early summers in. One photo of me was as recent as last year. I hadn't seen my mother for almost fifteen years, yet she had my photos.

That didn't surprise me.

But I felt a pang—quickly suppressed—for all the years I had spent without a mother. Even when she'd been around, my parents had spent most of their time together arguing or having intense conversations that excluded everyone else. We had never been a family. I was just a byproduct of their relationship, and far less than either of them. I had neither their vision, nor their intelligence. I was trained to fight and follow orders.

I followed the girl through wide corridors, interspersed with larger rooms filled with people. They sat, staring at dozens of screens, monitoring the city as well as the spaceships. Mother had the surveillance thing going on all fronts. No one was idle. And curiously, no one looked panicked. That did surprise me. Whatever my mother was paying them, surely no amount of money could compensate for the literal end-of-the-world.

As we got closer to what used to be my grandfather's study, I was annoyed to feel my heart beat faster. Even though my palms weren't sweaty, I felt the urge to wipe them on my jeans.

DOLLY GARLAND

The servant girl knocked on the study door, which was wide open; she motioned for me to go in, and without a second glance walked off in the opposite direction.

Mother sat behind what used to be Grandfather's desk, her hands on her temples, eyes closed. Her eyelids were flickering as if she was dreaming. I wondered if she was meditating.

Dressed in salwar-kameez with a Nehru collar, which took its inspiration and name from the clothing style of a former Indian Prime Minister, she looked just the way I remembered her. There were a few wrinkles beneath her eyes and a few strands of grey in her hair, but she certainly didn't look fifteen years older.

It occurred to me how strange it was to focus on her looks at this moment. Even without the aliens overhead, I was seeing my mother after a decade and a half. I should have had a more emotional response. But this was the cost of extensive training and control. Even as my mind, through psych training, recognised what reactions this scenario should trigger, my internal wiring prevented me from generating any of these expected emotions.

Mother opened her eyes. She was looking at me. Also not displaying a normal, human response. She was measuring me. Or perhaps waiting.

I stood silently. The gun felt heavy. No one had stripped me of it. I wondered if my mother knew why I was here. This was the day my father had prepared me for. A part of me had never believed it would happen.

It's not easy to believe that your mother is the mastermind behind an imminent alien attack.

At least not until the aliens actually show up.

I pulled the gun from its holster, unlocked the safety, and aimed at my mother's face.

She smiled. 'Can you really do it, Leena?'

I had seen enough action movies to know that when you start talking about your plans and wait for explanations at times like this, something invariably goes wrong.

So I pulled the trigger.

Something still went wrong.

#

I tried to open my eyes, screwed them shut again as the light blinded me. The ringing in my ears was giving me a headache. I pressed my fingers into each ear and shook my head to ward off the dizziness. Bad idea.

'Take a deep breath.'

My mother's voice. That was enough to snap me out of shock. I still felt sick and the noise was seriously pissing me off. Or perhaps anger was a psychological response, a way to avoid the real issue.

How in the world could I hear my mother's voice when I'd just shot her at a point-blank-range?

Something had gone wrong the moment I pressed the trigger.

I remembered being engulfed in light. Feeling as if I was floating. Then nothing but the humming noise that filled my ears, the very interior of my brain. Screams, which might have been mine, or someone else's. Maybe the aliens had attacked. But here I was, lying down, listening to my mother.

'I know you can hear me, Leena,' Mother said. 'The soundwaves have been regulated. They won't hurt anymore. And the shutters are down to protect against the light.'

I noticed then that the loud voices were gone.

My training took over. Assess your surroundings so you can decide your options. I accepted the fear. Fear was inevitable. But giving into it was a choice. Besides, I'd known the world was ending. What else was there to be afraid of?

My eyes felt like they had been glued shut and I needed to pry them open with the force of my facial muscles.

Mother was leaning over me. At such proximity, I noticed how similar our faces were. Same straight nose. A slight dimple in the left cheek. My eyes were the exact same shade of brown. She looked unchanged. And completely undamaged from the shot.

She reached out and brushed a strand of hair away from my face.

I flinched.

I couldn't remember the last time we touched or expressed affection in any way. I didn't know why she was doing it.

I looked around, but all I saw was a plain, circular room with seamless white walls. The flow of air and the way our words echoed made me think the walls were some sort of reinforced metal. The structure of the room seemed too slick, too smooth.

Were we on a shuttle?

Assess. Then decide.

I was lying on a white chaise lounge plucked straight out of a modern interior design catalogue. I sat up, fighting an unexpected bout of nausea.

'Where are we? How did we get here?'

'We are in one of the alien ships, orbiting over Gujarat,' Mother said. She was standing over me.

I looked at her. My mouth opened and closed, like a fish. No words came.

'Have a look.'

Mother walked over to one of the walls, pressed a button. It slid open, revealing a massive glass panel. Beyond it, pitch blackness. I stood up, though my knees wobbled, and I felt dizzy. I walked over to the glass panel and stood next to her. The last time we stood like this, I was several inches shorter than her. Now we were about the same height. I could have tried to kill her with my bare hands. I was certainly capable. But I looked out and it didn't matter anymore.

Earth, the blue-green blip of a planet, so brilliantly depicted in sci-fi shows and documentaries, was exactly as I had pictured it. With its oceans and greenery, bright and colourful against the black expanse of space. It was a view I had never expected to see. It was humbling, exhilarating. Sublime.

I pressed my hands to the glass, my nose almost touching the wall that separated me from the vastness of space. There was a tightness in my chest. Feelings I couldn't name.

'Do you know why you shot me?' Mother asked, bringing me back to the reality of where I was. She sounded sad.

I kept my eyes on the Earth, though I could see my mother's reflection in the glass like a cold moon in its orbit. The Earth...it was so weird. I had heard all my life people going on about climate change, saving the planet, pollution etc. But I guess I had never truly grasped the 'planet' part. Now, looking at it from the outside, I finally understood. When I visited the Himalayas for the first time, I realised what 'majestic beauty' truly meant. As I stood there, amongst the giant peaks of the Earth, cold and ecstatic, I learned that some things are beyond words. Beyond photos and videos. The vastness of the mountains made me feel tiny and insignificant but in a life-affirming, humbling way.

Looking at Earth now was that, but a hundred times more.

And now it would all end.

'You're responsible for this.' It came out as an accusation.

I hadn't meant to do that. I had meant to sound more businesslike. But training couldn't always control emotions. I was good, but not infallible.

'Dad told me what you were up to. When he died, he left me all the evidence. You spearheaded the project that brought the aliens here. You still act as their intermediary. I didn't put all the pieces together until the spaceships showed up.'

I didn't tell her that at first I hadn't believed Dad.

I had run away, using the very skills he had taught me, to escape the truth. I hadn't spoken to him for over a year. I had done many things during that time that I wasn't proud of and some that I was—all because I didn't want my mother to be even more of a stranger than she already was.

Mother's reflection tilted her head to one side. I remembered that habit from my childhood. Looking as if she was going to give you her complete attention.

'And you think if I die, they'll go away?' There was genuine curiosity in her tone, but the sadness lingered in her eyes.

'I don't know. Maybe they will. You've clearly played a big part in this. At the very least, they won't have their inside person.'

She tutted. 'We taught you better, Leena. If it was that simple, why didn't your father just kill me? Or have me killed. He had enough resources at his disposal.'

'He couldn't get to you. He tried. And failed.' I titled my head, mirroring her.

'Did you know Ranjit and I were equals when we played chess?' Mother asked, surprising me. 'You could never tell who was going to win. That's what made it so exciting to play with him.'

'Is this a game to you?'

'All I'm saying is that I admired your father's ability to anticipate my moves. But there was one thing he could not anticipate because it was beyond even his imagination.'

Our conversation was interrupted by a loud beeping noise. It sounded like an evacuation alarm. Except that my mother didn't look concerned. She glanced at the Cartier Tank on her wrist. 'It's time.'

Dread settled in the pit of my stomach. I continued to watch her through her reflection. 'Time for what?'

'Reckoning.'

Two bolts of white light beamed down through the empty space around the Earth. They crossed the planet from opposite ends. An explosion of light. There was no sound, but I felt the vibrations through the ship.

Then, nothing.

The Earth was still there. Just as it always had been.

'What was that? What happened?'

I must have closed my eyes because when I opened them again, the person looking at me from the mirror was wearing the same clothes as my mother and looked about the same, but she wasn't the same.

Instead of my mother, I was looking at an alien. Humanoid, but not human. There were ridges across her forehead. Her ears were smaller, pointier. She had a second thumb on each hand. I didn't know what other differences were hidden beneath her clothes, but what I saw was enough to feel nothing but a slippery surface, with no footing and nothing to hold onto.

I was on a spaceship. Something had happened to the Earth. My mother was an alien.

These three facts went beyond anything I was trained for.

'You are one of them?' It wasn't a question, considering what was standing in front of me.

'Yes, and so are you. At least half of you.'

'So Dad was human?'

'Yes.'

'But I'm not...different.'

'We have medical procedures that make sure that the child only inherits selective DNA. Our physiology is similar enough to humans that it wasn't that tricky. You still have some of my DNA but you are mostly human.'

'Did Dad know?'

'No. Only certain high level government officials know about us, and they weren't going to tell anyone the truth. We are not the aliens, Leena. They were the aliens. This was our planet. Our home. Then the humans arrived, tricked our people with their sweet words and offers of friendship. They stole the planet from us, then they tried to eliminate our entire race, so we wouldn't be a threat.'

I heard the words, but nothing made sense. 'Humans evolved here. We have centuries of scientific evidence. What about the apes, and Darwin, and that we've no space travel capabilities? We only went to the Moon, and nothing came of that.'

'That's because the people in charge didn't want to go beyond that. The space programme is a front to keep the population happy and satisfied that the human race is striving to reach the stars because most humans don't know their own history. But the leaders do,' Mother said, her face flushed...as if she was human. Her eyes sparkled with more passion than I had ever seen. Or perhaps it was anger. 'Humans cannot go further into space because they've made a lot of enemies. They looted, pillaged and tricked other worlds, and when they finally couldn't get away with it any longer, they found Earth and hid there. They have been here for two thousand years. The rest is a lie.'

She almost spat that last word.

'It's a pretty big thing to lie about,' I said, just for the sake of saying something because her words were creating fissures in my head, shaking up everything I knew, not just about myself or my own life, but literally everything.

'The early settlers did a pretty good job of covering their own traces. They pretended to be less technologically advanced than they were, and they charted a different course for their race. They would have succeeded if they'd managed to commit genocide like they had planned. But some of our people escaped on the very spaceships that the humans had brought with them.'

The fissures in my brain were getting bigger. It was good she looked different, because she was different. I didn't know how to associate this emotional, passionate person...was she a person?...with my pragmatic, efficient mother.

'We've been refugees ever since, trying to survive on the charity of other planets. It's taken us centuries to gather enough resources to return. We're not as blessed as the humans in terms of populating our race. It's been hard and hostile, and if our race is to survive and thrive, we need a home of our own. We need our planet back.

Even as I was struggling to comprehend, I tried to stick to facts and logic. 'But if it's been centuries, how do you know what you've been told is true? Maybe you've been brainwashed by your people.'

'We are genetically wired to hold on to the knowledge and history of our race. In each generation there are a handful of people whose brains retain all of our history. I'm one of them. I remember everything: all the horrors and atrocities committed against my people. I've known it all since the moment I was born. That was another loss we had to bear to hide here—miss out on a generation of children who could remember our past.'

'How have you not gone crazy then? Or perhaps you have.'

Mother's reflection smiled, and it looked more like her.

'The knowledge comes gradually as our cranial lobes grow. My people have ways to teach us to handle the weight of the history we carry. But even then, it was hard. Especially when I was younger. I did things I am not proud of. I fought wars I didn't need to fight. It took a while to keep the rage under control.'

I felt hollow in the pit of my stomach; my chest tightened more. Perhaps we weren't so different after all. I swallowed, pushed away the emotions.

'But you had parents on Earth. I remember them. You had a whole life.'

'I was adopted. I had a whole life, yes, because we needed to be sure that our attempt would succeed. There would be no second chances, so I was placed here to be a part of the world and learn everything. I can maintain the psychic connection to my people and feed them information. Your father found out that part. I realised through my life here that humans would never share this planet with us as equals. Either we would be their servants, or we would perpetually be at war.'

Finally, I asked. 'What have you done?'

Mother looked at me with sorrow in her eyes, but her voice did not waver. 'The biological weapon was fine-tuned enough that it should have only killed humans. There might be some other casualties amongst mammals, but no other animal or plant life would be affected. Earth will be inhospitable to us and humans for at least a year, until the poison completely clears from the atmosphere. But then we'll be home.'

'You killed billions of people who didn't even know what their ancestors had done. How is that different from what the humans did?'

91

'We can argue about the philosophy of it. It's not different, but also it is, because we wouldn't have had to do this if the humans hadn't done what they did. The reality is, it is about survival. This wasn't revenge. This was reckoning. And it was long overdue.'

This was the mother I remembered. Businesslike. Doing what had to be done. Always.

'Then why keep me? I'm half-human. I will always think of myself as human. What if I decided to avenge my race?'

'You're not the only one, Leena. There are others who are safe. Unlike the humans, we didn't want to commit genocide. You and other half-humans will be an equal part of our society because we don't want to erase the last 2000 years.'

I didn't know what to say. How do you process this kind of information? That your planet has been attacked by aliens, most humans are dead, your mother is an alien whose people were cheated by humans who were the real aliens, and now you and other half-humans are on spaceships on your way to be a part of an alien-human society. Thinking about it, it even sounds absurd. I wanted to feel the loss, the bleakness of what had just happened, but I couldn't even grasp it.

I am not very philosophical. I'm an army brat. I just do what's asked of me, and get on with the next task. But what do you do when there are no tangible actions to hide behind and all you've got to do is think existential thoughts, not just for yourself but for your whole race?

I finally turned to look at her. 'Do you have alcohol on this ship?'

Mother nodded.

She returned with a bottle of whisky and two glasses. Mortlach 25 year old. We sat there by the glass panel, watching Earth, and drinking.

The day of reckoning had happened. But if even our fake history was anything to go by, it was rarely the end of the cycle. Most often, it was just the beginning.

We moved towards a new reckoning.

MORE TROUBLE THAN SHE'S WORTH?

By
Cheryl Morgan

'There, that should do it. She'll be good as new after a little practice.'

Doctor Marpesia peeled off her surgical gloves and began the process of shutting down the equipment, leaving the patient to Tanais. It took a while for the anaesthetic to wear off, but soon Myrina opened her eyes and took in her surroundings. There was no question where she was. None of my other living quarters are so sparsely decorated, so wedded to an aesthetic of white and chrome.

I like the chrome in the sick bay, but am not convinced by the white. My crew have odd taste at times. I, by the way, am *Sagaris*, an Artemis Class cruiser of the Queen's Amazon Navy, General Thomys commanding.

This is not my story, though, so back to my crew.

Tanais moved into her patient's eyeline. 'How are you feeling?'

'Sick bay, huh? What have I done to myself?'

'Left arm taken off at the elbow. Whoever he was made a real mess of it. Doc's had to give you a prosthetic. Sorry.'

'Did I get the bastard?'

'Apparently so. Does that help?'

Myrina tried to raise her left arm. I saw well-honed muscles flexing beneath her olive skin. Tidy for a human. Belatedly she realised she was still strapped down for surgery and tried to raise her head to see.

'I can feel my fingers, but I'm not sure they're moving when I tell them to. I guess I'll need a bit of physio. Right's still working fine though, and that's all I need to paint a new kill mark on my helmet. Did I get any others? I can't remember a thing.'

Tanais shook her head sadly. A rarity among my crew, she is unable to understand where the thirst for killing comes from. It is a game to girls like Myrina, with their short, angular hair and skin inked to show the units they had served in, the battles they had fought. Killing is a game to me too, but I'm not as soft and squishy as a human, and much faster. Much as I tried to protect my crew, the game often got them killed. The pretty dyed-ash-blonde on the bed had a good chance of ending up as a pretty corpse before she hit 30. Tanais began unstrapping the girl.

'I'm sure that someone in your squad will have kept a tally. And yes, you'll need physio. Probably quite a lot if you want to be safe in battle.'

'There'll be time though, right? The General reckoned that Ionian ship was carrying something valuable. And if we're all still alive that means we captured her. With any luck we'll all be rich.'

Myrina grinned, and Tanais couldn't help but smile back. 'I understand that we have their cargo intact, including a number of prisoners for ransom.'

'*Yes!* Oww! Sorry nurse, shouldn't have done that. I promise to celebrate quietly until that arm is properly healed.'

'You'd better. It's not just the stitches you can see. There are lot of internal connections to the prosthetic you could rupture if you are not careful with it for a few days.'

'Yes nurse. Hey, do you think we've made enough for a year off? It's been five years since most of us have been able to breed. I bet you're itching to get back to your proper job, and Sinope has been ridiculously broody for the past few months.'

Tanais said nothing. Her brown eyes filled with tears. After a few seconds Myrina caught on and hers did too. Like I said, pretty corpses are a fact of life, or rather death, amongst my crew.

'Sinope bought it? Aw shit! This damn gig had better have been worth it then. Any others?'

'Five in total. No one else in your squad. Whatever was on that Ionian ship was well guarded. The General says there will be a formal ceremony tonight. She wanted to wait for you to be clear of surgery before we held it.'

Myrina nodded, grateful. She was sat up on the bed by now. Tanais give her a motherly hug and let the girl give vent to her tears.

#

The Sick Bay door irised open and a young ensign with starched uniform and ramrod-straight back strode in.

'Colonel Marpesia, ma'am?'

The doctor, who was just finishing cleaning up after her work, turned to the newcomer.

'What is it, ensign?'

'General's orders, ma'am. I'm to escort you both to the guest quarters.'

'Is that necessary?' Marpesia glanced over at her patient. 'Corporal Myrina has only just woken after surgery.'

'Not the corporal, ma'am. You and Nurse Tanais. It's the prisoners.'

Suddenly the doctor was all business. 'Is there a medical emergency? Will we need any specialist equipment?'

'Not an emergency just yet, ma'am. But it appears that we have captured an Ionian princess, and she's heavily pregnant. Likely to drop any day now, by the look of her.'

'Well,' said Marpesia, 'that *will* be interesting. Come along, Tanais, it appears that we have work for you.'

#

The ensign had been right, the Ionian woman was at least eight months gone. That, however, was by no means the most obvious thing about her. There was the long, white chiton, so impractical in zero gee but de rigeur for Ionian women everywhere, so legend had it. There was her pale skin, as if she had never been groundside on a planet, and her waist-length black hair so tightly oiled and waved its true length must have brushed her calves if left natural. Her face was immaculately painted, a rarity on fighting ships. And there was the jewellery. The woman was dripping in gold and gemstones. She was a princess, and she bore herself like one. Every inch of her pose, every facial expression, oozed command. Her entourage of maids watched her every move, ready to rush to do her bidding.

Marpesia had been left in charge. I haven't often seen the General irritated, but it was clear from her heart rate and skin hue she had been at the end of her tether with the prisoner and needed to calm down before she said something undiplomatic. I would just have vapourised someone, but the General keeps telling me that not all problems can be solved by extreme violence. Wiser in the ways of humans than me, she let the Doctor handle the rest of the conversation.

'Rest assured, Your Highness,' Marpesia soothed, inhaling deeply, 'our full hospital services will be at your disposal. While the *Sagaris* is mainly a military ship, we are an all-female crew. Childbirth is by no means uncommon on board. We even have a specialist midwife among the crew.'

The prisoner turned her imperious gaze upon Tanais.

'What is that creature?'

'Our midwife, Your Highness. As I think you have noticed, Nurse Tanais is an Enarees. We find them...'

'I thought has much,' snapped the Princess. 'Are you aware, Doctor, that it is contrary to Ionian law for a man to observe me in my current condition, let alone lay his hands upon me? That man's life is forfeit. Have him killed, *now*!'

#

Scuttlebutt among my crew has it that in their youth the General and the Doctor had been a couple. Senior officers, of course, are not supposed to have affairs with crew under their command, so if any flame had once burned it was now kept well hidden from everyone except me, and I don't tell tales on my commander. What keeps the scuttlebutt going is that whenever the General needs a sounding board, it is the Doctor she turns to. Thus it was that, later that day, Marpesia found herself summoned to the General's quarters for dinner.

'Well, that went well,' said the General, in a tone normally reserved for a particularly badly botched training exercise.

'Oh, I think we'll get there. This isn't the first awkward patient Tanais has had to deal with. We'll need to wean Miss High & Mighty off some of her ridiculous ideas about biological essentialism, but eventually I'm sure she'll see sense. When it comes down to it, having assisted with over a thousand live births is far better experience than having performed one. Ionians are supposed to be famed for their rationality, right?'

'That's the story that they like to put about, but Princess Prejudice is not top of my problem list right now.'

'Ah. Have we perhaps bitten off more than we can chew?'

'Possibly. Most of the time King Scylas is happy to go with plausible deniability. Behind the scenes he might get a little shouty, but the Queen will back us up and he's not going to risk an open row unless things get serious.'

Marpesia nodded. Most of the time my crew and I don't really care what our King says or does. Piracy is a way of life for us. As long as we don't accidentally provoke a war we can do what we want. Men, the crew tell me, have two main uses: making babies and providing extra troops in emergencies. The rest of the time they can be safely ignored. Personally I would add 'target practice' to that list of uses but, as I've noted, the General tells me I need more training in diplomacy.

'But you think it might get serious, Thomys, otherwise you wouldn't have invited me here. What's on your mind?'

'Well to start with, our prisoner is not just any princess. She's one of Theseus's wives.'

Marpesia pulled a sour face. 'The way that Ionians enslave their women into *matrimony*', she almost spat that word, 'is

99

bad enough. That the powerful among them should take many women captive in that way is just...just...Words fail me.'

The General let her fume for a while, then casually raised an eyebrow.

'If you are concerned about the birth, I've done enough tests to be confident that both mother and baby will be fine. Even if there is a last minute hitch, which I don't think is likely, the worst that she'll suffer is a scar on her belly. The child looks very healthy.'

'You know I have complete faith in you and your team, Marpesia. Our problem is elsewhere.'

This time it was Marpesia's turn to raise an eyebrow. She sat back, cradling her wine glass thoughtfully.

'Comms has detected some unusual emissions signatures back where we originally encountered the Ionian. Whatever it is appears to be heading this way, fast. Best guess is that it's a Dorian battle cruiser.'

'Bumfuck', said the doctor, using a word that did triple duty as an expletive, a description of the habits of Dorian soldiers, and a term for the preferred Dorian method of birth control. Marpesia has often said that she doesn't understand the Dorian fetishization of enduring discomfort, but at least they treat their women with respect the rest of the time, which is more than you can say for the Ionians.

'Exactly,' said Thomys. 'A bumfuck it most certainly is'.

'Can we outrun him?' Unlike everyone else in the galaxy, the Dorians gender their ships male. They even build them long and cylindrical, as if aerodynamics matter in deep space. It is a joke among my crew that Dorian ships can only fire forward, but even the Dorians are not that stupid. They have plenty of side-mounted weapons as well. And they are fast, very fast, which makes them honourable opponents.

'Unlikely. We are probably going to have to engage. Obviously I have battle plans for such an eventuality, but they involve...manoeuvres.'

'Ah, high G manoeuvres? And that's why you wanted to talk to me?'

The General nodded. 'Very high G.'

'That would certainly put my patient at risk. We'd have to turn off the artificial gravity on the ship. I remember last time *Sargaris* was hunting another ship at speed. It took weeks to remove the smell of vomit.'

I got him though, didn't I?, I thought proudly to myself. You can't scrag a target without wobbling a few crew stomachs. A little non-fatal discomfort does the little ones good.

'So it says in Regulations, but I wanted to confirm with you in person, just in case. Before taking action.'

'What action can we take?'

'There's a deep space rogue planet not far away. We have a supply base on it. I can plot a flight path close enough to it without looking suspicious. A shuttle is small enough to give us a good chance of cloaking it. I'll send a squad with you, and Tanais of course. We'll be back for you as soon as we've dealt with the dickship. And if we are not, you'll be good for six months which should be plenty of time for a rescue.'

'If we have to endure that stuck-up cow for that long,' muttered Marpesia, 'one of us is liable to kill her.'

\#

The rogue planet, without a star to warm it, was little more than a dark sphere of frozen rock. 'If you didn't know it was there,' the shuttle pilot had said, cheerfully, 'you'd never know it was there.'

Fortunately it did boast large amount of ice, both water and methane. Even more remarkably, there were substantial deposits of uranium, which were being used to power a small nuclear reactor. The general had sent an engineer down with the landing party, just in case, but everything appeared to be in working order and she was now busying herself going through all of the automated test reports in the hope of finding something she would need to take apart and reassemble. I had downloaded a small avatar of myself into the shuttle's tiny brain to keep an eye on what was happening. What follows is what I remember of the action there after I had re-integrated the avatar's memory into my main data repositories.

The base was entirely underground, which helped keep the heat in. There being no natural light, it was in many ways just like being on the ship, but there was a lot more room and a rather less military aesthetic to the decor. Someone had decided to decorate the interior with images of fields and forests to make it feel more like 'home'. If I was to expresses a preference, it would be for the clean white and chrome of the sickbay, rather than images of bovines on hills.

Myrina had been declared 'walking wounded' and was sent with the landing party rather than getting to fight the Dorians. With Sinope dead and three new kills to her name from the capture of the Ionian ship, she'd been promoted to sergeant and was now in charge of her squad, which should have cheered her up, but if her suit monitors were functioning correctly only made her nervous. Of course, being infantry the chances of them ever getting to board the Dorian cruiser were slim. The space battle was much more likely to end in one or other of us exploding in a massive fireball long before we got within a few klicks of each other. At least down here on the planet she had something to do.

The Princess, predictably, was not happy with her new surroundings. Lack of space on the shuttle had meant she'd only been able to bring her wet nurse, Khloris, from her throng of servants. She was not hesitant about letting Marpesia know her feelings.

'Why, exactly, are we being marooned on this gods-forsaken rock millions of light years from civilization?'

'Well to start with, Your Highness, there is steady natural gravity, which should make the birthing process much easier for you than if you'd remained on *Sagaris* in the midst of a space battle. In addition, as all of our bases are constructed with women's needs in mind, there is a variety of birthing equipment available for you to choose from. More, in fact, than you would have had on the ship. Do you have any preference? Water birth? A chair?'

For once the Princess looked less than confident. 'I'm not sure I understand your meaning?'

'How do women give birth in Ionia, then?' asked Tanais.

'Why, in a bed, of course.'

'No one had thought that other methods might be more effective, and place less stress on the mother?' Marpesia made a good show of sounding astounded, though I had heard her and Tanais planning this conversation as part of their strategy to handle their difficult patient.

'I'm sure that the method we use is the most effective, given that our doctors are the best in the galaxy.'

'You don't allow women to become doctors, though, do you?' said Marpesia. 'In Ionia women can only be nurses or midwives. They can't set medical policy. So although your births might only be attended by women, they are required to use techniques designed by men.'

'Goodness me,' added Tanais, 'next you'll be telling me that you don't use anaesthetic.'

103

'Don't be ridiculous,' snapped the Princess. 'We are not Dorians!'

'Thank goodness for that,' said Marpesia. 'Tanais, would you be so good as to talk our patient through the various options available? When she has made her choice we can start making preparations. My guess is that we'll see some action in a day or so.'

#

Myrina's stress indicators suggested she was finding command difficult. I made the assumption that her life had been much easier when Sinope made all of the decisions, and all she had to do was kill people. I felt for her. I'm much happier when I'm left to kill other ships and the General takes care of making sure I shoot at the right targets. I noted that Myrina consulted Regulations on her helmet display rather a lot, but at least the General wasn't there to see her struggle. I would keep her secrets to myself unless she messed up.

Colonel Marpesia was the ranking officer on the expedition, but she was busy with Princess Prejudice and had left everything else to Myrina. That included making good use of Merope, the engineer, and Nemerte, the shuttle pilot, both of whom would not normally have fallen under her command, and neither of whom seemed to have any understanding of infantry tactics. At least they could both shoot, with an acceptable margin of inaccuracy.

Myrina had left Creusa, her comms specialist, getting to grips with the impressive array of instrumentation in the base. Much of it was scientific, left there by astrophysicists who never seem to miss an opportunity to collect more data. There was, however, sufficient instrumentation to allow them to keep track of my ship body and the pursuing Dorian cruiser. 'At least that way,' Marpseia commented dryly, 'we'll know if we need to send out a distress signal.' Such little faith in me, Doctor!

'That's all set up, then,' said Creusa. 'They should be within shooting range in about twenty hours. I'll let you know as soon as one of them lights up.'

'And a general scan of the local area, please Creusa?'

'Is that necessary, Sarge? We're in the arse end of the back of beyond here.'

'It says so in Regulations, Private, and Hades take me if I'm going to fail to follow Regs on my first mission in command. Unless the Colonel says otherwise, we do everything by the book. It's better than being bored, right?'

Creusa sighed and set to work again. Code scrolled up screens, and she was soon fully absorbed in the task. I helped as much as I could, but I was finding the local systems very slow. Myrina, more comfortable servicing a laser rifle than a sensor array, stalked off to see what was happening with the prisoner.

#

On her way to the hospital—it was far too large and sophisticated to be called a mere sick bay—Myrina chatted to me about tactics. The base was much bigger than anyone had expected. My maps were years out of date and the engineering robots left to tend the base had been busy extending it since the last human visit. Was it in their orders, Myrina asked, or had they just got bored being stuck out here alone? Boredom, I assured her, is endemic among us digital folk.

Myrina's team didn't have enough troops to construct a viable perimeter if we came under assault. They could probably defend the hospital, but that would mean sacrificing other parts of the base, most importantly the communications centre and the reactor, neither of which they could survive for long without. I got to work running some simulations as best I could on the local hardware, while Myrina headed on to the birthing suite.

'Thank goodness for signage,' she commented along the way. 'These corridors are all alike. It's a labyrinth in here; I'd need that proverbial ball of twine to find my way out again.' That gave me an idea.

Tanais was in the process of explaining the birthing pool when Myrina arrived. 'Ah, here's an expert on the subject. The sergeant here has only birthed one child, but she did it in a pool and it all went swimmingly, so to speak. Isn't that right, Myrina?'

'Easy as anything, Nurse. You just lie back in the nice, warm water. Get whatever aromatherapy treatments you want added, and let yourself be pampered by the midwife. I'd love to do it again.'

'I don't think that's entirely appropriate,' snapped the Princess.

'Well the pampering is entirely optional,' said Tanais. 'Or I could ask one of our soldiers to do it. We train them all in massage therapy. You never know when they are going to get stuck in a firefight unable to exercise properly.'

'That isn't quite what I meant.' For once the Princess looked somewhat shamefaced.

No further information was forthcoming, so Tanais decided to ask. 'What did you mean, Your Highness?'

The Princess looked down at her extended belly. Carefully not making eye contact with anyone, she muttered, 'I can't swim.'

Tanais considered the depth of the birthing pool, which had more in common with a bath than anything you might swim in. Then again, then patient needed to be happy and relaxed. 'No pool then,' she said.

'Oh, well in that case,' said Myrina cheerfully, 'why not go for the chair? That's what the General uses, and she's had six kids. Being sat up there sounds right up your street, Ma'am, if you don't mind me saying so.'

Tanais flashed a warning look at Myrina, but for once the Princess did not seem to mind.

'The chair it is, then,' she said. 'And I have a question for you, Sergeant.'

'Yes ma'am?'

'What happens to your babies once you have birthed them?'

'We get a year to raise them. Some women choose to leave service at that point and work in childcare instead, but many of us are career soldiers and if the kid is a boy he'll be given over to the men to raise soon enough anyway. I chose to leave my daughter in care. She'll be better looked after by professionals than I ever could. But I visit when I can. Judging from what I've seen so far, in 12 years time I'll be proudly watching her graduate from military academy.'

'That seems...rational,' said the Princess. I had learned to recognise that statement as high praise from the Ionian woman. 'You do care for your children, then?'

'Of course we do!'

'Good. I had heard tell that you were more...mannish in your attitudes.'

'I can assure you, Your Highness, that your child will be entirely safe with us,' said Tanais.

'Will you swear that to me, in Hera's name?'

'Yes Ma'am, of course. Is there some risk of which we are unaware?'

The Princess drew herself up, having let her usual rigid posture lapse somewhat in planetary gravity thanks to her condition. She coughed.

'I have informed you, Nurse Tanais, that it is taboo for one such as yourself to observe me in this condition. Even more so for you to lay hands upon me. I have permitted these outrages because, in our current circumstances, it is the only way to guarantee the safety of my child. My husband may not be so forgiving. If he learns of the circumstances of the child's birth, he may order it killed.'

'*What?*' Marpesia stood in the doorway, having just returned from the mess hall where she had been organising a menu plan for her patient.

'That's barbaric!' said Tanais and Myrina in unison.

'It is the Law,' said the Princess. 'Men's Law, anyway, to which I am subject. Tell them, Khloris.'

The little wet nurse, whom Myrina had likened to a pet mouse, so silent had she been since her mistress was captured, piped up.

'It is true, my ladies. We must obey the dictates of our Lords. My own child was a girl and deemed surplus to requirements. King Theseus had her killed so there should be plenty of milk for his own child. A royal child is more valued, even if female, but Theseus would not hesitate to have one killed if he thought his Law had been transgressed. After all, he has plenty more, and is still virile.'

The effort of speaking, and being forced to remember her personal tragedy, brought Khloris to tears. Tanais wrapped her arms around the girl in a motherly hug. The Princess took up the story.

'It was convenient, in a way, that so few of my entourage could accompany me to this planet. Some of my servants are spies for Theseus, but Khloris is loyal. She will swear that only she and Doctor Marpesia assisted me with the birth. If you Amazons are defenders of the rights of women, as you claim, you will swear to me by Hera, Queen of the Gods and Protector of Mothers, to support my story and keep my child safe.'

'You have our word,' said the Doctor.

'You poor dear, of course!' said Tanais.

'Go Team Hera!' said Myrina, punching the air with her good arm.

'Thank you, on my own behalf, and on behalf of the life within me.' The Princess seemed suddenly tired, as if a great burden she carried had just been put down.

'Sit, please, Your Highness,' said Tanais. 'You will need all of your strength soon enough.'

'And we will support you in that as well,' said Marpesia.

An alert bleeped in Myrina's helmet and she gestured to receive the call.

'Er, Colonel, Ma'am, I think we have bigger problems than that right now. That was Creusa. We have incoming.'

#

'They'll come in on the main landing strip because it's about the only place flat enough to do so,' said Myrina to Marpesia. 'Sadly we don't have artillery covering it, though they may airdrop a few troops first on a flypast to check that out. Our own shuttle is safely underground so they can't disable it from the air.'

'We don't have enough troops to hold the base.' She gestured at the map displayed in the communications centre. 'We can, however, confuse them. This place is a rabbit warren of corridors. I have Creusa reprogramming the signage.

They'll catch on eventually, but before they do we should be able to lure them into an ambush or two. Here. And here.

'If it is a standard Dorian shuttle there will be twelve men on board. There might be fewer as they are notoriously overconfident when fighting us. Our ship was smaller. We have only seven fighters, including Merope and Nemerte who aren't combat specialists, and Creusa who will be busy managing comms. The Princess and Khloris can't fight, and Tanais may be busy by then. Anyway, she can't shoot straight to save her life.

'So we hit them hard in the ambushes. With any luck we can even up the numbers. We put the reactor in shutdown so it protects itself with the blast doors. I have turned off all power to the shuttle hanger in the hope that they won't find it. That means we only have this room, and the hospital, to defend. We have two days of battery power. Do you have any suggestions, Ma'am?'

'You have far more combat experience than I do, Sergeant,' said Marpesia. 'I defer to your judgement in these matters.'

No one thought to ask my opinion, though to be fair, once I had given her the idea, Myrina filled in all the detail herself. Her stress indicators were abnormally high, but I had confidence in her. Besides, hobbled as I was, I was not going to be much help.

#

'Breathe deeply, and push again when you have your strength back,' said Tanais. The Princess was applying the same steely dignity to giving birth that she seemed to apply to everything else in her life. Tanais and I have seen veteran soldiers reduced to gibbering wrecks at this point

110

in the process, yet the Princess was as calm and poised as always, despite the occasional sound of blaster fire from elsewhere on the base.

'Tell me, Tanais,' said the Princess, 'what made you become a midwife? Is that part of being Enarees?'

'Traditionally, yes. We Enarees have been involved in medicine since time immemorial. But tradition is all about stereotypes, is it not? Real people don't fit into neat little boxes. Yes, good. A few more like that and you'll be done. Khloris, can you dampen that cloth again, please? Your mistress is working hard.'

'So if you are not a stereotype, what are you? I had met none of your people save diplomats until recently. You seem so much more, well, traditionally feminine, than most of your...ahhhhh...excuse me...your colleagues.'

'I'm a woman, Your Highness. A woman unlucky enough to have been born without the ability to bear children of her own, but who loves babies so much that she wanted to help other women make them. Good, good. Almost there now.'

'And how does that fit in Amazon society? Isn't the fact that we Ionian women devote our lives to raising families the reason why your people look down on mine? Shouldn't you be a soldier, like young Myrina?'

#

The solider in question was busy watching her plan unfold. The Dorians had landed a full complement of twelve space marines, all armed to the teeth. We'd taken two in an ambush at the entrance to the base, but now the Dorians were inside it was harder to keep the corralled. The plan involved spreading out to draw them away from the comms room and hospital, but it inevitably risked the enemy chasing one group down with overwhelming numbers.

Plus the Dorians seemed perfectly happy to bring the entire base down on their heads if that was necessary. Burying your opponents in rubble was safer than engaging in combat. One on one, my crew was more than a match for any man.

#

There was the sound of an explosion from somewhere nearby. Khloris squeaked.

'Concentrate, everyone, please,' said Tanais. 'Baby first, battle later. And no, Your Highness, Amazon women don't have to be soldiers. We can be anything we want: doctors, engineers, lawyers, shopkeepers, childminders. All of these things are valid. We are soldiers first and foremost to allow us to be those things. Our histories say that had we not been soldiers our menfolk would have enslaved us as we believe yours have done to you.'

'In defence of my sisters, I hold that we are far less servile than you Amazons believe. Our battles are fought in other ways, and with other weapons. Oooff! And sometimes we fight the same ones, in the same ways.'

'And are no less brave, Your Highness. One more push, please.'

#

Crouched behind a pile of rubble, Myrina was weighing options. She had two kills to her name now, but her prosthetic arm was starting to give her trouble which made using a rifle difficult. She'd kept Merope and Nemerte with her to protect them, but the Dorians were pressing her uncomfortably close to the hospital. Time to take some risks. Breaking cover, she laid down a broad pattern of fire.

#

There was a loud scream from somewhere close. The Princess screamed too.

'I'm not sure if that was one of us or one of them,' Tanais remarked conversationally. 'However, all our troops are equipped with plenty of these painkiller patches. They are very fast acting. If I place one just here…'

The Princess, who had been just about the scream again, opened her eyes in surprise.

'Another push, please, Your Majesty.'

#

Three down. Back in cover, Myrina consulted the tactical map Creusa was broadcasting. Three more Dorians in her section of corridor. There was a branch available so they could split up. She'd have to take the one leading to the hospital to have the best chance of keeping it safe. Merope and Nemerte could take the other. Then it was a matter of where those three Dorians chose to follow.

#

Now she had the painkillers, the Princess was back to her regal and rational self, though I could tell by now when it was natural and when forced, and so could Tanais. This was very forced.

'Given your experience, Tanais, is my experience normal?'

'You are doing very well, Your Majesty. I've seen people struggle much more. And the first birth is generally the hardest. You'll doubtless be expected to have more, but they will be easier.'

The Princess grimaced. Possibly she needed another painkiller patch.

Also the sounds of gunfire were getting closer.

'One of the things I have always admired about the Dorians is that, if one of their women dies in childbirth, they bury her with the same ceremony they give to a man who has died heroically in battle.'

Tanais shrugged. 'That's as maybe, Your Majesty, but as far as I'm concerned death, whether in battle or childbirth, should be seen as an avoidable disaster, not as a noble sacrifice. I've never yet lost a patient, and I don't propose to start now.'

Myrina crashed into the room, rolled twice and took up a position behind a bench covering the door. Her battle armour was covered in blood and blaster scars.

'Tanais, grab that pistol I left you and be ready to protect the Princess. Don't forget to take off the safety, and for the sake of all that's holy try to shoot a bit straighter than usual!.'

'I'm a bit busy right now,' said Tanais, 'and besides, my job is bringing life into the world, not killing people. Can't it wait?'

'*No!*' yelled Myrina.

Two men in red battle armour charged through the door. Myrina fired once, taking the lead man through the chest. The other was across the room before she could re-target. He smashed the rifle out of her hand and raised a vicious-looking electrosword.

Across the room, Khloris screamed and dived for cover. The Princess closed her eyes and pushed. The bright gleam of laser fire lit the room. Briefly my circuits were overloaded and I had a horrible instant of shutdown. It was over in seconds, but when I recovered my sensors, there was blood everywhere.

#

'Would you look at that?' said Myrina. 'Concealed laser cutter in my new prosthetic. Small but perfectly functional. Cut right through his throat guard.'

No one in the room was listening. The Princess, mission accomplished, had allowed herself to collapse with exhaustion. Tanais was dealing with the afterbirth. Khloris was still shaking with terror, but found enough courage to stand and hold out her arms for her new charge. The baby, a healthy looking child who would be assigned male by his parents, announced his arrival in the world with a blood-curdling scream.

When the smoke of battle had cleared, Myrina found that she had lost only one of her squad. Creusa had died at her post. I couldn't keep track of all the Dorians fast enough on the crappy base hardware so she had to help. When a fire fight broke out in the communications centre we were both distracted. I will have those engineering robots given orders to do something more useful than build housing in future.

#

Two days later my ship body was back. Yeah, I scragged the dickship. Mess of quarks everywhere. It's my job, and I take pride in it.

The General expressed surprise and approval at how cooperative her prisoner had become. Negotiating a ransom went very smoothly. The evening before the exchange was due she held a farewell dinner for the Princess. Marpesia, Tanais and Myrina were all invited. It was a very pleasant affair, for all concerned. The Princess proposed a toast to Creusa, then took off her necklace and asked the General to have it sent to Creusa's family.

After the meal, the Princess took Tanais aside.

'Thank you, again, Nurse. That was a birth experience I do not intend to repeat, but one I shall remember for the rest of my life.'

'Many women claim that they were in such pain that they remember nothing, Your Highness.'

'I remember more than you think, Tanais. When Myrina came into the room with those two Dorians on her heels she ordered you to take up a gun to defend me. You refused.'

'I did, Your Majesty.'

'But you moved. You put your own body between me and the door. You would not have shot anyone, but you would have given your own life to save mine, and that of my child.'

'I am a midwife, Your Highness. Saving mothers and babies is what I do.'

'I see that, and I see that the courage of Amazons is measured in ways other than their willingness to throw themselves into combat.'

'The courage of Ionian women is likewise measured in ways too numerous for any but the Gods to count, though those ways may be invisible much of the time.'

The Princess took Tanais by the hand and placed something small into it.

'My name is Lysistrata, and this is my token. Should you ever be in danger in Ionian territory, find a woman and show her this. I will aid you if I can.'

'Thank you, Your Highness, I am deeply honoured.'

Lysistrata drew herself up and, to the utter astonishment of Thomys and Marpesia, embraced Tanais. They did not hear what she whispered in the midwife's ear before she left, but I did.

'Fare you well, sister.'

CIVIL WAR

By
Juliet E. McKenna

'The king is dying.'

Whoever spoke didn't mean to be overheard. Unfortunately every other voice in the long servants' hall fell away at that moment. What had been a natural lull in the bustle of conversation during the midday meal became frozen, horrified silence.

'Who said that?' the Mistress of the Keys demanded with icy precision.

She rose from her chair at the head of the senior table. As she looked around, everyone seated along the low benches stared at their pewter plates. Not a single sideways glance betrayed the unfortunate speaker.

The Mistress of the Keys laughed, harsh and humourless. Easily half the assembled servants were startled into looking around, wide-eyed with alarm. Someone knocked over a beaker. It fell to the flagstones with a clang.

'Your loyalty to each other does you credit,' the Mistress of the Keys observed. 'I expect you to display equal devotion to Queen Heritha in this time of trial. If I hear there is so much as a whisper of such despair beyond these castle walls, I will be sorely displeased.'

Picking up her silver goblet, still half-full of ruby wine, she nodded at the Mistress of the Wardrobes.

As the Mistress of the Keys stalked out of the hall, statuesque in her black silk gown, her lean and sharp-eyed deputy took her place at the head of the table. She glanced at the great clock above the entrance, opposite the vast fireplace where smouldering logs warded off winter's chill.

The Mistress of the Wardrobes clapped her hands. 'You have seven minutes to finish eating and clear your tables.'

Maids and lackeys sprang to their feet. They carried their plates, beakers and dirty knives to the wooden tubs held by waiting scullions before hurrying away. Anyone who hadn't finished eating lost their chance to take anything more. Baskets of bread and platters of meat and roasted vegetables were whisked off the tables by kitchen porters. Only the most senior servants were still seated when the great clock struck the first half-hour of the afternoon. The Mistress of the Wardrobes stood and nodded to the Mistress of the Kitchens, and to the Masters of the Halls and of the Cellars. They rose and departed to their various duties.

The Mistress of the Keys hadn't gone far. She was watching through the narrow, angled aperture in the inner wall of the Chamberlain's Office. The Chamberlain could stand there and survey the servants' hall if he wished without being observed himself. Every scullion and maid of all work was warned on their very first day to assume he was watching them at meal times. He could also appear unexpectedly at any other time of the day or night, anywhere within the vast castle's encircling wall. So it was whispered, anyway.

'You didn't say what would happen if you were displeased,' he remarked, spearing a round of sausage with his knife and folding it inside a slice of bread. He had shed his black doublet with its gold embroidery and brass buttons, sitting comfortably in his shirt and breeches while he ate.

'I never make a threat I'm not prepared to carry out,' the Mistress of the Keys said drily. She drank the last of her wine and walked over to set the goblet down on the table. 'Word will spread, whatever I say. The vermin in the wain-scotting have doubtless smuggled out their notes. The best we can hope for is a few days' delay while those messages are passed from hand to hand to their masters and their ciphers decoded. It won't be long before the breeze blows this sad news along the city's streets and no one will be able to say where it came from.'

'It'll be a chilly breeze,' the Chamberlain said through his mouthful. 'People from highest to lowest will be shivering, even if only greybeards remember King Matil's bloody reign.'

'With the incomplete and confused memories of chil-dren, so their tales of those days will be all the more terri-fying.' The Mistress of the Keys helped herself to a spiced biscuit from a silver dish. 'As well as inaccurate.'

The Chamberlain heaved a sigh and tossed his knife onto his plate. 'Cassin has been a gracious and generous king. He doesn't deserve this.'

'Fate and twilight fevers have never respected rank.' The Mistress of the Keys shrugged. 'If they did, King Serlan would have succeeded to the throne while his loyal brother Duke Cassin now guarded the northern marches.

'I take it there's no chance Queen Heritha...?' The Cham-berlain didn't look hopeful.

The Mistress of the Keys shook her head. 'Alas, no.'

'This will throw the Councils of the Realm into turmoil.' The Chamberlain looked grim. 'At least our duties within these walls are clear. We had better do what we can to make ready for whatever is to come.'

'Indeed,' the Mistress of the Keys agreed. 'There is a great deal to be done. Please excuse me.'

#

'The king is dying.' The count smiled with vicious satisfaction. 'Without a son and heir, leaving only three useless daughters. Forgive me,' he added hastily. 'Daughters are undoubtedly a blessing in the general sense. I'm sure you will make good matches for your girls to secure their future comfort well before your cousin's son takes your place. You can offer him Zela's hand to splice the branches of your family together. But the king's situation is different.'

'Zela is my second daughter. Ireth is my eldest.' The count's sleepy-eyed companion lounged in a high-backed chair well supplied with cushions. 'Your man is sure of this? That the king's illness will be fatal, I mean.'

Count Forsel gazed across the gables and ridges of the capital's rooftops towards the distant castle's towers. The early dusk was deepening, but he had dismissed the maid who had come to close the brocade curtains at these windows. 'He has not left his chamber for nigh on twenty days. Serlan pissed and puked himself to death in less than ten. Of course, apart from the queen, only the king's doctor and his apothecary are admitted to the royal chambers. The physic-slingers don't say a word, but no one can hide fouled linens and endless chamber pots being carried out.'

Turning away from the shadowy vista, Count Forsel clenched his fist to screw up a slip of onionskin paper. He hurled it at the fireplace. Unfortunately the translucent scrap was so lightweight that a gust of warmth swept it back into the luxuriously furnished room. As it bounced across the silk-fringed rug, the count was forced to bend down, snatching at empty air until he recaptured the evidence of his spying. Red-faced, he walked to the table and held a corner of the paper in the candle flame. Realising the burning message would soon threaten his fingertips, he hurried over to drop it into the hearth.

'Let's not be too hasty.' Lord Radest shifted in his comfortable chair. His dark eyes were thoughtful.

'Heritha won't whelp some late pup.' Count Forsel shook his head, adamant, as he adjusted his doublet. 'My informant says the queen's women know she cannot carry another babe to its first breath. Not after the travails of her last childbed.' He grimaced with distaste.

'That's not what I meant.' Lord Radest rested his elbows on the chair's arms and steepled his fingers. 'You must surely realise your son will not be the only claimant to the throne.'

Forsel's round face grew even redder, now with indignation. 'Jaquin's claim is undeniable. His mother is the king's aunt as well as the firstborn of King Matil's grandchildren.'

'No one can dispute that,' Radest agreed, 'but the Great Charter of the Realm is clear. The crown passes from king to king, whether that's from father to son or grandsire to grandson as was the case when King Matil died. If the direct royal line fails, the succession passes to uncles, cousins and nephews as the case may be, but still through descent from father to son.'

'King Matil put paid to that,' Count Forsel snapped. 'Seeing treachery and conspiracy in every corner. How many executions did it take to satisfy him there could be no rival to his precious heir? The villain even grew suspicious of his own younger grandson. Even though Duke Nathin was barely out of his tutors' care. I'm still not convinced the old monster wouldn't have moved against the boy, if he hadn't choked to death on his own bile first.'

'I think—' Radest began.

'That's by the by,' Forsel continued briskly, 'since Duke Nathin was careless enough to fall off a horse and break his stupid neck, leaving no children. As the only male cousin of our beloved and soon to be lamented King Cassin, Jaquin will inherit the crown. As his loyal and loving father, I will guide him through the early years of his reign.'

Forsel smiled at Radest, triumphant. Radest gazed at the count, unmoved. 'Only if the Great Charter is amended to allow Jaquin's claim by virtue of his mother's royal birth.'

Forsel was unconcerned. 'The Noble Council must confirm an amendment to the Charter in these exceptional circumstances. The Guilds Council will have to do the same. The temple elders won't even be asked to do their usual wheedling and bargaining to secure agreement from both sides.'

He was growing impatient. 'What's the alternative? We sit on our hands and stare at an empty throne while the Egressi sweep into the borderlands of the south, and the Thruli raid our ports in the west? The realm cannot be left defenceless because we have no king to order troops mustered to fight invaders.'

'I'm sure Count Wyden will agree.' Lord Radest nodded.

'Wyden?' Despite the heat of the fire reflected back from the polished oak panelling, Count Forsel paled.

'His grandsire was King Matil's younger brother, and his mother was the bloody king's eldest niece. Wyden is older than your son, and he has healthy sons of his own. Jaquin isn't even married.'

'That's not a valid argument,' Forsel objected.

'Says who?' Radest raised his bushy dark brows. 'I'm sure Count Wyden will argue his case convincingly as soon as the principle of inheritance through a mother's blood is agreed. I expect Count Sacher will support him.'

'Why would Sacher do that?' Forsel protested. 'They can barely stand to be in the same room.'

Radest sighed. 'You forget Count Sacher's mother was daughter to King Matil's eldest sister. He has his own dog in this fight.'

'No. No. No.' Count Forsel waved impatient hands. 'Sacher can have no claim to the crown through successive women. Jaquin is only one generation removed from the direct male line.'

'You think your proposal will muster support in the Noble Council, when everyone sees you inventing rules solely to favour your son?' Radest was sceptical. 'Wyden and Sacher will be as quick to point out that if Jaquin dies without an heir, the realm will be landed in this selfsame fix. Meantime, if the rumours I hear are true, we will see Sacher's two elder daughters wedded to Wyden's sons before the year is out. One way or another, the noble count will hope to see his grandson crowned.'

Appalled, Count Forsel stared at his sister's husband. 'Shit.'

Radest heaved himself out of his chair. 'If you're determined to pursue this, I suggest you start rallying supporters to your cause. Now, if you will excuse me, my lady wife expects me for dinner and she will have spent a sad and wearying day trying to comfort the queen.'

#

'The king is dying?' Lady Annire of Barine sat up abruptly. She had been reclining on her silken pillows with the bed's sheets and quilts tossed aside in expectation of her husband's arrival. The delicate lace and gossamer of her chamber robe ornamented rather than concealed her splendid breasts. 'Truly?'

'There has been no official announcement, but there can be no doubt. The moon has come and gone and come again since he last left his chamber.' Lord Barine heaved a sigh as he unbuttoned his doublet and dumped it on the floor.

'My poor Heritha.' Lady Annire brushed a hand along her cheekbone, as though wiping away a tear. 'Cassin is truly the love of her life. She will be bereft.'

'Forgive me, dearest, I should have broken such grievous news more gently,' Barine apologised as he shed his boots, stockings and breeches. 'I assumed the queen would have told you in her letters—'

'Wait—beloved—there is no prince to follow Cassin.' Annire looked at him, artlessly wide-eyed. ' There is no heir.'

'No indeed.' Lord Barine heaved a sigh as he dropped into a spindly ornamental chair which creaked alarmingly. 'As you might imagine, that's the talk of the smoking dens. Forgive me bringing their reek home, sweetheart, but the dens always have the latest news.'

'You can wash away the taste at least.' Annire swung her long alabaster legs over the side of the bed and went to a side table to pour him a measure of burnt wine. She diluted it with spring water. 'So what's to become of the realm?'

'It's pretty well agreed that the Great Charter must be amended to allow for succession through the female line.' Barine grimaced as he took the glass from Annire's hand. 'Jaquin of Forsel seems to think the crown will be tossed straight to him by virtue of his mother's blood. Menit of Wyden is strutting around the cockpits loudly confident of his father's stronger claim. That will make him the heir presumptive with his pustulent brother at his shoulder in case of need.'

Annire wrinkled her nose. 'The Council of Nobles might as well choose between the stink of the slaughterhouse or the stench of the dunghill.'

'That's a little unkind.' Barine's protest was half-hearted.

'Truly?' Annire challenged him. 'When Jaquin of Forsel is an arrogant bore who reeks of horses and endlessly boasts of butchering stags? If he's not up to his elbows in some deer's innards, he's idling around the cockpits or cheering at a bull-baiting. He mocks anyone, man or woman, who shrinks from the sight of blood, or even so much as protests at a dumb animal's agonies. As for Menit and his brother, they prefer to hunt in the corridors and gardens, whenever the great and good of the realm gather to enjoy music and dancing. They are scum, my love. Villains without honour or conscience. The flame of life can't scorch their hearts black for their sins soon enough.'

Barine stared at her, bemused. 'What do you mean, sweetheart?'

'Not every noble lord is as diligent as you in serving his liege men's interests. Think back to the entertainments we have attended in and around the palace.' Annire sat down on the edge of the bed. 'Did you never notice girls huddled in tears in corners, or being bustled away red-faced by their mothers and chaperones?'

'Girls have their quarrels and rivalries.' Barine waved a vague hand. 'I just assumed...'

'You would know better if you had any sisters.' Annire said curtly. 'Ask those of your friends who do.'

'I know Lord Menit and Lord Tefir of Wyden like to flatter and flirt with the younger girls, and especially with newcomers from the country. So do all unmarried men. How else are good matches to be made?' But Barine looked uneasy.

Annire pursed her plump lips. A moment later, she swept her golden ringlets back over one shoulder. 'That's as far as honourable youths will go, with no harm done. But Menit and Tefir lure innocents away from their friends and trap them in dark corners. They force rough kisses on them, thrusting their hands up their skirts or down their bodices. They whisper filth into their ears and promise to use them like whores if they ever catch them alone.'

'Surely, they don't...?' Barine swallowed hard, aghast.

'No, they don't. They're not such fools.' Annire wriggled backwards to lie against her pillows. 'But it amuses them to see their victims' ashen faces when they next encounter them. Watch and you'll see them laugh as frightened girls scurry away. That's their idea of sport.'

'I had no idea.' Barine glowered. 'Were you ever...?'

'Oh no.' Annire laughed without much humour. 'They never venture near the queen's attendants, or accost girls they can see will fight back. I told you. They're not fools.'

'Wherever did they get such notions?' Barine was appalled.

Annire shrugged. 'No one has ever told them they may not do whatever they wish, or that they may not take whatever they want. They have that much in common with Jaquin of Forsel. Unlike your father of blessed memory, not every noble count takes the time to teach his heir to respect the balance between duty and privilege. That at least was a lesson King Cassin was quick to learn.'

'True enough.' Barine drank down the last of his amber glassful. His expression turned sorrowful. 'This is hateful. Cassin has always been a true friend and an excellent king, honourable and kind.'

'Come to bed, beloved.' Annire pulled at the ribbon that had been attempting and mostly failing to hold her chamber gown closed. The sheer fabric slid back to leave her all but naked in the seductive candlelight. 'Let me ease your cares for tonight at least. You can decide who you might favour as the realm's next king tomorrow.'

'Some choice,' Barine muttered as he pulled his shirt off over his tousled head and joined her.

#

'The king is dying.' The bearded man shook his head. 'There can be no doubt of it now.'

'We have no official word from the temple elders,' protested a stout woman sitting on the far side of the polished table.

The clean-shaven man in the upright wooden chair beside her grimaced. 'The elders will cling to hope as long as they think they see a spark of life in his eyes.'

'As is right and proper, Master Tanner,' another woman said, reproving, as she smoothed her widow's cap over her grey hair.

'Of course, Mistress Weaver,' he said hastily.

She acknowledged his concession with a polite nod, and looked at the bearded man. 'Please continue, Master Glover.'

'I take it we all have heard the same grim news from our various guild members who supply the royal castle.' The bearded man looked for reluctant nods of agreement from the ten or so men and women gathered in this small chamber built onto the side of the Fishmongers' Hall.

Satisfied, Master Glover went on. 'And we are also aware of the edict of amendment that seems likely to be proposed to the Council of Nobles, and to the Council of Guilds?'

The men and women nodded again. These artisans and merchants were much of an age, well into their middle years. Their gowns or doublets and breeches were tailored from good broadcloth, though their clothes were more practical than ornamental. They dressed to spend their days busy around their workshops or warehouses. Half of them looked impatient to get back to the commerce that filled their coffers and paid their taxes. Mistress Weaver considered how soon one of them would insist this meeting drew to a close.

'What's to discuss?' a pock-marked man demanded. 'There is no heir, but we must have a king. Therefore the crown must pass to a new monarch by right of a mother's blood. An innovation to be sure, but one that we cannot oppose.'

'Why can't we propose a solution of our own?' the stout woman who had spoken first countered. 'I was my husband's partner in our business, and I took charge when he died, just as Mistress Weaver did, and countless others before us. I am as skilled an apothecary as my Tomare ever was. Our colleagues freely acknowledged that when they chose me to represent them in the Guild Council. Why should we not see Queen Heritha take the throne?'

Mistress Weaver's expression did not alter as the other women seated at the table looked startled at that outrageous notion. She was content to let them assume Mistress Theriac had come up with this idea on her own. Though surely she wasn't the only one who occasionally proposed an obviously unacceptable option as tactic in business negotiations.

Master Tanner cleared his throat and took refuge in fireside wisdom. 'The Great Charter safeguards the rights of those who guard the realm. The common law safeguards the poor. It is not our place to propose mingling these ancient traditions.'

Everyone around the table nodded hasty agreement, though none of this gathering could be considered poor, even if they had not been born into wealth.

'I concede the possibility that this sad day may soon be upon us,' Mistress Weaver said with distaste. 'When it comes, it will be in everyone's interests to see the succession settled as swiftly as possible. Uncertainty is bad for business. We can agree on that.'

'Each of us represents men and women who live and work in the borderlands, loyally paying their guild dues,' a previously silent man observed, 'as well as many who trade through the ports of the west. We must consider which of these rival claimants will be most widely respected. A king has to enforce the rule of law along our roads and rivers. We need a man whose resolve this realm's neighbours will think twice about testing with raids.'

Mistress Weaver wanted this meeting focused on threats closer at hand. 'We should also consider how these claimants are likely to take defeat,' she said bluntly. 'Lord Jaquin of Forsel has a taste for bloodshed. That is very well known.'

'In the hunt and for sport, perhaps.' The pock-marked man looked uneasy. 'You cannot think he would take up arms to enforce his claim?'

'I wouldn't bet against it,' someone said, unguarded. Mistress Weaver resisted the urge to look around the table to see who that unexpected ally might be.

The widowed apothecary shrugged. 'Who can know what either noble claimant will do? These are unprecedented times.'

'Count Wyden is a man who holds a grudge,' Mistress Weaver observed. 'We all know folk who can attest to that.'

The gathering nodded grim agreement. The silence lengthened.

'But we must have a king,' Master Glover said eventually. 'Which means we must set the Guilds Council's seal to this edict of amendment. We have no choice.'

'We should give more thought to whose claim we might choose to support.' Mistress Weaver folded her hands in her lap.

The pock-marked man nodded. 'We must see what we can learn about these rival lords beyond street corner tittle-tattle.'

A woman in a creamy gown spoke up. 'I believe my guild has members well-placed to gather reliable information.'

'And mine,' another woman said.

'Thank you, Mistress Miller. Mistress Brewster.' The lines furrowing Master Glover's forehead eased a little.

\#

'Good morning, my lords.' Count Krisen looked down from the high-backed chair on its plinth, set beneath the stained glass window. That depicted the sacred flame of life in countless shades of red and gold.

His voice echoed back from the bare stone walls of the royal castle's great council hall. Few of the noblemen sitting on the benches to his right looked in his direction. No matter. Krisen could read their faces regardless. A good many of his lifelong friends were still guiltily relieved that fate hadn't landed them with the task of presiding over this debate. Krisen could hardly blame them. His heart had sunk when his name had been read from the slip of paper drawn by the temple elder who had opened this assembly's first day. Getting this lofty chair with a back to lean against rather than a seat on those humble benches couldn't possibly be worth the burden of this so-called honour.

The temple elder had opened these proceedings with fervent prayers that the flame of life would shed the light of divine wisdom on the assembly's decisions. Krisen hadn't see much sign of that so far. Every day's arguments saw feelings running higher and higher. Such deep divisions had been revealed that he doubted they could ever be bridged. He couldn't recall such a fraught and uncertain time in the four decades since he had first attended a noble council as a youth at his father's side.

Krisen wondered glumly how many enemies he had made for himself, for his sons and for his daughters, and most likely for his grandchildren too, by simply doing his duty to the realm. Count Wyden's adherents were gathered together at the far end of the rows of noble benches. Several were looking at him, silently accusing, while the rest glowered at each other in mutual resentment.

Thankfully it appeared these noble lords would not be coming to blows today. An undignified brawl had seemed all too likely yesterday, and evidently not only to him. Krisen realised the non-aligned lords must have arrived early this morning, determined to separate the rival factions by taking up the seats between them. Those men who had argued long and loud in support of Lord Jaquin were now sitting on the benches closest to his lofty chair.

At least Count Forsel's allies didn't seem to blame him personally for not handing over the crown without further debate. Their sour glances directed elsewhere suggested they were saving their ire for the nobles who had agreed this new principle of inheritance by right of a mother's blood, but who stubbornly refused to take the next step of agreeing which claimant's lineage was superior.

Count Krisen turned to the men and women representing the guilds of the realm, who were seated on the benches to his left. 'Good day to you, honoured masters and mistresses.'

Like the nobles, they were dressed in sombre colours even though no official announcement of the king's death had seen mourning declared. Unlike the nobles, there were no obvious factions supporting Count Wyden or Count Forsel. Some of the guild masters and mistresses had nodded, approving, when aspects of both claims had been argued. Then as far as Krisen could tell, they had changed their minds the next day.

A few murmurs in reply to his greeting rose to the black hammer beams of the ancient roof. Movement up aloft caught Krisen's eye. The king's war banner hung from the central span, high above the table where harried clerks recorded the past six days of repetitive and bad-tempered debate. A momentary breeze unexpectedly stirred the banner's blue and green folds.

'Who wishes to speak first?' Krisen coughed. He was hoarse after days of repeatedly pleading and even shouting to demand civility.

One of the clerks hurriedly filled a copper cup with water. He came up the three steps of the plinth in a single long stride. Krisen gratefully accepted the cup and took a drink before he spoke again.

'Who has fresh wording which we should consider for this edict of amendment to the great charter of the realm?'

Despite his best efforts, his voice cracked as he contemplated another day of pointless bickering. A day that would inevitably end with every proposal discarded for lack of sufficient assent.

'I do.' A stout woman stood up in the middle of the guild benches. 'Mistress Weaver on behalf of the Clothiers.'

Krisen saw interested faces on both sets of benches. He shared their curiosity. This woman hadn't spoken thus far.

The clothier looked across the hall. 'My noble lords, forgive my bluntness. The artisans and traders of this realm have chosen us on this side of the hall to safeguard their interests. We need to get back to work. No doubt you also have responsibilities which you would rather not neglect any longer.'

A murmur of agreement from the guild benches interrupted her. Krisen saw more than a few nobles nodding with equal fervour. The clothier went on.

'This great council of the realm has agreed that inheritance through the female line will be valid in the absence of a direct male heir to the crown. Let us put our Council seals to an edict of amendment that says that much and no more. As for who should wear the crown next, surely that need not be discussed until King Cassin is dead.'

She sat down, taking everyone by surprise, including the clerks at the table. For a long moment, no one spoke. No one rose to their feet to be heard. Krisen saw the entire gathering was confused. So was he. Was it remotely possible that the clothiers' guild mistress was the only person in the realm who didn't believe King Cassin's life was as good as snuffed out?

Krisen decided he didn't care. He got to his feet so fast that he nearly lost his balance and fell off the plinth. If this simple edict could be agreed on, it could be written up and formally sealed before midday. Before the wax had hardened, this assembly could be declared over and he would be free. More than that, his name would be removed from the next drawing of lots. Some other luckless wretch could try to stop Count Wyden, Count Forsel and their rival factions ending up at daggers drawn, once the king succumbed to his lingering illness.

'You have heard the proposal. Is there any dissent?' he demanded.

No one spoke. No one got to their feet.

'I call for a show of consent.' His wrinkled hand shook as he raised it.

The men and women of the Guilds Council were quick to agree. The noble lords were slower. Krisen's breath caught in his dry throat as Count Wyden and his supporters huddled in hasty consultation. Count Forsel's allies were more discreet, but Krisen could see them exchanging nods and glances. Fingers pointed, indicating various men on the central benches.

The non-aligned nobles began to raise their hands, led by the youthful Lord Barine. A few moments later, Count Forsel's scowling faction joined them. Once the first of Count Wyden's adherents nodded and assented, the rest swiftly followed.

Krisen could see Count Wyden's allies were studying the non-aligned lords, and so were Count Forsel's friends. He realised each faction had decided to settle for getting half a loaf today rather than risk ending up with no bread at all. As soon as this assembly was over, he had no doubt those undecided lords would be besieged with arguments and inducements. Each side would be determined to secure their backing, before the council was summoned again. Would enough noblemen openly support Count Forsel to convince Count Wyden to back down, or vice versa? He had his doubts.

No matter. He would be on the road to his family lands in the east before sunset today, never mind the hazards of winter travel. He would return for the interment of the king's ashes, of course, but that would surely be delayed until the succession had been agreed.

The clerks were busy tallying the hands on both sides of the hall, to confirm the necessary numbers had been reached to confirm official assent. Like everyone else, Krisen could see that was a mere formality. He breathed a discreet sigh of relief and sat down in the high-backed chair.

'Very well, my noble lords and honoured masters and mistresses,' he announced as the clerks returned to their table. 'You may take your ease while the edict is prepared for both council seals, and—'

The sound of an opening door interrupted him. Krisen's heart plummeted into his hollow stomach as he saw the temple elder in her deep red robe approaching. There could only be one reason for her return. There would be no end to this assembly now. The question of the succession would have to be settled once and for all before anyone could leave.

The temple elder halted between the furthest benches. She looked calmly from side to side and then at Count Krisen. 'My noble lords. Honoured masters and mistresses. The king is here.'

What? For an instant, Krisen couldn't believe his own ears, and not only because the elder's last words were drowned out by plaintive, pointless denials on both sides of the hall.

Those protests turned to confusion, and just as quickly to relief and delight. King Cassin joined the temple elder. He stood beside her, smiling. Now everyone was on their feet, cheering and applauding, including Krisen, though he had no recollection of standing up.

He stole a quick glance at Count Forsel's sons and saw their smiles were as fixed as a death's head's grin. He couldn't see past the jubilant crowd to pick out Count Wyden, but he was sure he would see the same. Before Krisen could decide what that might mean for the realm, the hubbub subsided. King Cassin's gestures were calling for quiet.

There could be no doubt he had been gravely ill. Cassin was pale, gaunt and hollow-eyed, walking with a stick for support. He had lost so much weight that he could have been wearing a shirt and doublet tailored for some stouter relative. His breeches hung loose and his stockings sagged around his ankles on his bone-thin legs. But the resolute glint in his eye was familiar as he surveyed both councils. His voice was strong when he spoke, once everyone had resumed their seats.

'My noble lords. Honoured masters and mistresses. You have earned the right to be the first to see that fate has not yet cast its dread shadow over me. I stand with you in the blessed light of the flame of life.'

Most of those in the hall cheered again, though Krisen could hear a questioning undertone in those congratulations. He wondered if the course of the king's illness would ever be fully explained.

Cassin's raised hand asked for silence again. 'Forgive me. My doctors will soon insist that I return to my chamber to rest. I am here to thank you for your diligence and wisdom as you have debated the best way to safeguard the peace and stability of the realm, now and for the future. Thank you, from the bottom of my heart, for decreeing that the crown will be inherited through the female line. It eases my heart to know that rule over this realm will pass to my daughters in the fullness of time.'

Cassin swept a low bow with an elegant flourish of the bony hand that wasn't holding his stick. Krisen nearly choked as he stifled an unguarded laugh. That bow handily meant that Cassin did not—could not—see the blind fury on Count Wyden's face or Count Forsel's apoplectic indignation.

Plenty of other nobles noticed though, and they clearly didn't like what they saw. Lord Barine was the first on his feet, waving a hand to secure the king's gracious nod of permission to speak.

'Quite so, my liege. As soon as today's edict of amendment is prepared and sealed, let us set a date for a celebration when we can pledge our fealty to Princess Dithra.'

As Barine looked around the hall, most of those assembled on both sides agreed with loud enthusiasm. Count Krisen had to pretend to smooth his beard with a hand to hide his grin. He nearly laughed out loud when the chief clerk stood up from his stool, holding a sheet of vellum.

'My liege.' He bowed to the king, before addressing everyone else. 'My noble lords. Honoured masters and mistresses. I have the edict ready.'

Well, it wasn't as if he'd had some detailed proposal with multiple clauses and caveats to copy out. How many words had there been in that single sentence? No more than thirty. Krisen resisted the temptation to make an accurate count on his fingers. Then he realised the clerk was looking expectantly at him.

'Let us see the edict sealed and this assembly can be concluded.' He didn't hold back his smile now. His old bones need not be jostled along rutted roads as he fled the capital in search of peace and quiet.

At the clerks' table, one of the lesser scriveners was opening the box that held both council seals and the sacred sticks of scarlet wax. The temple elder who had accompanied the king took flint and steel from a pocket of her robe. She prepared to light the holy candle that would sanctify the seal with the flame of life. Nobles and guild leaders mingled as they clustered around the table, eager to witness the procedure.

Krisen came down from his lofty seat to join them. As he did so, he realised King Cassin had already left the hall, unnoticed.

'The king is sleeping.' The queen closed the door slowly and quietly as she entered her private parlour, as if her husband was in the next room rather than in his own apartments on the far side of the castle.

'Oh, Heritha.' Lady Annire sprang up to embrace her. After a long moment, she stepped back to hold the queen at arm's length, smiling and damp-eyed. 'How is dearest Cassin, truly?'

'Very tired.' Heritha accepted the glass of wine that the Mistress of the Keys was offering. 'But he is well, truly. It will be some while before he regains his full strength, but there is no doubt that he will make a full recovery. Thanks in no small part to the Apothecaries' Guild.'

She raised the glass to salute Mistress Weaver, Mistress Miller and Mistress Brewster. The small table in front of them offered the queen's guests a decanter of pale golden wine and a silver basket of honey cakes.

'I will convey your gratitude to Mistress Theriac. Though we all played our part.' Mistress Weaver raised her own glass to the Mistress of the Wardrobes and the Mistress of the Kitchens. 'Some of you had far more onerous duties. We three merely had to drop the right words into the right ears in a timely fashion.'

Lady Annire returned to her seat beside Countess Radest. 'How did you convince so many different spies that the king was deathly ill?'

The Mistress of the Wardrobes shrugged. 'The sneaks were so concerned with chasing after whatever left the king's chamber that they paid scant heed to what might be taken in. The castle's laundresses answer to me, so I know who to trust with such secrets, as well as who is reliably loose-lipped.'

The Mistress of the Kitchens laughed. 'Quite so, and with the midden buckets at my disposal, making sure no spy would want to examine the soiled linens too closely was no great challenge.'

Countess Radest chuckled. 'My husband tells me Lord Barine was lightning fast, jumping up to support your proposal, Mistress Weaver.'

'My darling lamb.' Lady Annire smiled fondly. 'I wish I could have been there to see it. He's so proud of himself. He's convinced that was all his own idea.'

Countess Radest sipped her wine. 'My husband says at least a handful of others were ready to take the lead, after he pointed out to them that an edict to guarantee the crown passes to Princess Dithra ensures they can never be lumbered with Jaquin or Menit as king.'

'Are we going to do anything to repair the reputations of those young men?' The Mistress of the Wardrobes looked around the room. 'We have cast a great deal of shadow over all three.'

'Let them strive to ensure their deeds stand up to scrutiny in the cold light of day.' Annire was unsympathetic. 'We said nothing that wasn't true.'

'No, but we did nothing to stop people imagining the very worst that their conduct might imply. We encouraged the spread of those rumours as fact,' the countess pointed out.

'There's nothing to say those scoundrels wouldn't have done the worst that we feared, if one or other of them had been handed the crown.' Mistress Weaver looked for the other guild mistresses' agreement. They nodded, emphatic.

Countess Radest shrugged. 'Ah well, I'm sure the experience will teach those young men some valuable lessons.'

Queen Heritha settled in a chair with a honey cake in one hand and her wine glass in the other. 'How soon do you think your husband will let it be known he considers Ireth is now heir to Radest in her own right?'

'I imagine he will let someone else make the first move. Our lands border Forsel after all, and the noble count will be in a foul mood while he's licking his wounds.' The countess was unconcerned. 'We won't be waiting long. Radest says a double handful of noble lords will seize the right to pass their lands and wealth down to their daughters rather than see the benefits of their life's endeavours handed to some distant relative whose only merit is possessing a cock and balls.'

The queen raised her glass. 'Then let us offer thanks that the future peace and prosperity of the realm has been secured without a single drop of blood being shed.'

Lady Annire smiled sunnily. 'Without those ambitious lords having the faintest idea who has defeated them.'

LADY CONA

By
Anna Smith Spark

'Have the dogs been fed?'

Her servant, Kriran, nodded eagerly. 'Of course, my lady. Raw meat, but half rations only, as always.'

'Good.'

'They looked well,' Kriran said. 'Eager.'

She thought: They are the finest dogs in this kingdom. They look more than 'well'.

Kriran said, 'Shall I bring you your spear, my lady?'

'No. No, it is polished and sharpened enough now.' The most beautiful boy in all Elorn, his hair like sunlight on new fallen snowfields, his eyes like the night sea as the storm breaks, fairer than roses are his lips and the curve of his mouth when he smiles, his fingers long and clever, his arms strong as the summer wind, all day this boy who served her so faithfully had sat silent with the whetstone on his white knees, in a tent of green silk for him alone and no food or drink must pass his fair red lips until the point of her spear was so sharp it could cut the petals of a budding rose, it could cut the night sea or the summer wind. As the sun set he had come to Cona's tent bearing the spear before him, music played as he hung it upon the wall there above her bed. And now it was only a time for waiting. The spear waited, the dogs waited, the boy in his beauty, Lady Cona—waited, waited, waited, wait, wait, wait.

Kriran wanted something to fuss over, some distraction from her fears. A new servant, untrained in these long dull white hours before brilliant red war. She fretted, fussed over a cloak hanging on a peg but hanging slightly crumpled, not even a cloak Cona liked to wear. 'I'll refill your water cup, my lady, here, it's on this table; would you like—I could fetch your armour if you wish, my lady, give it a final polish to make it shine better, comb your helmet plume.'

Comb my helmet plume? Did someone just actually say that? But most things sound like dirty jokes when you're thinking about the most beautiful boy you've seen since the last one. (The last one had eyes like a moth's wings and hair like dark wine and was the most beautiful boy not in one kingdom but in all the world, but he was dead.) Cona said kindly, before the girl's fussing drove her to shout, 'I'm fine, I don't need anything, Kriran. Thank you. In fact, I think I might go to bed.' The girl was fussing with something so intensely she didn't hear the command there to stop fussing. Cona said gently but pointedly, looking at the bed: 'If you could...'

'Oh! Yes, yes, my lady, yes!' The girl turned down the covers, plumped up the cushions. The coverlet was fur from a bear that Cona had killed herself; the cushions were from the black iron throne of the God King of Thearanor Land of Twilight Meadows, taken as loot the previous year. Very comfortable, as she had hoped.

She hadn't gone to war for those cushions, to clarify. Taking the God King's head off with one—okay, okay, three—sword strokes (He had a thick neck and a thick beard), holding His head up proudly by His greasy hair, sticking His head on a pole on the back of her chariot; that was why she had gone to war last year. Grinding the walls of the God King's temple to dust beneath her chariot wheels, sowing the ruins with salt so that nothing would grow there: that was why she had gone to war last year.

But the cushions had been a very nice bonus. She slept better now than she had all her life.

'Your sleeping gown, my lady.'

Cona held up her arms, let Kriran slide her day robe off her, drop the sleeping gown down in its place. Kriran smoothed the furs around Cona carefully. 'Good night, my lady.'

'Good night, Kriran. Oh, Kriran: leave the lamp burning tonight, please.'

The servant girl looked anxious at that. Do you expect bad dreams, my lady, the night before battle? You cannot be...afraid? I had heard that—the stories they tell of you, at least—they had to wake you from your slumbers, I thought, the morning of the battle of Geranish, so I thought—you'd sleep...And in the girl's face also: does this mean I will have to sit up all night myself, not get any sleep?

'I like to see my spear and my armour the night before a battle, Kriran. See the lamp light on them. That gives me sweet dreams, good sleep.'

The girl blushed, seeing Cona had guessed her thoughts. 'Very well, my lady.'

To be kind to the girl, who was new as her body servant, Cona said, 'It's natural to be anxious before such a battle, Kriran. My last serving girl was the same, fretting too much the night before, worrying too much. It will be a great day tomorrow. Don't fret, Kriran.'

Pleasing, to see the girl smile, look reassured.

The servant girl disappeared through the doorcurtain into the tent's outer room, although Cona could hear her fussing out there too, tossing and turning in her own bed. Cona could almost hear the girl listening out in case Cona needed her, called her back. A little reassured. But then, if Cona died tomorrow...yes, it's true, be fair to her, she has a right to feel anxious about what will happen to her tomorrow.

Forget her. Ignore the noise she made pretending she was still and silent and asleep. Lady Cona had slept...three times in her life, perhaps, without a servant so close at hand she could hear their breathing. Beneath the warm furs, she forgot the girl's fears now in perhaps three heart beats. Fixed her eyes on the spear hanging above her bed. The lamplight on the long ashwood shaft, painted with flowers. If she blew out a hard breath the lamp flickered, the flowers seemed to dance. Like flowers in a meadow, in the first grey light of morning, in a cool fresh spring...

She blew out another breath, it was beautiful, making the light dance so. Tomorrow, I will make the sunlight dance so in dying men's eyes, she thought. Flicker, dance bright, go out.

Then she laughed and cursed together, because Kriran had left the lamp slightly too near her bed, and too hard a breath made the lamp blow out.

They did not need to wake her the next morning (that story was just that, a story! No one would dare wake Lady Cona from her sleep!) although the sun was well up in the sky by the time she was up and dressed (She was nineteen! She needed to sleep late!) She breakfasted outside the tent in the spring sunshine. If she had woken earlier it would have been too cold and damp out on the grass. Thus a good reason to sleep late.

White bread fresh from the bake oven, spread thickly with yellow honey from the high heather-clad uplands of Anderal her home kingdom where her father was a king and her mother was a queen. An apple, the last of the barrel and thus the very last of the last year's harvest, it had made it all this way from Anderal without a single blemish, a dried leaf still proudly clung to the stem, but unluckily she dropped it after a few mouthfuls and had to watch it roll off down the slope, after all that trouble to be the last of the last, a thousand miles from the orchard it could have fallen in. White milk to drink, rich and creamy, and a single cup of dark wine because that was a necessity on such a day. Cona raised the cup, poured the wine out in offering. It spattered on the ground, not dark, but brilliant bloody red.

Above her tent, a gust of wind caught her banner. It too was, as it must be, blood red. Cona threw down the empty cup. A peaceful, pleasant breakfast, if perhaps the morning was little cold still, a nasty nip in the air. Now the time for war was come.

Back in her tent, she sat impassive while Kriran dressed her. Bronze corslet, studded at the neck and the waist with balas rubies, flowers worked in silver around the neck. War leggings with bronze plates to cover her thighs and knees. Bronze greaves, worked like the corslet with silver flowers; bronze arm guards; thick leather boots. Kriran must leave then: the beautiful boy came into the tent dressed in cloth of gold and cloth of silver, a collar of yellow diamonds glittering around his white throat. He lifted high Cona's bronze helmet. The sides and back of the helmet were decorated with golden figures of women dancing. Her childhood friends, she had asked for them to be set in gold on her warhelm to be always near her. The cheekguards and the noseguard were covered in gold leaf. The plume was black horsehair coated with lime so that it stood up in a high spike.

There was a fine mirror set on the wall of her tent opposite her dressing chair. Cona watched them dress her, distant in the mirror, murky as if underwater, as if she was watching a scene from far away and long ago. She saw her face in the bronze mirror discoloured, blurred and thus not quite her own—and the look in her eyes, cold and waiting for the slaughter, almost made her frightened. Then the helmet went on, the beautiful boy moving fluid and graceful, and there was indeed her golden war face. He let out a deep breath of fear when it was done.

'Take up the spear,' Cona ordered him. She said loudly, 'It is time. Take me to my war chariot.'

The bearer entered the tent with eyes averted—no man could look now upon Lady Cona in her glory without trembling. Huge, strong as oceans, his hands huge. He lifted Cona with such delicacy he might be lifting one of the apples her mother had sent. Carried her in four smooth steps out of the tent. And there, there, outside the tent waiting now, the sun flashing upon it, so beautiful it made her catch her breath with delight...her war chariot!

Pear wood, warm and golden, oiled and polished until it gleamed and until it felt like silk to the touch, plated in thick bronze. Like muscles, she thought, great muscles beneath a shining skin. Her muscles, for the chariot was a part of her war body as much as her armour and her spear. The seat was padded in red leather, the hide of two great fire-breathing bulls her mother had once killed. A strong leather harness to hold her secure, also scarlet, crossing her chest and studded with bronze spikes because...just because. Oaken wheels, studded to help it grip and move even if the earth was churned to mire, even if her enemies' blood ran like a river around her those cunningly wrought wheels would grip and turn and let her move. Long blades were set in each axle—in a charge, they could sever a man's legs clean through. Her spear was set on a gilded mount, easy for her turn and stab and twist and thrust.

There were more spears waiting at her right hand should her favourite spear break in the fighting, and a dagger should it come down to close work like that.

Although she was the Lady Cona, greatest warleader in all this great first dawning age of all the world, and it never had and never would come down to close work like that.

The chariot was drawn by the two war dogs, Kharlie and Lira, resplendent in bronze armour. Slaver dripped from their mouths, they were hungry and they could smell man flesh on the wind. They let out a great howl when they saw Cona, louder and longer and more beautiful than the belling of a whole pack of hounds when the quarry is sighted. The bearer slave held Cona so that she stroked each one before he placed her in the war chariot. Their beautiful silken ears, their wet noses nuzzling her hands with love.

'Good Lira. Good Kharlie. Fine girls, both of you.' They tugged at the reins now, so eager for battle. Hungry for it, to show their strength. Tongues licking their huge teeth. 'Patience a little longer, girls. Soon.' They bayed joyfully. Fell silent, contented now Cona was there and all was set. Such fine dogs. So clever she barely needed the reins to guide them. So strong they could pull the chariot through anything, mire, standing water, the fallen bodies of the dead and the dying. Their teeth could tear a man's arm from his body. Bite through leather and bronze. They were braver than any man: they had once fought a dragon, Cona and her two dogs alone against a black dragon from the northern mountains. Lira had torn off the dragon's right foreleg. Kharlie had torn its throat open.

In the valley below Cona's tent her army had been assembling itself for battle. At the sound of the dogs' baying, every face turned to look up.

Oh, the smiles, the shouts of wonder, from the soldiers looking up!

A little time fussing, smiling at the dogs, and then... At Cona's command a trumpet rang out. A single note of triumph. Hiera, Cona's lieutenant, brought forward the war standard. Set it rising above Cona's chariot.

And now she must address her army. Rally them, before the battle came and they would be free to kill. Get them as hungry as her dogs to kill. She thought briefly of the slaves slaving over the cookfires. The agony in the ranks if there was a problem with the supply carts: '*Three days with only bread and water. We're not having it. Three days!*' If only not feeding them the night before had the same effect on warriors as it did on Lira and Kharlie. Men and dogs. Dogs and men. The warleader's silent prayer: *send me to war next time with an army of dogs instead of men.* Ideally ones with long floppy furry ears and spotty tummies when they roll over for belly rubs.

Cona looped the reins lightly around her wrists. The dogs yelped joyfully, recognising the movement. 'Lira. Kharlie. Let's go, then.' She turned briefly to smile thank you at Kriran who stood watching in the doorway of her tent.

Goodbye, Kriran. Have a hot bath waiting for me when— if—I get back.

A short run down the hillside, and the army parted before her, flowed open before her like a body opening to a tearing spear thrust. She drove through the ranks of her warriors, and they were cheering and cheering. (Also (ignored), cooing and oohing about the lovely dogs—and the dogs, being dogs, loved that). The army was forming itself: like a tent being raised, like a house being built, ten thousand people setting

149

themselves in order, a chaos and a trembling in the air all sweat and thighs and swords and last moment no time now errands and then, like great wild magic: an army! Bronze-clad, fire-eyed, blood-lusting; it faced her there in the green fields and the army was hers to command and hers alone. Shaking of spears. Clashing of swords on corslets. Stamping of feet. And her name, such love in the chanting of it: *Cona! Cona! Cona! Lady of War! Lead us!*

The trumpets rang to call them to order. Three times, loud and long and terrible, the trumpets rang.

(Well...pretend they rang three times for the pleasure of hearing trumpets ringing: but an army is, in truth, less easy to train than dogs.)

Fine silence. Cona drew breath.

Her own voice was quiet. *'Like the rustle of new spring leaves in the aspen'*. (That's poet-speak for a whisper of a voice.) Oh, a lovely voice for some things. Discussing the plan of battle, telling a man he must lead a charge that is clearly suicide for him and all who follow: so reasonable, so appealing, so unarguable, in that meek quiet gentle voice. Oh, most pleasing when accepting a city's surrender, *'Unconditional, my lords. That is my condition. Your unconditional surrender, your gates not just opened but torn down for my soldiers to enter, the royal family and other dignitaries prostate beneath the wheels of my chariot—or else I do not accept your surrender, my lords, and the battle continues. Which?'* all spoken soft and gentle in a voice like new spring aspen leaves rustling, so gentle that my lords, trembling like aspen leaves themselves, have to lean forward to listen, and she says in her gentle soft quiet voice, *'I will count to ten, my lords, if you have not decided by then I will set my dogs on you,'* her dry meek little voice so quiet they have to strain to listen. Oh, yes, a lovely voice for some things—many things. But not, alas, for giving great speeches to ten thousand battle-hardened (that's poet-speak for trumpet-deafened) warriors, their ears covered by bronze helmets. So Cona spoke, and Heira, who alongside many other sterling qualities had a voice louder than some trumpets, shouted it to the soldiers.

'My people! You who follow me! You who will fight and die—for me! The enemy is massed on the plain before us. They are gathered because they think they can destroy us. Destroy—me! A weak creature, perhaps, they think me, here at your head to lead you, high in honour and glory only, surely, because I am my parents' daughter, a king's daughter and a queen's daughter, not because I myself have any power in me. You follow me, they think perhaps, only because you fear—not me, even, but my parents' anger, you fear, and that alone is why you follow me—out of fear! Because you are but craven! A weak little thing I must be, needing another even to shout my words for me. And you—weaker, lesser than I, if that were possible, because you fight for me. Would die, for me. The enemy has only to show you the blades of swords and you will flee the field—because you fight only—for such a weak young petted thing as me.

'Such is arrogance, the cruelty, of our enemy!

'I know the truth, my warriors! You know it! You are the greatest army that walks the earth in these bright new days we live in! We fight together as one being, you will fight and die for me, each one of you, and I—I will fight and die for each one of you!

'And we will be victorious!

'For days now, the enemy has taunted us. Sat on the plain before us just out of reach of our arrows, refusing to fight, waiting in his arrogance for you, my warriors, to break with me. His spies have crawled into our camp—like lice, they have crawled over us—speaking ill words of me, of those that follow me, speaking honeyed words to tempt you to leave me. 'Come over to us,' the enemy's spies have cajoled you. 'You see what your lady is, and what she does. You see it is not right.' Tempting their words. Honeyed their voices.

Sweet, I know, the gold they offered as a gift to those of you who would go over to the enemy.

'Not one of you have done so. Not one warrior in this camp has left to join the enemy. Those spies, every one of them, lie dead now, cut down by your blades even as they spoke such ill things of you and of me, your captain! How little does the enemy think of me! How little does the enemy think of you, my warriors! How wrong the enemy is!

'And now, today, my warriors, my friends—at last the battle is joined and the enemy can no longer hide away from us! Today, you and I together will fight side-by-side, and the enemy will learn what strength we have!

'Today, now, in this bright morning—we will fight!

'To battle!

'To battle now!

'My friends! My companions!'

Cona's gentle voice shook, and the tears ran freely down her face beneath her warhelm. Heira shouted loud the words with a voice so filled with emotion that the words came raw and cracked. Such a small thing before ten thousand armed warriors, Lady Cona seated in her war chariot drawn by dogs. Dogs! Not dragon or giants or wild stallions! Two fine bitches, wiser and more beautiful than stallions. The trumpet sounded, the war drums beat out the war march. Cona shook the reins and her war dogs let out a growl.

She led them. The great host, one being, marched with one mind to battle.

A long march across a green plain, the grass smooth beneath the chariot's wheels. The sky was very blue, that good spring blue that has a promise of the summer to come. And Cona was young enough to think of childhood days with such a blue sky above her, endless, and to think with pleasure of lazy summer days with friends to come. Festival days.

But tiny shadows fell over her and danced and darted, raced across the green before her. All the carrions birds of half the word, coming drawn to the slaughter-feast. Cona raised her head to smile up at them, as she might smile on a summer evening sitting talking with her friends around a campfire and in the dusk the swifts come flitting. Kharlie looked up, sniffed the air, gave a friendly yelp at the carrion birds. When a battle was over, Kharlie liked to chase them.

The plain dipped down, then rose again. A low rise, the dogs taking it easily not changing their pace. Their tails wagged. Crested the rise and there, there before them....

The enemy. The enemy ranks, already waiting.

Spear forest. Ripe cornfield of men. And Cona's hand held the axe to fell them like dead trees. The scythe to reap them like dried yellowed wheat.

Fifteen thousand, she had been told by her scouts. Yes: looking at them assembled before her, yes, fifteen thousand was near enough right. A few more, perhaps, than fifteen. (There were two kinds of scouts, Cona had very quickly realised: the gloomy ones who over-counted, 'It's hopeless, a flood of them, they overwhelm us, outnumber us twenty to one,' to make sure their mad-for-war war leader truly understood the gravity of the coming battle; and the gloomy ones who undercounted, 'A mere handful, we'll crush them in ten heartbeats,' with the more sophisticatedly gloomy idea that their mad-for-war war leader would not welcome bad news such as that she was outnumbered. They never learned to tell the truth, either kind, no matter how many times she told them.) Twenty thousand of them, she'd guess.

To her ten thousand.

Nine thousand.

Yes, alright, yes.

Eight thousand. Maybe eight and a half.

'Spear forest' was not really in all honesty quite accurate either: the enemy's front ranks held spears, but behind them were peasants with sharpened farm tools and angry faces, untrained for war. But therefore the cornfield description fitted perfectly at least. A fine pretty field of poppies and cornflowers and ripe wheat. For they were a bright host in many colours, banners flying green, blue, red, silver, the warriors drawn from all the villages and towns for miles and miles and miles, woodlanders with skin like oakbark, farmers smelling of manure, fisher-folk from the coast gilled and with webbed feet. Drawn all together to resist the Lady Cona and her army, those cruel plunderers. Their faces were set hard, teeth clenched, determined. Even from this distance, Cona could smell the hate for her, rising, stinking off them. As the mist rises from the river, as the dew rises in steam from the grass on a summer morning, so rose up her enemy's hate. Untrained as they were, these peasants in their gaudy clothes more fitted to a may day feast, they would fight to the very last, down to the close knife work, to their dying breaths with the blood running freely down slicking their weapons. For Lady Cona had burned every village for twenty miles. Taken great plunder. Butchered all that lived. So bright, so righteous, her enemy's hatred.

Outnumbered, hated—that was how Lady Cona had been taught to fight! The best way to fight!

She gave the nod to Hiera. Hiera gave the shout, and the trumpet sang the order: 'Form up there. Foot soldiers: to the front. March!' And her army was a spear forest, truly. Perfect order, spear shafts stiff upright as tree trunks, as they began their march. Slowly. Not rushing undisciplined like peasants. Slowly, as one being, five thousand foot soldiers advanced to meet the enemy ranks. There Roza, captain of the foot—the yellow plume of her helmet picked her out. There, marching, leading them.... And the enemy ranks waiting, waiting. And the enemy ranks wait, wait, wait. There, see them, still, just,

154

from Cona's low vantage: there Roza with a single beam of sunlight briefly flashing on the yellow plume of her helmet, there the ranks of our soldiers, there the enemy ranks.

And there...in a shaft of light, with the carrion birds wheeling, there...

there...

there...

there...

...the spears meet....

...the front lines meet.

She could not see. Low and seated as she was, even on the raised seat of her chariot but it was only drawn by dogs, it should be vast drawn by dragons, monsters, high and huge with wheels that could crush down the walls of a city, but she was in the end only woman sized, sat low so she could not see. The warriors marched out of her vision. Beyond her helping. Nothing she could do now for them. As sometimes she will watch her friends swim against cold waves of a cold sea, or run fast whooping out of her sight. She can imagine, but not really imagine, what it is like for them. She has watched it from a high distance, a mass of lives indistinguishable, nothing, the thin line of different colours where they meet, the line pushing, holding, thrashing like a ribbon when a child plays waving it behind them, she had clenched her bones in some attempt to imagine how they feel, her soldiers holding, gripping their feet bracing their knees clutching their great spears rigid. But she could not watch today from her low vantage, she must only sit, listening to her dogs bark, to wait. A long time sitting waiting. Shouts, rumbles, weariness, dust, from the battle front.

Then Heira said, 'I think it's time, my Lady.'

'Have they dropped back holding, as I ordered?'

'Yes. They are holding still just, but a gap is about to open.'

Cona smiled. 'Well, then. So then.' She shouted, thought it strained her voice and would leave her throat sore, but some things she could not leave to Hiera, she must shout herself: 'Horses! Now! Horses!'

A slight jerk of the rein with her left hand. So little. The dogs howled with joy.

The dogs began to run, with the war chariot smooth drawn after them.

Behind her, at her summons, two thousand warriors wrapped in bronze armour, mounted on great white horses.

Before her, her own army, and they opened to let her rush through, and beyond, at last, awaiting her spear, there the enemy ranks.

She held her spear. She was the spear. The spear point, honed and polished.

A weak, small thing on its own, a single bronze spear point. It rests in a man's hand, a little, pretty, shining thing. But with the weight of the ashwood shaft and the well-trained arm and the will behind it, it can pierce armour, pierce flesh and bone, rip a life out. The spear trembled in her hand for one brief moment of fear that was her heart being only human. It sang and leapt forward as she sang and the dogs leapt.

Her own army before her, tight packed, herded together, folded up into themselves. The enemy, far outnumbering, pushing them and shaping them, surrounding them. Stretching out to overwhelm them. Her army was a solid mass like a stone. Her enemy was water poured and flowing over the stone, drowning it.

No...not like that. That's not it. Struggle to describe it. Think! War is hard to put into words sometimes, it really is.

Her army was...a line of men six warriors deep. The enemy had almost overwhelmed it. Holding, just, but moving backwards at the flanks, pulling apart, a gap opening in the middle where the thread of her army's strength was frayed so close to snapping.

Gods, these metaphors get tangled! Lines, men, flanks, words, water, threads...So...so...let's try...arghh! So...Ah! Yes! Imagine a child (that's the enemy) taking a stick (that's us). One end in either hand, pushing the stick backwards into a curve, until the midpoint of the stick is under such pressure it splits. The child crows, thinking he's done something really strong and clever and grown up.

The moment the stick breaks in two, that's the opening. Cona charged through the break with two thousand horses behind her, before her her war dogs with gnashing teeth.

A n old battle strategy. Two men, great kings and conquerors both, did it just like this. She's read accounts of all their battles (one book at least is quite well-written, if you like that kind of thing). She's not imaginative in her battle strategies, to be honest, is the Lady Cona. Just bloody good at getting them to work in practise. Why re-invent the wheel if some big hero man's already done it? The trick, as always, is to do it twice as well as he did. The enemy's cheering and pushing her army on all sides, confidently stretched out surrounding her army. Some might even say...overconfident...and...even...over...stretched. And at just the moment when their overconfidence outweighs our danger. At just the moment before the overstretching becomes obvious at just the moment she knows it must happen—her army opens a gap to let her through, going very fast with a spear and two war dogs and scythed wheels on her chariot which is heavy with bronze plates. So she rushes out faster and heavier and far less anticipated than any big strong hero man. Straight into the surprised overconfident overstretched enemy ranks. Straight out with a whoop of joy and maybe a little human fear, straight into the enemy ranks.

Red murder. Red killing. Red the dogs' panting mouths. Red her great joy whoop.

Spear point. Scythed wheels. She can take men apart without the need to do anything but point the spear. Without needing to think.

On each side of her she mowed them down like cutting corn.

Literally like that. Literally literally like that. Her scythes scythed through them.

Her cavalry fanned out behind her, a great wedge driving deeper and deeper and wider and wider into the enemy ranks. Rushed through out into the back of the battlefield. She gasped fresh air, bright light. A touch of the rein and the dogs knew, they turned a tight circle, brought her back faster and faster into the back of the enemy ranks.

Her cavalry spilt perfectly into two smaller wedges. One charged left, one right. Into the back of the enemy ranks.

At the far flanks of the battle, horns blew in the distance.

More cavalry appeared. Two more wedges.

Charged into the side of the enemy ranks.

Her foot soldiers roared with one voice. Held their ground, stopped shrinking together backwards encircled. Held their ground and pushed out into the front of the enemy ranks.

The enemy dissolved before Cona's spear. She trampled them like they were flowers in a meadow, delicate flowers beneath her scythed wheels. Blood red, bone white, grief green. The dulled bronze of weapons. The bright new gold of death-screams.

Their leader, like their screams, was golden. She had seen him from afar, now she sought him out, steered her chariot with a touch of the reins, twisted her head to find him left and right. A roar: his roaring war cry, her roar when she saw him. 'Lady Cona! Face me!' He waded through the slaughter seeking her just as she sought him. 'Face me, war bitch!'

Language! He should wash his mouth out.

It made her smile. She must (as she knew) be winning.

A man before her, her spear took him, cut him open at the throat. Then a woman—came at Cona wielding a great two-handed sword, furious; Cona's spear slipped harmlessly away over her; her sword came down over Cona's body and the shadow of it was vast, the sword had more weight and strength to it than Cona had in all her body, the dogs yelped turned trying to bite but the woman pressed in too close. Cona ducked her head down to make herself tiny in the war chariot. Too small for the blade to cut. The shadow of the blade, knowing it was coming. Through the crash of battle she could hear the blade's rushing, killing wind. It met her shoulder, clashed down there and she saw pain sparks fly up in her mind. White pain fires in her mind quickly kindled. The noise of it, hurt and fury together, sent her reeling back. Blinded. Deafened.

Then nothing. A shriek. The war chariot shook beneath Cona. Kharlie yelped. The chariot rushed forward. Cona squinted through the pain to see the enemy woman had vanished behind her. Lira sank her teeth into a man's arm. Cona twisted the spear with her left hand, caught an enemy warrior on the thigh. He gasped, his eyes met hers. Then he too was gone, and the man Lira had bitten, the chariot rushing on across the battlefield. Cona blinked heavily, shook her head to clear the pain. A horseman drew up beside her, a man's helmeted face dripping sweat: 'I cut her arm off, my lady! Are you hurt?'

Yes, gosh, you think, I might be hurt? Her right shoulder was pure pain. She risked a glance at it: the whole right side of her corselet was damaged, the bronze caved in against her body at the shoulder. Her whole right side would be black and blue by tomorrow. But she didn't *think* the skin beneath had been broken. Beyond cuts made by her own armour, at least. She shook the rein to make the dogs slow a little, calm the chariot's jolting mad rush. Closed her eyes, took three long breaths, opened them.

'It's not so bad. I'm alive.' The dogs had run the chariot almost out of the back of the battle, the sound of fighting crashed behind her now like sitting on a beach with her back to the sea. 'Another moment and I'd be dead. Thank you.'

The horseman saluted. 'We're winning, my lady.'

Cona said with deep relief, 'We are, yes.' She took another deep breath, pushed down the pain fires in her shoulder. 'We are, yes!' The spear and the spear-bracket holding it on the chariot were undamaged. Kharlie and Lira were scratched and filthy but pricked up their ears and looked up bright-eyed at her voice. All would be well enough to fight on. She touched the rein and the dogs bayed. The horseman kicked in his heels so the horse reared up. The chariot turned in a tight circle, rushing back into the heart of the battle.

The battle was almost won now. Cona's warriors surged forward, driving the enemy before them. The chariot jolted heavily over the thick-piled dead. Cona craned her neck in search of the enemy leader. He was still looking for her: she heard him bellow, 'Cona! Face me!', turned the chariot towards him.

His name was Lord Morren. A mighty and valiant warrior. Paladin of light. Leader of men most high regarded. Many the songs that praised him. Cona had long desired to face him in battle, test herself against him and best him. One of the few, the very few, who could. But now it was almost strange seeing him close up and real, now at last when the battle was almost won against him. A great, tall, strong man, very handsome; his hair and his armour both gleaming gold. She could imagine the girls at her parents' court squealing if he strode through the hall all smiles; had to admit she'd not be entirely and utterly outraged herself if he gave her a smile with those big eyes and those pink lips. One of those people who wore his armour lightly: pitched battle, savage fighting, his side about to admit defeat, and he moved across the battlefield with his warcloak like a flame and the light glittering on his muscled breast-plate. He shouted, 'Cona! Face me!'

Shook his great sword—killed one of her warriors, casually, barely noticing. His thighs rippled. His shoulders rolled. 'Cona! War bitch!' Her warriors and his warriors drew back, a space opening between Lady Cona and Lord Morren. He saw her. Finally. Raised his sword in radiant challenge. His voice came louder and slower as he shouted right at her, 'Cona! Face me! Fight me, bitch!' He shouted very loudly, 'Come and fight me like a man!'

He stopped and looked embarrassed.

'I'm here,' Cona said.

The space around them widened. His warriors, her warriors, all drawing back. This should be something to see. Cona jerked the rein and the dogs stopped with perhaps two spear lengths between her and Morren. He fixed his eyes on her, looking down his nose, his expression something between a frown and a sneer.

She thought with weary irritation: *he thinks he's so bloody exhaustingly literally good*.

Morren waved his sword, Cona shook her spear and her dogs barked at him. She said: 'Your army is destroyed or fled. Here I am. Fight me? You should surrender now.'

He shouted, 'You burned every village for twenty miles around, Cona the war bitch!'

He seemed so...upset, saying that.

Cona said very reasonably: 'I did, yes.'

'I swore on my sword that not a drop of water will pass my lips until I have killed you, Cona the war bitch!'

Still very reasonably, she said, 'So you can drink through your dick can you, then?' Such a handsome man—and goodness but the testosterone reeked off him. But obviously also more than a bit mighty-man-of-war-warleader-heart-of-solid-oak thick. He'd be saying he'd sworn on his honour next.

Now that would be serious: if he said that, she'd be in danger of wetting herself laughing.

'I've sworn—'

Cona shook her spear, which made Kharlie and Lira bark. 'Yes, yes: so: are you going to fight me like a man or not?'

Morren gave her that look, confused, panicked, annoyed. Raised his sword mightily. 'I have sworn to kill you and I will, Cona the war bitch!'

She said with a smile, 'Come on, then.'

Morren balanced himself in a war stance. Sword ready. Sunlight caught the blade. He was a man of gold, all glorious shining, the light was on his hair, his skin, his greatness; he was the light, radiant, longing, carved from sun and flame. As a child dreams of being the hero, built of summer days, of hope and glory, tall enough to reach the sky, strong enough to break the earth apart. A tree with leaves all

dancing. A landscape spread with fields, flowers, forests, clear
lakes. He threw back his head and roared his war cry: poetry!
He jumped, flexed his great sword in his great sword-arm,
with a radiance now in his eyes, eager now for battle, daunt-
less, the true hero, with a cry of joy in his own prowess he
leapt furious in daylight running on to fight. His shadow was
golden, and his armour; golden warm and like music was the
hiss of his blade when it fell, and it fell in beauty like a star
falling at first twilight; and he leapt like a second brilliant
rising golden sun.

Cona touched the reins and the dogs were running. In
the charge they had been fast, but now truly freely they ran.
Head-foremost, headlong, both together; one being, daunt-
less, of their own lives uncaring, as water flows, as wind flows.
As a rock is rushed by winter torrents, the snow-melt and the
storm-swell darken and make wild the river, on-run of wild
water bearing down sharp with rocks and broken branches,
and the green bare banks are burst. As the lightning flashes
faster than thought in the blackened clouds and the sky
opens; the people run to shelter with the flash still burning
on their soaked eyelids. As fire is running through a house
unguarded, the dry wood that is all a man possesses rising
ruinous smoke stained, falls burning broken faster even than
his frantic tears can fall. Faster than speech. Faster than bird
song. Faster than any man, the dogs, the dogs ran! The chariot leapt with Morren leaping, Morren's sword came down
like thunder with all the might of his arm behind it, struck
only the earth and the dust stirred up in the chariot's wake.
Turning, hurling forwards, fast away from him then fast
toward him into his bright stance. His sword high, crashing;
Cona's spear thrust, twist: and he fell back, mouth open,
wounded, a shout came from him as the blood burst fast as
the dogs from his left hip. Cona was past, herself laughing;
the chariot turned, the dogs bayed joyful, fast as his blood
they rushed. And Morren's sword of gold this time caught

the high side of the chariot so that the sparks flashed, bronze on bull's hide thickly gilded, and the crash of their meeting made the earth shake. And Morren spun, all of gold in his fury; and the chariot turned; and again they met. His blade took Cona's arm, cut it, her blood on the floor of the chariot, on the spear shaft, on her lap. Her spear tore his knee, cut skin and bone open. Then on, each turning, turning, turning, the charge to meet, the sword hissed, the spear searching, then on, turning, the dogs panted, the chariot carrying Cona flowing past him, the dogs baying red. Cona almost dizzy, so fast was the chariot moving. Morren spitting, cursing, leaping the scythed wheel like he was dancing, panting harder than her war dogs.

The sparks! The blood! The fury! The clouds of dust kicked up when Morren leapt! The battle was won for Cona and had been won since she began it, there was no fighting left now and no pursuit either, the vanquished fled wild into safety, for all left in the place with eyes to see could only stare, wondering, at this one great terrible fight. Lady Cona held the killing ground amid much slaughter—but her army was heedless of their victory, too dazzled by the beauty of the fight. Flecks of gold from Morren's fine armour made the dust glitter. As fireflies in the dusk make the air glitter. His beautiful hero's body rank with his sweat. Again the dogs rushed and again he met them, his sword clattering against the chariot's bull-hide sides, Cona's spear shrieking against the greaves that shielded his long well-muscled legs. Again she sped past and he leapt up and back.

'I swore I'd kill you!' Morren's voice was a croak. Mouth dust-clotted. They paused perhaps three spear's lengths apart, both breathless. The man gasped, sagged on his feet. Exhausted. And very thirsty, too, no doubt.

'So fight me until you kill!' Cona was nauseous, her head spinning from the endless turns, bruised and shaken about so hard she had bitten her own tongue. The dogs panted, they were wounded and tiring. But Cona shook her spear at her enemy, he ran at her, a slow run, half-falling, she had only to whip the reins to make the dogs pull her out of the reach of his blade. They were close enough almost to touch hands, but Morren only turned very slowly, grunting for breath.

'I...swore...I'd...kill...you...'

'So kill me.' Cona's voice was brighter—sounded brighter, even if she did fear she might be sick. 'Shall we fight on, then?'

Morren raised his sword with a howl. The stink that came from his armpits was something else. Black liquid ran down his arms and dripped at his feet: sweat mixed with dust. Oh, yes, and blood. He roared, staggered at Cona. Cona sat perfectly still in her chariot. Morren's sword smashed down at her. Blunted and dented. She moved slightly, very slightly, just twisted her body, Kharlie and Lira pulled the chariot just one or two dog steps. Cona leaned sideways, lashed out a flick of her dagger, caught Morren's sword hand. Not a deep wound, but he let out a yelp of pain, oddly like a dog's yelp, dropped his sword.

Her warriors all around with swords drawn. He groaned aloud. Not used to defeat.

The greatest fight in the oldest of stories—the great hero man of that, he broke and ran rather than stand and fight. His enemy, the greatest hero of all of them, pursued him. When both were exhausted, they threw their spears, and the greatest hero man of all, he cheated, and the great hero man fell dead.

Hiera said easily, 'Shall I kill him?'

'No. Leave him.'

Half sat, half lay in the dust by the chariot, dripping with sweat, filthy, covered in blood. He stared up at her. 'Ruthless evil war bitch, are you?'

Cona stared back at him. 'Oh, yes.'

She clapped her hands for attendants. 'Kharlie and Lira are exhausted and wounded. Take them away to the kennel, tend to them. A meal and a wash, play with them.' The dogs had sunk down on their bellies, panting; now their ears pricked up and they yelped happily. Hiera herself unfastened their harnesses, eased off their armour. From out of the bronze, two beautiful dog faces nosed at Heira, licked her hand, then both ran eagerly to Cona. She rubbed their ears, kissed them. 'Oh you wonderful good girls you. Thank you, Kharlie, thank you, Lira. Good girls. The best. Nice Hiera has some meat for you, you go with nice Hiera, girls.'

'Come on Kharlie. Come on Lira.' The two trotted after Hiera with tails wagging. Cona sighed. 'Oh, they are the best dogs.' She clapped her hands again for her daily chariot to be brought up. Kriran was there with it, blood on her lip where she's been biting it in terror for the whole battle. Very carefully, trying to avoid cutting themselves on Cona's battered armour, two slaves lifted her from the damaged war chariot. Cona sighed again, this time with pure pleasure. The joys of sitting in something not bashed up and soaked in sweat.

Kriran said with a kind of gasp of relief, 'There's a bath waiting for you, my lady, and some food.'

'Yes. Good.'

'My lady: what about the last of the enemy?' That was a new junior commander Hiera had appointed, who obviously couldn't think for himself. 'The enemy has fled. All the ones left here alive have surrendered. What do you want us to do?'

Sitting in the nice clean comfortable not-made-for-war-made-for-nothing-but-comfort chariot (made of pearl looted from the Temple of the Spider Lady With Ten Thousand Faces, eyes averted least we invoke Her presence, cower in terror, mortal, cower and fear Her wrath! and the hide of a red sea-dragon spewing poison from its maw into the waters ever hungering, and gold melted down from the queen's throne from High Semyran City of Singing Flames, but honestly it was very comfortable despite all that stuff), the dogs being tended and safe, Cona felt she could fall asleep in her armour. Do I care anything about some bunch of defeated cowering peasants with broken farm tools? No. 'Pursue anyone worth pursuing until nightfall. The ones who've surrendered here on the battlefield...' Her eyes were heavy, now the battle joy had worn off her own body was beginning to howl back at her worse than the enemy did. (Two days in bed resting? Three days? Small price, yes, for a massive victory— okay, yes, a right pain in the arse, but also a real pleasure, three days stretched undisturbed in bed eating and sleeping and giving orders, *Oh woe weak me what suffering I must endure for my battle prowess.)* Can I bothered with this stuff now? No. 'Just...kill them or something.'

The junior officer nodded, although he looked a bit shocked. 'It will be done immediately, my lady.' The 'or something' was the key, of course—he could do a lot with that 'or something' if he had it in him, like set them all free with a purse of gold each. He wouldn't, because he didn't quite have it in him, and next battle she'd make sure he was right in the front lines with a slightly less than perfectly sharp spear, and they'd see if he could get it in him quick before he got it in him quick.

Cona gestured in the rough direction of the camp. 'It's done here. Let's go.' The trumpets began to ring for her final victory, ringing her home in triumph to her tent. Her army stretched out before her, filling the battlefield, to us was kept the place of slaughter, they looked up from corpse-looting to shake swords, cheer, Lady Cona! Lady Cona! Victorious! The chariot, lighter than the great war vehicle, creaked uncomfortably over the piled bodies, the slaves cursing under their breath as they pulled. If the dogs had been less valiant in battle she should have taken her war chariot back to the camp, she thought. A horrible noise as the left wheels went over someone who wasn't strictly quite dead until she went over them. Whoops.

Kriran said, 'My lady...?'

Cona gestured for the chariot to stop again. 'Yes?'

'The...um, the enemy leader, my lady.'

'What? Who? Oh, yes, him.' Actually, she'd been watching him out of the corner of her eye, greatly enjoying the look of bafflement on his face that he, the great shining golden hero was being...was being...ignored by everyone. 'Do you know, I'd sort of forgotten about him. Should have made more of a fuss and got my attention, not just sat there, should he?'

She looked down at him now. 'What shall I do with you, Morren? I've defeated you. Shall I kill you?' She smiled at him. 'Or shall I leave you here to make excuses to yourself for how I came to beat you? There's always some excuse. Bit too sunny for you today, maybe, or really you won you were just very briefly unlucky?'

He tore his helmet off and covered his face with his bloody hands. Bent his head and then fell forward, weeping. His vast body shook with his sobs. Oh how fair, and how ruined. As a palace that stands deserted, the dust fills the rooms where stately kings once walked. As a fine tree is cut for mere kindling, as the rain tramples down the golden crops. And the beast lies dying in the field, and the bird cannot fly for its wings are clipped. As a child sickens and will never know the pleasures of its body, as clouds cover the moon and the sun. The mould is broken open after much toil but the casting is flawed and the bronze is cracked. His hero's beauty shrunken, grieving, all his pride and his bright honour forever tarnished. He sobbed out, 'I swore.... Dead... dead...'

'Am I even revelling in my triumph that I beat you? Right now: maybe not.'

'I swore it...I swore on my honour...'

Cona turned her face away. 'Oh, just leave him. I can't be bothered with him. Leave him.'

Kriran said, 'My lady?'

The man raised his head. Now gore-stained as well as sweat-stained, which was a shame as his hair really was very nice. 'Cona! War bitch! I swore not to leave this field of battle until either you or I was dead! Come back and fight!'

'We've burned down every village for twenty miles, butchered half the people who live here, taken everything here there is to take. Every single part of me hurts like a bitch, I've got a hot bath and a meal to look forward to, then I want to go home and see my parents. We fought, he lost. He wants to hang around here crying and making excuses, that's his problem. I won.'

'But...you could kill him.'

She thought: Honestly, Kriran, look at him. The hero. The bright shining light.

I can't be bothered to kill him.

The chariot jolted back to the camp. A hard pull up the hill to Cona's tent. Almost died with pleasure when they stripped her filthy armour off. Bath or food, bath or food? such a difficult choice.

'That was a good battle.'

Kriran said, 'I watched from a distance. You were amazing.'

'And the dogs. They were amazing, amazing. The darlings.'

She chose the bath first because hygiene. Closed her eyes as Kriran poured almost too hot water over her head. Oh, that's good. And a warm towel to be rubbed dry, and a woollen robe perfumed with thyme and lavender, and a chair piled with cushions, and a plate of bread and honey and one very, very last home-scented apple they'd lied about earlier and kept back. It was dusk, growing cold on these spring evenings, the lamplight drew in the first early moths. The doorcurtain was closed tightly against the darkness, but a wind blew and made the tent shiver so that Cona's shadow was alive on the wall. The slave boy, beautiful, crept in a little later: 'My lady: your war spear. It is mended and polished, and it gleams brighter than before the battle.'

'Good.'

A messenger, a little later again, casting envious glances at the food and the cushions: 'My lady: the pursuit caught most of the survivors in a valley, trying to cross a river there, killed many of them. But we left off there at nightfall as you ordered; half of them perhaps, got away over the river.'

'Good, then.'

He frowned: 'My lady?'

'They can rebuild their villages. After a few years they'll be ready for a raid again from Lady Cona the war bitch.'

He frowned. Then he smiled. 'Yes, indeed. Good.'

When he had gone, Kriran insisted she sleep. For, yes, she was as exhausted and aching as Kriran said.

'You can put out the lamp tonight, Kriran.'

'I will yes, you call me if you want it relighting. There's water there, my lady, just by your hand there, see it? Call me, if you need anything.' And a final fuss over the cushions and the quilt.

Cona sunk down into the bed. In the dark the spear gleamed faintly, half-visible, like music almost heard at a far distance. She stared up at it for a while, trying to sleep. The worst of it was her hands. It took days for them to relax from holding the spear and the rein, she kept almost falling asleep and her hands would jerk to wake her up. Exhausted and aching, but hard to sleep. The dogs barked, a happy barking, they had had a good day also. She thought to the dogs: but we'll go home and rest a bit in peace now. You have a sleep, girls. She thought briefly of her enemy, great golden hero, out in the cold dark...sulking? Still shouting for her to come back and fight him? Learning to drink with his dick? Behind the doorcurtain Kriran fussed, unable to settle down, made a long loud sound of trying to breathe like someone deeply asleep.

Cona thought briefly: I could have kept him as a slave, I suppose. Him being so strong and handsome.

Cona stretched out her hands, felt the God King's fine cushions cradle her head, fell asleep.

In the morning she played fetch with the dogs for a while, before she started for home at the head of a great column of loot. Dozing, aching, in a litter carved of dragon bone, hung with white samite, born by ten slaves in diamond collars. Well content.

READY FOR COMBAT

By
K R Green

Shannon scanned the hall tables, already assuming they wouldn't be here. Even extending her magic, she could tell Rowan clearly wasn't in the building. Checking that she wasn't being watched, she slid out the side door into the courtyard, wrapping her arms around her coat against the wind. Rowan stepped off the terrace opposite, landing on the balcony just above Shannon. Chestnut hair falling flat against their ears, green eyes set on the wall opposite. Their necklace chain of rings shook under their boho-style tunic, their boot squeaking on the tile.

She tried to keep her voice to a loud whisper. The last thing she needed was for someone to hear them and investigate. 'Row, get down.'

Rowan smirked down at her. 'Oh, like this?' Her best friend lifted a foot off the edge, as if about to step off the low wall at the edge of the balcony.

She knew it was a joke. Really she did. But the squeal came out involuntarily, before she covered her mouth with her hand. 'No!'

Rowan giggled, jumping to the roof opposite. 'I can't help it. I'm clearly made to fly.'

Shannon shook her head, looking behind her to check the door to the hall was shut. 'Climb more like. You don't have wings.'

'I can do both.' Spreading their arms like wings, Rowan grinned down at Shannon, who shook her head and rolled her eyes.

'You know what I mean. You shouldn't be out here when there's no tutor around.'

Rowan's smile fell away. 'It's just a bit of practice. I have to be ready, you know?'

Shannon closed her eyes, trying to understand why Rowan didn't feel enough just by being allowed here. 'What makes you feel you should be the one to do this anyway? You're strong enough, as you are.' Kai had stolen fire from the gods—they didn't need to prove themselves as warriors anymore.

But Rowan shook their head. 'Because in this culture, I have twice as much to prove.'

Shannon's heart skipped a beat, remembering the threat Rowan faced. Even here, they were not safe to be themselves. 'I hear you, but you know what the Elders would say about you being out here without their supervision.'

Still, Shannon knew it went so much deeper than just a rule. This was Rowan's life. Day in, day out. The lump in Shannon's throat solidified as she heard the door behind her creak open.

'Shannon.' His voice was deep, and she let out a silent sigh. Elder Karunajala. She'd tried her best.

'Sir.' Shannon tried not to wince, knowing it futile to claim ignorance. She tried to shut her ears, knowing what was to come, as they deadnamed Rowan, but the look on their face was painful enough to see. It really wasn't hard.

Rowan climbed down from the awning of an entryway, hiding their face in the plant strands from the trellis.

'You know the penalty for breaking the rules.'

Rowan stepped up beside Shannon. 'But Sir—'

'I have told you. Your beliefs do not exempt you from our rules.'

But Rowan's voice only rose. 'I am at risk every time I leave this place. Sometimes, I wonder if I'm even safe within these walls.'

Elder Karunajala let out his own sigh. 'I hear your concerns, child. And I come to ask once more for Shannon's skills, but also, this time, for your experience. If you would be willing to accompany her?'

Shannon stepped forward, beside Rowan. 'What is our assignment?'

'There is a protest in town that we need you to oversee. I wonder if...Rowan...would be a useful ally to have with you.'

Well that was unusual. Elder Karunajala was one of the more understanding Elders, but none of them used Rowan's preferred name.

He met Rowan's gaze. 'It is a protest about gender identity rights.'

Well that explained it. Pride marches were often good places to find those with magic—outcasts often allied together. Rowan would be there as Rowan, to show that they were safe people to approach. And Shannon was there to shift their mindsets, to tug on their feelings, and to ensure that no one with magic was left without guidance. Especially in such a heated environment.

Shannon waited for Rowan's response, aware that the danger they feared was more likely at such a rally.

Rowan's eyes narrowed, and they bowed their head. 'I can be ready in half an hour.'

#

S hannon tied the rainbow flag around her neck, considering her attire options from the bag they'd brought and looking around at the others preparing to counter the protest. The sight of so many rainbows and flags specific to people's identity filled her soul with hope, and her heart with joy. How the hell could seven billion people fit into two oversimplified boxes, after all? It was such a ludicrous idea.

A man in a fluorescent jacket nodded his head at them as he approached. 'Morning. You here for the rally?'

'Yes. What time will things get moving?'

'Around 10am. It's such a shame this is still needed in the modern day.'

Shannon nodded, sighing at the pavement. 'I hear you. Sometimes I just despair at the amount of hatred people feel towards those they do not know.'

'Tell me about it. Can I check your bag for weapons?'

She kept her face neutral. 'Of course.' She unzipped her cross-body bag, careful not to let any of the zipped compartments show, lifting a water bottle out so he could see the bottom. Rowan held open the cloth bag containing their rainbow fishnet gloves, bandana, and non-binary coloured mini flags. 'Thank you. You stay safe out there.'

When he moved away, Shannon let herself exhale, swallowing back anxiety. She was trained to alter mindset, not hide a whip from an inspection.

175

Rowan's voice brought her back to the present moment. 'Ready?'

Shannon forced a smile. 'Of course.'

They walked up to the crowd of other gatherers, forming part of the line that would travel to the protest site together. One thing the community did well was include everyone and seek safety together.

The walk was uneventful, and she found herself searching the crowd for those with a magic signature. There were definitely one or two people here using aura magic, and maybe one or two with some level of elemental magic. They'd have to mingle so she could focus in on the right people at closer range.

The pride flags, with their 6 stripes across the rainbow colours filled the gaps between people, adorned skin in the form of face chalk, wrapped around them as capes, and were held up on signs. And then, opposing them, slogans of fear and anger.

Shannon narrowed her eyes across the park, her stomach tensing at the chants of protesters. The protest was around the same size as their counter rally, with people shrieking about women's rights and how transgender people did not belong in the community. Shannon felt the unease in the pit of her stomach and her chest at the same time. This was not what being a woman was about.

Living in such a city, she couldn't really be surprised, but in a way, it being known as the 'gay capital' really should suggest that protesters against the community weren't welcome. Still, even in such a place as Brighton, the counter protest was a dangerous place to be.

She thought of Clarissa, grateful she was not here to see the blind hatred these people had for someone they had never met. Shannon was lucky, able to blend in when the radicals came to judge her people. Her partner's beauty was clear from across the road. Her graceful height, the strength in her shoulders, and the curve of her throat. There was a depth in her eyes that shone a light across a room, and while it led the way for those lost in the darkness, it also made her a target.

A target specifically from these protesters. First, it had been the male gays. Then the laws against 'pretend families,' as they called it. Even after civil partnerships were legalized, the fight against the transgender community soared.

And that made it all the more important she attend these rallies—not just as a Circle member—but as a person fighting for the rights of every human being to feel safe in their own skin. She was not new to these gatherings, yet the sight on one edge of the protesting group made her physically bend over; as if she'd been kicked in the stomach. Her mouth went dry, her heart speeding up.

Even she had never seen such disrespect at one of these rallies before. The pride progress flag; noted in its progression by five arrow stripes, a yellow triangle, and purple circle had been deliberately, openly vandalized. Someone had cut the arrow shape from the 6 main rainbow stripes: separating the old pride flag of the lesbian, gay, and bisexual folk from the more specific flags represented in the arrow. Cutting the transgender, intersex, black, mixed race and HIV-positive queer people from the rest of the community was such a symbol of ripping apart her population that she didn't even realize the shriek came from her own mouth.

How dare they?

Her eyes shut of their own volition and she felt the ripple of magic tremble at the wave of emotion she felt.

The warmth of a hand on her wrist brought her back to the present moment, but also pulled her watering eyes back to the shredded material, the person proudly holding up her work of mutilation, then to her friend who had reached out.

177

Rowan's face was red and wet. Shannon twisted her arm so that she could grasp Rowan's hand with her own, squeezing it tight. They shouldn't have to see this. No one should be subjected to this.

Shannon swallowed, grounding herself with some deep breaths. 'Let's get some space.' She met Rowan's gaze and turned away from the sight of desecration.

'Oi! Tranny!'

Her breath stopped in her chest, tightness spreading through her neck. She tried to exhale, she really did. But her body had taken over, instinct still in control, just as it was when the shriek left her lips. She felt Rowan's hand tighten on hers and with her best friend in the firing line, she felt the strength of her wildfire rise.

Shannon turned her head to face the abuser, remaining silent. It was a woman clutching a placard about women's genitalia above her head who had stepped forward to specifically target them. She felt the wave of power from this woman's hatred, and had to stifle her own power striking out.

'How can you touch that filth?'

Shannon twirled to face the person, placing herself between Rowan and the offender, spitting her words at the protester. 'The only filth here is currently hurling abuse at innocent human beings.'

'I'm not the one forcing our kids into sexuality.'

The roar of her own anger flared at the injustice, the gall, of this person. 'Look, lady. My friend and I don't have anything to do with children. We work in finance. I don't come and protest how you dress, what name you asked to be called or which bathroom you use. It would be polite if you would have the same common decency for us.'

'You're hanging around with *him*. That makes you just as bad.'

The lightning erupted inside her, the storm of her magic ignited and ready to strike. But she was not here to attack these people. As much as they might deserve it after the suffering they were causing. But there were no rules against telling this person exactly what she thought.

'For fucks sake, what planet are you on?' Her body stepped forward, although she had no memory of choosing to move. Her arms raised in frustration, and the woman stepped back. 'I'm just as bad as a kind, compassionate human being who has the same rights as you? Damn right I am. I'd rather be on the side of equality and compassion than even be associated with your nazi hate group. Anyone who hangs out with you clearly doesn't care for the safety of other humans, so I'm very happy with my place. Now I must ask you to stop harassing us, else I will involve the police.'

Shannon felt the spark of her power at the edge of her aura, and wrestled to pull it in. But she felt the reactionary spark of others gifts ahead of her. This crowd had magicians within them. How was that even possible?

The sudden Scottish accent yelling at her side startled her, and she had to clamp down on her power before she lost control. The man's gruff voice was stern and powerful. 'Leave these ladies the fuck alone.'

'Oh, of course you've got *another man* to defend your stance. I'm not at all surprised. Maybe you're right. You even fight like a little girl would.' It was this venomous spiel that Shannon felt the tug from. This woman was using the gift; trying to bend her will to match her view. Of course such a strong counter protest would have tricks to get more people involved. She'd need to report that.

The Scot didn't back down, his voice booming across the park. 'When you grow a heart, we'll have a chat. Until then, mind your own fucking business. Whether I'm male or female doesn't matter—I don't tolerate bullies and fascists like the likes of you. Get back behind your tape, bitch.'

Rowan pulled Shannon backwards, and the next thing she knew, they were slipping into the crowd so that others could step forward to argue with their oppressor.

An adult with two teenagers wearing nonbinary flags came up to them. 'Are you okay? I'm Ruth.' The woman glared at the crowd now standing by the accuser who had yelled at them. 'And I can't stand the way they treat us.' She put a hand on Shannon's shoulder. 'Are you alright?'

Shannon nodded, but Rowan was practically blind with tears; their cheeks bright red and blotchy, eyes full of water. 'I think we need a moment to regroup.'

'Of course, dear. Come this way. We've got a little wind breaker you can sit inside and gather yourself. It's horrific the things we have to experience just to exist.'

The wave of exhaustion was too strong, and Shannon found herself spinning through various thoughts. She was here to find those with magic; to invite in anyone who might need shelter with their powers, and to keep Rowan safe. That woman misgendering Rowan was a deliberate act—they didn't even look male, just like a tomboy.

Shannon was used to this treatment in some places. After all, her girlfriend was openly trans and didn't 'pass' as a woman at first glance. And the first thing anyone noticed in this society was someone's apparent gender.

But if there was one thing Shannon knew, it was that Clarissa had been female all along. In her mannerisms as a teenager, her emotional literacy, the way she felt and shared that power people often attributed to the 'womb.' Clarissa hadn't known she was female until her thirties, but Shannon had known her at eighteen, and the signs were always there. Whatever these people thought made a 'woman,' they clearly didn't have a fucking clue if they excluded trans women.

As Rowan was hugged by one of the teens, Ruth kept watch from the other side of the little rainbow material screen, and the second young person sat cross-legged in front of Shannon. Long red hair reached below their chest, and they used their nails on one hand to remove some dirt from other the nails on the other. Being so close, she felt the little ripple of the child's wellspring.

She looked more closely at her mental space, and realized she'd been emitting her own waves of power, almost calling for those with similar signatures to come to her. 'I'm Shannon. She/her.'

'Lark. I'm not sure, yet.'

Shannon smiled. 'I'm very glad your family came to support us, Lark. It feels like you could sense we needed help.'

The teen tilted their head to one side a bit, and Shannon smiled. So they were aware of their power, at least. 'I guess you could say that.'

Shannon glanced over at Rowan, who seemed to be calmer now, chatting with the other teenager. She didn't feel safe to stay here much longer, but she had a job to do.

'I also have a kind of...sense, I guess you could call it. I can't use it when I'm all emotional like I was then, but I feel like I can sense it in you. Does that sound crazy?'

She'd learned that talking with young adults was much more effective if she was straight with them. They could smell bullshit a mile away.

Lark pursed their lips, clearly not sure how much to share. 'I guess not really.'

She was losing them. She pulled out a business card with her name and number on it. 'If I give you my card, would you be willing to chat with me a bit via the phone? I'll let you text me when you're ready. I work with people who can help with this...sensing thing. If you ever need a hand or want to meet others...Just give this number a message. If you don't,

FIGHT LIKE A GIRL VOLUME 2

feel free to just keep the card in case anyone you know needs help.' She swallowed. Usually she was more succinct than that but, oh well. It was done now. 'Does that make sense?'

Lark nodded, taking the card and frowning at it for a moment, before putting it in their little hip bag.

Shannon stood, turning to face Ruth who was distracted by another part of the crowd. 'I feel Rowan and I should get moving, maybe speak with our friends before we step back to the front. Thank you so much for your hospitality.'

'Oh, any time, dear. Those bullies are nasty pieces of work. Why they can't just mind their own business or target actual predators, I'll never know.'

Shannon offered a hand to Rowan, who took it, and helped lift them off the ground. 'I want to speak with Clarissa. Did you want to come with me?'

Rowan nodded. 'I'm sorry. I thought I could do this, but I don't think I can.'

Shannon hugged her friend tight. 'Of course. Let's get to safety. Then we can plan what the next step looks like.'

#

Shannon sat with her hand in Clarissa's lap, their fingers interlinked, as she explained the events of the protest. A few arrests had been made by the local police, and various stories were trending on social media. Thankfully, magic had not been exposed to the public, even after Shannon had left.

Clarissa stroked Shannon's hair behind her ear, kissing her cheek and resting her head on Shannon's shoulder. 'I'm sorry you had to experience that. I don't understand why they hate us so much. We're not hurting anyone.'

Shannon sighed. 'It feels like I can't rest, even here. If they can protest your existence in Brighton of all places, what hope does anyone else have?'

'Rest is crucial. Else how will you be strong enough to stand with our siblings next time? Remember that the space between the trees makes a forest.'

She sounded so wise. 'I just don't know where I'd be without you.'

'You'd still be trapped in your old patterns, and I'd still be lost.'

Shannon laughed a little. 'Alright, fair point. I guess we know full well where we'd be.'

'What are you going to tell the Elders?'

'The truth. That it is hard to manage my own feelings, that as a female-only circle we should be doing more to protect those at risk from society, and that finding people in those spaces is hard with the level of mental conflict going on.'

Clarissa squeezed her hand. 'And what about the protestors magic?'

'I didn't get a very clear reading because of the environment.'

'But surely that's important for the Elders to know?'

She tried not to let the anger in her voice come out as tears welled in her eyes. 'Yes, Clarissa. I'll tell them. I just...I need to process it for a moment.'

Clarissa's arms came around her, and she let the comfort of being home soothe the unease that had been growing since this morning. People could judge and they could hypothesise, but when they were together, she felt like she was actually alive. Like her fire ignited and she could control it. Like she was just meant to be alight in this moment, and that with Clarissa, she could burn brighter.

After a few moments, letting herself ground in her partner's energy, Shannon felt the tug of duty and pulled out of the safety of her lover's arms. 'I better go report my findings. See you soon, okay?'

Clarissa kissed the back of her hand and squeezed her fingers before letting her get up. 'We can do hard things.'

Shannon followed the winding paths from her accommodation to the main complex, and knocked on Elder Karunjala's door.

'Come in.'

She stood in the doorway, waiting for him to turn around from his desk. 'Sir, I have some concerns from the rally today.'

Elder Karunajala frowned, turning from his chair to face her. 'Do come in. What did you see?'

'The protesters, the anti-trans people; at least one of them was using magic to influence the crowd. I felt multiple threads of magic, but it was so hard to actually pinpoint. I became overwhelmed by the woman using magic—she targeted Rowan and myself so it was a very focused experience.'

His eyes softened, lips pursing. 'Are you both okay?'

'Rowan is taking some time alone. I've had a debrief with Clarissa.' They wouldn't let Clarissa fight, but she helped in other ways. Shannon tried not to overthink that too much, especially since she was sure Clarissa's hormones were more in range of a female than some of the well-trained cis-women in their group.

'What can you tell me of this group?'

It hadn't actually occurred to her that they were specifically interested in the hate group. 'Around three hundred people, at a guess. The woman who spoke with us; she was using a mindset shift like I have. I also felt other ripples but it's very hard to tell what's from their group and what's from ours. I met a teenager who has the gift, and gave her my card.'

The Elder closed his eyes. Shannon bit her lip. 'What haven't you told me, sir?'

His sigh told her she was on to something. 'The group at the rally today. Kai, your circle's founder, fought with some of the members. We've been watching them since, and with Kai's disappearance last year, many eyes turned on this cult as suspects.'

Shannon swallowed, anxiety in the back of her throat. Kai, along with two others from the original five, had taken fire from the Buddhist centre in the cliffs just outside the city's perimeter. The Circlet had always spoken of this being their proof of female power and cunning, and they had created a haven for females with magic to practice combat in safety. Being hosted here, in Brighton, they had accepted anyone who identified as female.

In her eyes, that's what made their crew so successful— the balance of all energies and access to the whole spectrum of magic and experience. Those who didn't fit inside the simple boxes of two genders, or two sexualities, knew how to experience the world outside of the lines society tried to draw around it. She had always wondered what meant that Karunajala could be so involved, but that was not for her to understand.

Karunajala looked down at some paper on his desk. 'We believe this group are trying to steal the fire back.'

Of all the things Shannon had expected, that was not one of them. 'But even we don't know where the original Circlet hid it.'

'I know that. I presume this is why they took Kai last year. She likely does know. And the fact they are here now suggests they may have found out.'

Why hadn't she been told this before? 'What of the others?'

'Mairi is still safe. Aileen is now considered missing. It's hard to know if she has ducked out of the public eye to stay safe, or if she has been taken.'

Shannon hadn't heard the names specifically before, but she felt some level of reassurance that someone was keeping an eye on the original Circlet members. But where did this leave them now? She frowned at the floor, picking at the skin on the back of her hand. 'What happens next?'

The Elder sighed again, and looked down at his hands. 'I think I need to share this information and ask...Rowan?' He paused, clearly checking the name with her. Shannon nodded, tilting her head to one side at this change in behaviour. 'For their view on how the march felt.' He met her eye contact, as if hearing her question. 'I appreciate that not everyone supports the openness of the circle to someone nonbinary and I myself struggle with the name changes, but the original Circlet were clear that this is a space for feminine energy however it may present.'

Shannon nodded, trying to work out the appropriate response to such a human comment. But the Elder stood up and she instinctively did the same. 'Thank you for the feedback. I'll go speak with the team immediately.'

Assuming herself dismissed, Shannon bowed her head and stepped back out into the sunlight, head spinning with concerns about this hate group in her city. They were here for her, for Rowan, and for Clarissa.

This was getting beyond personal.

#

The sunrise was hidden behind cloud as the pebbles clacked together under her boots. There was a group of them invited to this briefing; close to where the old Community Centre had been. Shannon tried to calm the apprehension in her gut, but the fact Clarissa was with them made her instantly cautious. They had not let her be a fighter because of her assigned gender. Yet, they were here to be briefed on this hate group, and her partner was with them.

Rowan was not.

She glanced at Melody and Charlie who had also been instructed to attend, and tried to keep her voice low. 'Do you know what this is about?'

Charlie shook her head, clearly uncomfortable with the question, eyes still on the beach beneath her feet. Melody just mouthed back a silent question in response. 'Do you?'

Deciding to mouth her own answer rather than try to project it mentally, she moved her lips. 'I'm not sure.'

Melody nodded, her focus on the path ahead. Clarissa's hand squeezed hers, and Shannon tried to take comfort in the fact they would get through whatever this was together.

At the base of the cliff edge they stopped. An Elder dressed in red robes stood in silence to greet them. She was a lama, one of the Buddhists who tended to the centre.

'Welcome, initiates.'

Initiates? What was this? The panic was already spreading through her, melding with her magic as the fight or flight system kicked inside her.

'Please follow me. There will be time for your questions once we are seated.'

The lama led them up some rough stone steps, into a room adorned with a couple of chairs and a simple burgundy rug in the centre. 'Do you know how girls fight?'

Shannon wasn't sure if that was a rhetorical question, or if she should try to venture a response. She swallowed, trying to lubricate her dry throat. Glancing at the others, she noted Melody's wide eyes and Charlie picking at her fingernails. Whatever this was, it was clearly something none of them had prepared for. Just as she opened her mouth, not even sure what she might say, the robed woman continued.

'Strategically. Forcefully. With purpose.' She paused, making eye contact with each of them. 'The original Circlet were physical fighters. They used cunning, extrasensory abilities, martial arts to achieve their aims.' The woman paced from side to side in front of them. Although there were chairs, none of them moved to sit. 'They were seen as cursed—where men gain superpowers, women are afflicted or possessed by the power. And they were on a mission to disprove that stereotype.' She sighed heavily, and Shannon could feel the power of grief from the ripple of power that exhaled with it.

'We fight very different wars now. We fight to feed our children as food banks rise. We struggle to balance time with community and support each other with getting enough sleep in the evenings to function each day. Our combat is within our own minds.'

Clarissa's hand tightened on Shannon's, and she squeezed back, sending a flow of calm and love to her partner. Again, she debated speaking, but that didn't seem to be what this lady wanted of them.

The Elder finally seemed to take notice of her audience, gesturing to the chairs. 'Please, take a seat.' She stood, waiting in silence for them to move. Clarissa took her seat and Shannon moved a chair closer to Clarissa's, so their knees could touch as they sat. She put her hand on Clarissa's thigh, and Clarissa interlinked her fingers with hers.

'You have not been told why you are here, is that correct?'

The four of them shook their heads. This seemed to be the correct response.

The lama looked at some art on the wall. It seemed to be a figure sitting in lotus position with one hand on their knee, the other touching the earth. 'What do you know of the original Circlet?'

This time, Shannon was sure they were meant to speak. 'The five who began the circle, women who felt they had something to prove.'

'Not just women, child. Witches. And humanity was taught to fear the witches, the magicians, the spiritual, and to celebrate those who burned them alive.'

Like the protesters, Shannon thought.

The Elder's eyes met hers. 'Exactly, child. Like the protestors you met.'

Had she projected that thought?

Again, the woman seemed to smile, and Shannon tried her best to shut down all thoughts she might be having. She imagined the ocean, hearing waves, seeing its colours and smelling the seaweed to block out any thoughts this woman may be able to read.

'I will not intrude again, child. Your barriers could do with strengthening though.'

Clarissa raised a hand beside her. 'They had to fight to prove they were worthy.'

'Aye, the original Circlet did, yes. These days, that is not the combat we are in need of warriors for.'

Shannon squeezed her partner's knee as Clarissa continued to offer a reply. 'We need to fight the misinformation, the attempts to silence us, and the demands that we be placated.'

'Indeed. You have each been trained specifically to fulfil a role in the Circlet, if you are willing to make the oath. To

189

protect our sisters and show that fighting like a girl means so much more than what society has been wrongly taught. We are fearsome. We are careful. We are capable of holding the fury and the power of life and death within us.'

Finally, Melody spoke up. 'You mean because women can bring the next generation of life through pregnancy?'

As she spoke, Shannon noticed how young her voice sounded. She meant well, but Shannon felt Clarissa's leg grow clammy against hers, her hands shaking a little in her lap.

Shannon glanced over at Charlie who seemed to be equally distressed. The unease grew, and she addressed the comment directly. 'We are creative, we have a spark that cannot be extinguished no matter how hard they try. We, as women, radiate our power, we bring light to each others' life, and we can choose to annihilate those parts of the world that do not serve us. This is so much bigger than pregnancy. This is at the essence of existence; fuelled by our feminine fire to bring whatever change we deem fit to the earth.'

The lama smiled, bowing her head in response. 'Yes. There are women who never get pregnant, who cannot, who may have but didn't want to, who became pregnant but did not carry to term or give birth to a life, and women who do not have wombs at all. They are no less women, for the spark of wildfire is innately what makes us who we are.'

Charlie's voice was quiet, lower in pitch than Shannon had expected. 'What happens next?'

'We test your abilities and if you meet the requirements, we offer you a space to train them here, as the newest Circlet members.'

Melody tilted her head. 'What about the old Circlet members?'

'Mairi will be your fifth, if you all pass. The others have retired from Circlet duties at this point.'

Shannon swallowed. That wasn't necessarily a lie but it didn't exactly share the truth that she knew of. Again, the Elder women's eyes met hers and she quickly looked to the floor; saying nothing.

Charlie spoke again. 'What does this test entail?'

'Each of you have different skills. We basically ask you to demonstrate them.'

Clarissa was still shaking a little beside her, and Shannon squeezed her hand before her partner spoke out loud. 'And what would the expectations be, as Circlet members?'

Melody spoke before the lady could answer. 'What if we fail your test?'

The robed woman smiled. 'If you do not meet the requirements, we simply ask you to practice and to try again at the next opportunity.'

Shannon waited a few beats for the answer to Clarissa's question. When the Lama didn't seem to have anything else to say, she asked again. 'And what do we need to do as a Circlet member?'

'You would guide trainees and complete your own outreach projects. This originally was designed to be missions to fight other groups, but these days, fighting misinformation with social media campaigns, writing real experiences online, ensuring that truths are exposed and generally fighting for the wildfire of women everywhere is the main focus.'

Shannon had expected something about training, about harnessing power, and about fighting the enemy. A social media smear campaign was not exactly what she thought of when she pictured the Circlet. Even sacred circles had to move with the times, it seemed.

After a long period of silence, the Elder stood up. 'Who would like to come through first?'

Shannon stood up without even thinking about it. 'I'd like to go, if that's okay.' Waiting always made her more nervous, and thus likely to mess up. The lama smiled her little smile and bowed her head, gesturing for Shannon to step through the curtain into another room.

The shock of a force field made her shake her head as she stepped into the next space. Even after what they'd just heard, the laptop and headphones shocked her, in this rustic cavern made out of the rock. They weren't kidding about modernizing the Circlet.

'Please take a seat, apply the headphones and listen to the instructions. We'll be monitoring your powers as you complete the exercise. Please feel free to use your powers as you see fit. This room is shielded.'

With that, she walked over to another part of the room, a little alcove that seemed to be outside the force field.

Sitting in the computer chair, swivelling it a bit until she felt more grounded, Shannon put the headphones over her ears and closed her eyes. The screen was black anyway.

An automated voice told her to listen, to feel, to exist in the next few moments.

Well that's not at all creepy.

The music was gentle at first. A pretty classical piece she vaguely recognized. Then lyrics appeared, a voice haunting her with words about facing fears and trying their best. Then the sound of chanting; from a rally not dissimilar to the one Brighton had seen.

She felt the ripples of her magic connecting with the mourning in the singer's voice, the hatred in the shouts at the rally, the softness moving into a wave of symphony of the classical background music. More layers of experience were placed into the mix. Gunfire. A scream. A howling dog. A baby crying.

She didn't know what her powers did in between the spaces, but when the shriek came into the track; a recording of her own shriek from the rally; she lost control and let out a wave of feeling across the room.

Instinct kicked in, and she clenched her fists against her thighs. *Pull it back.*

No need. You may remove the headphones.

Her head snapped up at the voice in her mind, and she was back in her body. Her cheeks were wet with tears, her hands marked by her own nails from clenching so deeply. A few items in the room seemed to have been knocked over by her expression, but the voice seemed calm.

The Elder came back in, smiling. 'You are strong and capable of controlling that strength. You are welcome to join us.'

She was ushered out into the previous room, and Clarissa stepped forward before the woman could ask for her next candidate. Shannon watched the love of her life enter the room, and instantly began to wonder how they tested all the different skills. Was that the same track? She knew their magic was connected through emotions, but surely it wasn't that simple.

Clarissa's powers were less active; not able to influence others mindsets, but rather in her words, her logic, her ability to feel for solutions others may not be able to see. She made connections others just didn't know how to even connect.

But Clarissa also had a wellspring that she was only just discovering how to access. Being trans meant she had been actively discouraged from accessing that fire inside, she had spent decades trying to hold her emotions in her head, under control, instead of feeling the cyclic nature of who she was beneath the surface.

Whatever the Elders back home had thought, they must have felt they were all ready to send them without explanation or training. He could easily have got them to practise a bit more this week if he'd wanted to, and she doubted any of them would have questioned it.

Thankfully, Clarissa came back while Shannon was still caught in the distraction of her thoughts, and from the relief in her face, it had gone okay.

Charlie went next, but Shannon knew so little about their gift that she focused all of her attention on Clarissa.

'Are you okay?' She grasped both Clarissa's hands in her own, needing the stability of their connection.

'Yes. It was weird but not difficult.'

'Did you listen to sounds?'

'No, I was shown puzzles and then video clips of animals solving mazes'

Shannon frowned. 'How does that test you?'

'I then recreated the paths with my mind. They said I passed, so I presume I did okay. I'm not sure how I feel about joining the Circlet though.'

Shannon strokes her hand. 'I know. I don't either. But this might be exactly what we need to give us the ability to reach more people'

Charlie came back, and Melody went through. Again, Shannon stayed focused on their conversation. It might be considered antisocial but she didn't care. She was here to shine with Clarissa. That was her role in this world, and whatever this was about to become, she wanted to be fully present.

And nothing would stop her fighting to keep their wildfire alight.

When the women came back in, she seemed to almost be beaming. 'Welcome in, initiates. We cannot wait to have you on board to help us develop as a protected space for those in need. You may not be physical fighters, but you are ready for combat training on a whole new level.'

Handing out a silver hairpiece to each of them, she grinned. 'You are ready for combat. The Circlet doesn't just fight like girls. We fight like women.'

#

There was something particularly stupid about holding multiple rallies about the same thing, in the same place within a month of the last one. At least for gender-related rallies with no clear audience and no evidence. The big stage across the road, set against the backdrop of the beach and ocean, dared to have lines of pink, white, and blue against it. Shannon really had thought that the Lemkin Institute publicly stating the gender critical argument was officially genocidal, the same as the Nazi's, would have got some of these fascists to quieten down. But no.

They felt threatened that women weren't all wearing heels and makeup in the kitchen, raising babies like in the 1950s. And they were angry about it.

Shannon recognised the tension in her jaw and shoulders, and forced herself to exhale. People called this a march, and a protest, but it was a bunch of insecure bullies who needed therapy, hurling abuse at innocent people. And that made her teeth grind together again.

Shannon tightened her grip on Clarissa's hand on one side, and Rowan's on the other, scanning the crowd for signs of magic, but also the vibe of this gathering. Something felt tenser than last time. She swallowed against her sore throat, focusing on her breathing as the anxiety pounded in her chest.

195

Part of her worry came from how quiet it was. There were a lot of people on her side, and not too many of the oppressors. Yet, the oppression from the signs and yelling of 'women have wombs' and 'stop child abuse' was definitely louder than any counter-chanting they had going so far. 'Protect Trans Lives' didn't sound quite as sensational. Partly because it wasn't. Unlike their chants, which manipulated the truth, the pro-rights group were stating facts.

Clarissa's hand squeezed hers, their fingers interlinking. Shannon let her eyes close for a moment, feeling for the stability of her partner by her side. It was in the clarity of her slow, deep breaths she felt a familiar energy signature approaching them.

Turning to check her recognition, she smiled at Lark, and Ruth waved, looking excited. 'I wondered if we'd find you here today!'

Lark was staring at Clarissa. Not staring. Gazing. The awe was utterly clear across their face. 'You're so tall!'

One side of Shannon's lips curled up in a smile, and she looked up at her girlfriend's face, watching her features as she spoke. 'I am. And I love your flag.' Clarissa tucked her hair behind her left ear, briefly touching the silver headpiece that kept them connected to the Circlet.

Lark looked down, smiling. 'Thanks. I sewed the edge on myself.'

The megaphone tannoy screeched, breaking the concentration, conversation, and sanity of all close to the front of the group. No sooner had the feedback cut out, that she heard the music coming from Hove to the west, and saw the double decker open top bus bringing the celebrity who had made a name for herself in her intolerant ideology.

Shannon felt Clarissa's chin on her hair, her partner kissing just above her ear. 'Calm down love. You need to ground.'

She became aware of her body again, and only then recognised the heat in her palms, warming Rowan's and Clarissa's hands as her own sweated. She had to keep herself in check. Especially now they were in the Circlet.

Shannon's throat went dry, remembering the campaign buses that this emulated from the referendum. The literal steamrolling of evidence, science, and rational discussion had many similarities with these TERFs. Rowan's hand began to shake in hers, and Shannon tightened her grip on her friend as the bus with its music, singing something about freedom from oppression, pulled up in front of them, and the main organiser of this hate group took the stage with her loud ass microphone.

Kathleen-Jane always looked the same: zebra print skirt with clashing bright blouse, and even less coordination in her accessories. She'd begun as an academic, not a fashion icon, that much was clear. Moving over to politics when her fragile ego decided to take on the LGBTQIA+ community hadn't helped her sense of style any more than her IQ.

Because all humans must surely fit into one of two boxes.

Shannon huffed, gritting her teeth. 'You'd think someone who studied technology, requiring maths, would know how to count above two.'

Rowan's face remained stony, but their response still made Shannon laugh. 'Maybe she only studied binary, that's only two states of existence.'

Kathleen-Jane's hoarse voice overpowered that of the crowd, and silenced those chanting on her side of the road. 'Biological sex is science. It is a communal definition. And you, supporting those who live in fantasies of being someone else, are only supporting mental illness.' Clarissa's voice was hushed in Shannon's ear. 'Is she using magic?'

Oh fuck. She mentally sent out her tendrils of energy, reading the space ahead of them. The propagandists better not be using magic to bend the wills of the public. Although it would explain why so many people, journalists, and companies had bought into the horseshit that gender critics spouted.

Her shouting continued, and Shannon felt the power being pushed behind the words. 'I am not saying all of you are abusers. But your movement gives those who do somewhere safe to hide. And that is what I cannot allow.'

Mutterings began in the crowd behind them, and people began to hold hands along the human fence they'd begun to form. Solidarity was a huge symbol for their community, and the physical connection was a particular sore point to the bullies who basically believed in the cooties of playground children. Shannon smiled, grateful that here she and her partner could feel at least some kind of safety, knowing they were not instantly feared and hated just for existing.

The energy signature next to her grew, and she felt Clarissa lending her strength. But then, on the other side, she saw Lark, and felt the ripple of power from them too. 'Lark, are you trying to focus energy somewhere?'

It was perhaps stupid to ask out loud, but Ruth was on Lark's other side, and Shannon wasn't here just to shut down bullies, but to help empower those in her crowd to stand up for truth. Lark tilted their head at her, and shrugged. That was about as much of a yes she'd expect from a teen. 'Want to hold our hands and boost my energy so we can protect the crowd? It's something I can do, but I need help.'

To her surprise, Lark looked back Ruth, who smiled. 'You know we find others like us sometimes.' Lark held their hand out to Clarissa, who grinned and took it. Clarissa was used to being a conduit for Shannon, and she felt the trickle of energies around them as she raised the shield across the front of the crowd; focused on reflecting back anything Kathleen-Jane's people were sending their way.

Time to see if this new technology worked. Shannon closed her eyes, pulling on the wellspring inside her. The silver hairpiece on the right side of her head was fashioned into a branch and stems with small flower shapes, similar to baby's breath. She felt for the little magnet points at the end of each flower cluster, and pushed the energy from those holding hands along their line up through her shoulders and neck, guiding it into the hair clip.

The pain in her head shocked her, but with Rowan and Clarissa holding her steady, and Clarissa's hair clip close to touching her own, the invisible spider web of energy began to pulse.

And there, she felt the amplification.

There was no one else from the Circlet here, but many people involved in human rights had a sense of conviction that connected them to the energies around them. And like Lark, there were definitely others attuned to magic in the crowd. She could feel the threads of energy, as each individual wished to protect those on their side of the road.

Some wanted to harm the others, especially knowing the damage they were causing, but those with magic knew better than to indulge such desires. Besides, a reflection spell was going to do plenty considering the amount of hatred and ill-intent in Kathleen-Jane's cult.

But even she did not expect the fucking ground to tremble.

People shrieked on both sides; a crack forming in the road between the two groups, sounding like thunder booming through the neighbourhood. Shannon tried to hold the energy steady on their side, to keep her concentration while the groups both split into smaller groups, spreading out.

Brighton was not, oddly, on a tectonic plate, or used to earthquakes of any kind. And watching the women drop her mega speaker to grab hold of the stage behind her gave

Shannon a huge sense of satisfaction. Then the back of the stage fell over, thankfully onto empty pavement behind, and Kathleen-Jane herself dropped to her knees.

It only lasted for a few moments, and Shannon bit her lip as she saw that their side of the road hadn't been damaged at all.

But the public were panicked now; and Ruth pulled Lark away from them. 'I'm sorry, I have to keep them safe.'

Clarissa already had a business card in hand. 'Never hesitate to contact us.' She was so damn practical. It was one of the reasons Shannon had fallen for her.

The police presence had doubled, and people were being evacuated from the area.

Ruth rushed off, and Rowan's voice pulled Shannon's attention back to the crowd. 'Did we do that?'

Before she could answer, Kathleen-Jane was up on her stage again.

Her screams sounded eerie; much more panicked and delusional than Shannon would expect, even after such a scary moment. 'God has spoken! You must all repent for your crimes! Surgery on our children is just the devil's witchcraft, and you are his hands!'

The disgust rose in her chest like a wave of tightness, fury at this woman, so desperate to feel superior that she would see her stand and 'protest' literally torn up under her feet and decide that a god had struck down in upset at the group who remained unharmed.

The turbulence ricocheted from her, and the shield of protection almost glowed around the human's rights activists on her side. She hadn't meant to do anything, but the ripple seemed to affect those outside the sphere of her magic, and even police officers held on to trees or each other to fight the sudden wind that accosted them. The rain followed swiftly, a soft drizzle to her, but seemingly lashing down on the other side.

And that's when the shouting back raised in volume; as if enhanced by some invisible loudspeaker. Was no one seriously questioning this incredible feat of nature and clearly supernatural experience? But she looked back around and the trans flags, pride flags, placards, and rainbows were only waving faster, their bearers seemingly caught up in how the other side were, for once, having to back down.

'I'd check which side you're standing on!'

'God loves all his children!'

'History will remember you, Fascists!'

Shannon swallowed, looking at Rowan. 'I think the Circlet might be more powerful than we realised.'

'You know what they say. Hell hath no fury like a woman scorned. And I can assure you…' Rowan's eyes narrowed at the people being escorted off the beach area by police in fluorescent tabards, rubbing a silver hair piece in their hands. 'What that person thinks of as a 'woman' is so narrow; they would barely fill a single level of the inferno.'

Clarissa's arm came around Shannon, her hand resting on Rowan's shoulder.

'The number of true women will always be an overwhelming force.' She gestured to the bus where the protesters had retreated. 'And they stand on such thin ground; our voices alone could knock them over.'

WE HAVE ALWAYS BEEN HERE

By
Julia Hawkes-Reed

I paused at the base of the steps that led to the door of the experimental station to fiddle with my skirt for what felt like the twentieth time since leaving my car. The slide-show of awfulness in my head was currently featuring a shot that featured the rest of the staff crowded along the second floor windows, pointing and hooting at me. I looked up to see that the windows were, of course, empty.

I clattered across the ancient parquet in the entrance hall, cursing my decision to wear the boots, even if they did look better with this skirt than a pair of trainers, which would have probably made rubbery-squeak noises instead. I hoped that the comedy duo in the porter's cubbyhole were brewing tea or staring at the sports pages of the Hookland Messenger.

'Here we are, look!'

Ha. No such luck.

'M...'

Say 'mister'. I dare you. Or mate. Either, both. Mate mate matey mate.

I started reflexively cringing, and tried to think of something funny to say, so as to get the first boot in myself.

'...iss Whichford, we've had your new pass made up.'

Oh.

My hand barely shook as I scribbled in the box on the clipboard and tried not to smile too much as I read 'Margaret Whichford. Paraphysics/F.' F for field and F for the other thing. I looked up to find Bill and Dave beaming back at me.

Oh. I can absolutely do this, can't I?

#

My office was the same as when I left yesterday, an entirely alien territory filled with unknowables and a room of glowing possibilities, all at once. It felt uncomfortably blokey, then I felt uncomfortable at feeling that because, dear god, where was that going to lead?

I made myself tea and then realised that I would quite like to see the entire top surface of my desk.

I had scaled the long bookshelf that was at right-angles to the window, so I could file Hatchjaw's guide to Hookland folk music in its proper place, when there was a tap and a cough from the doorway. I peered over my shoulder to find Dr. Hearthstone regarding me with mild amusement. There was no dignified way of returning to ground level, so I spidered sideways to the windowsill and jumped moderately gracefully into the clear spot in front of my desk.

By this time, Dr. Hearthstone had pushed a pile of Flight International magazines to one side and parked himself on the clear end of the sofa. I scooted my chair to the near end of my desk, sipped from my mug and wondered what sort of impression I was giving off.

He waved the file he'd been carrying at me. 'This one's just come in from the short-wave section, and it's got your name all over it, M... Oh. Would you prefer "Miss Whichford" or "Margaret"?'

'Margaret is fine. Thank you for asking,' I said.

He beamed at me. My existence did seem to make people happy.

I nodded at the file in his hand. 'What's got the wire-less-intercept people excited?'

He slid the file towards me along my now clean desk. 'You know HM Gov have decided to re-activate RAF Nook?'

I grimaced. 'Yes. Against the express advice of some of our people and their own experts, as I understand it.'

Hearthstone looked pained. 'Apparently the UFO flap was long enough ago that it has fallen out of institutional mem-ory, and the local MP has found a tame boffin to make all the right noises in front of the select committee about bringing jobs and cutting edge science to Hookland.'

If there was one thing the Hookland Experimental Station did not lack, it was institutional memory. The section of shelf behind and to the right of me was largely about the airfield, the area round it, its history and its phenomenology. My own half-dozen papers about the UFO flap were at the far end of that section. If I wanted more depth again, or a different perspective, I had only to walk over to the post-structural-ist folklore group or find someone in the laser archaeology block and offer them tea and biscuits. I often felt that my own speciality, asymmetric paraphysics, was the least weird thing in the place.

I leafed through the file. There were two pages. One boilerplate - date, time, document status, moon phase, computational tarot index, Orgone readings—the usual office sludge. The second page was a waterfall frequency analysis that looked quite benign. I looked at the frequency ranges themselves, then back at Dr Hearthstone.

'Yes,' he said. 'Apparently short-wave wasn't interesting enough, so some bright beggar decided to have a poke around in the Ultra Low Frequency bands, using the fence round the estate as an aerial. Good improvisational skills, but asking for trouble if the wrong people found out. And, as if that wasn't bad enough, some back-of-envelope calculating reveals that the shape of that fence is an almost perfect directional antenna.'

'Which, if you're asking about Nook, means the grey barrows. They're going to be super annoyed if they think we're eavesdropping. Which set of idiots are poking them with a stick... Oh! This is about the re-activation, isn't it?'

Hearthstone nodded along as I catastrophised.

'This establishment used to be RAF Whiteley Grange. It was requisitioned at the start of the war for signals research. Specifically radar.'

I put the folder down on my desk and gave him my full attention. 'I did not know that.' I'm one of the outdoor people, not an archivist, but discovering I'd missed something still didn't sit well.

Dr Hearthstone is in charge of the research group because he knows how his people are. He gave me a sympathetic grimace.

'Given the shape of the hole in the official records, I would imagine there was a D-Notice involved.' He pulled a folded sheet of paper from the inside pocket of his jacket and handed it to me. 'This is a chit and a sigil that'll allow you access to that end of the archives. Let me know how you get on.'

205

#

CL Nolan's guide to the notable buildings of Hookland contains a single paragraph on Whiteley Grange. 'Built 1644. Extensively modified 1840. Caught fire 1841. Rebuilt 1901. Requisitioned WD 1936.' That there is a folly in the grounds that resembles a small masonic temple, or that the place is very haunted, is obviously considered normal for Hookland and not worth a mention.

The neo-Palladian front elevation of the Grange handily disguised the west wing, which looked like someone had bolted a workhouse onto an unsuspecting country house and staggered into the night to sleep it off in a hedge. The west wing was given over to the archives because it's not the sort of place that anyone can stand to work in.

As I approached the door, my skin prickled and the temperature around me dropped. A chit/sigil enscribed by Dr Hearthstone was the functional equivalent of an access all areas pass, but the feeling of being inspected by something non-human still gave me pause.

The door swung open silently.

There isn't a section or shelf marked 'Ministry cover-ups, 1940-1949', so I dug in the index cards for 'RAF Whiteley Grange'. This led me to the military history of Hookland shelves. I was staring up at a row of box files, wondering if I'd seen a stepladder on my travels, when one of the files tipped away from the shelf and fell towards me. It seemed to float rather than plummet, so I fielded it as if this was a normal phenomenon.

'GREEN CHAPEL.' I read it aloud, more or less to myself. There was a shuffling and a thud, from the shelving somewhere to my right. I backtracked and found another box file at my feet. It seemed to have come from the 'Radio frequency phenomenology' section, and was labelled 'White-ley Grange'.

I had an idea that I knew what I was expected to do next. I stared at the ceiling, for want of anywhere else to look.

'Ok. What else do I need to know?'

There were three more thumps. I went in search of a sack truck.

#

It was the middle of the afternoon when I finally pushed my chair back and swung my feet onto my desk, so I could more easily lie back and address the structure of the building.

'I'm sorry. I didn't know. It must have been hard for you. I mean, is there anyone that does know?'

I didn't know what I would get by means of a reply. Conversation with non-corporeal entities wasn't part of the on-the-job training. Recognising, avoiding and/or containing same—yes. Anything more complicated was theoretical at best.

I continued, 'I mean, I hesitate to resort to ugly cliche, but one signal for no and two for yes?'

One thing you learn in field-expedient paraphysics is how to read a room. Not just the attitude of the people in it, but how the actual structure of the built environment might be feeling about what is going on. In this case, if an office could have been said to have rolled its eyes and glared at me, then that's what happened.

'Understood. So, um, would an ASR33 teleprinter hooked to a ouija board and some strain gauges work for you?' It would be the sort of hardware hackery that the particle demonology group would have done before. Keeping it electromechanical felt like a sensible security precaution.

This time the room settled back and propped its notional feet on its own desk. *Go on then*, it seemed to say. *In your own time.*

#

— is this thing on?

— testing 1 2 3

— shit piss wank fuck cunt bollocks bollocks bollocks

It was much like watching the sweary version of the full-time scores.

'Yes, that seems to work. Is that frustration or a parity error?' I said.

— sorry. it has been a few years. men are causing trouble again.

'I'm sorry. What can I do?'

— i said men.

I smiled to myself, and didn't try to argue the point. It was a lovely thing to be told. The printhead clattered again.

— you have read the material from the archive?

I glanced at the pile of folders on my desk. 'Yes. GREEN CHAPEL was an experimental terrain-following radar being tested on a bearing between RAF Nook and here, the former RAF Whiteley Grange. As bad luck would have it, the transmitter was sufficiently powerful to literally wake the dead.'

— yes. i am glad to have been awoken, but the method was... unpleasant. i would not wish shock therapy on anyone.

'How do you know about..?'

— it has been a few years. i have read the entire archive several times. your theories about the ufos are... interesting.

It was my turn to roll my eyes at the room.

'Anyway. After exorcising the apparently possessed and grounding out the affected airframes, the ministry decided to contain the problem by erecting a cold iron perimeter around Evie Barrett's Tump, dropping further work on GREEN CHAPEL and papering over the cracks with a D Notice.'

— yes. contain. they were told how best to proceed, but ignored that advice in favour of that given by men. i/we prefer the company of women. i/we would not have talked, had i/we been asked.

I stared at the printout for a while. There'd been something in a report on the progress of the wind-down of the RAF station, before it was handed over to the Hookland Paraphysical Research Group. I rooted through the pile of reports until I found it. 'Detachment of admin personnel seconded from Station X, demobbed or posted to Oakley Priors.'

'Codebreakers?'

— yes. go up onto the roof.

'Why?'

— you are welcome to ignore the advice you are given. again. you may need binoculars.

I took the hint, and some binoculars, and steamed up the stairs to the roof.

#

There was still a well-maintained Observer Corps bunker on the eastern roof end of the main building. The wartime brickwork and concrete slab roof was weathered in an oddly comforting way. There was a double layer of sandbags facing the glassed-in cupola that provided a light well above the central staircase, and moss was starting to take hold among the rotting fibres . I planted the binoculars on the post plotting indicator that lay next to the entrance to the bunker and waited for something to happen. I could hear the house martins nesting in the eaves below me, and further away someone running a mower over the croquet lawn. I felt that the fabric of the building was fully aware of the situation, but had decided to see if I could work it out for myself.

I heard the distant scream of jet engine, and pointed the binoculars in that direction. A TSR.2 in anti-blast white dropped into the groove in the landscape between RAF Nook and us, and howled in our direction at zero feet. It was an impressive sight, presumably part of the re-activation that Dr Hearthstone had mentioned.

As the aircraft screeched over my head, I realised that the bomb-bay doors were open and it was carrying a full load. I wasn't entirely sure about the relevant safety protocols, but wading in like you were going to drop heavy ordnance through the skylight seemed a bit previous.

I felt that the building desperately wanted to leap into the air and swat the aircraft away, as if it were a wasp.

I turned west to watch as the TSR.2 pulled up into open sky and banked right, hard enough to generate vapour trails from its dropped wing-tips. I had the impression that it was determined to have another try at removing the Experimental Station from the map with some vigour. At the same time, there was a flash from behind me.

The aircraft exploded into two pieces, twisted apart by a great yellow-orange fireball. I ducked reflexively behind the sandbags. There was a gust of hot air and a weird spanging of what could only have been shrapnel from the remains of the airframe.

If nothing else I was going to do some swearing back at the ASR33. Just as soon as my legs stopped shaking.

#

I stopped outside my office when I saw my shadowy reflection in the glass door. I looked like someone who'd just witnessed an aircraft exploding and then been showered with shrapnel for their trouble. In a previous life, charging into a room looking like that would have demonstrated that I was a person of action. Right now though, I felt I should go and dust myself off somewhere with a full-length mirror. I turned, and paused again. That was a wicked stereotype, too. Women were not people of action and should be immaculately turned out at all times.

Gah. Fuck it. I decided to go with woman-of-action who has at least made sure there were no sharp objects, sandbag-detritus or concrete particles adhering to her dress, and who has had the sense to go and get a calming mug of tea from the canteen before laying into the spirits haunting the fabric of the building she works in, via a teletype connected to a ouija board. Going to fetch myself tea also allowed for a diversion via the short-wave section, who had prompted my involvement in the current situation. By the time I returned to my office, I was less in the dark about the latest developments.

'Did you know they were going to shoot one of their own aircraft out of the sky?' I gestured expansively, trying to indicate that the whole room should be paying attention. Maybe I should just plant a jack o'lantern on top of the teletype, so I had a face to focus my ire upon.

— no. we can feel the shape of our sibling's anger. they did not anticipate that. they have learned, however. you are safe here.

'Safe? How?'

— i/we prefer the company of other women. this space is safe for you.

I glared at some cornicing. 'That's not an answer, but I'll take it. Also, thank you. Would I be in the right area if I opined that in re-activating the work at RAF Nook, they've also re-activated GREEN CHAPEL. Only this time with supersonic nuclear strike bombers and a lot more power and brains in the transmitter?'

— yes.

'And the response is still 'burn the affected components, fence off the contaminated bits, nothing to see here, nice cup of tea and a sit down'?'

— yes.

'Well. Bugger.'

— yes.

'Before the explosions and fiery death, you talked of not being heard by the men, yet someone did listen to you. The women codebreakers from Bletchley Park. Can you tell me what you told them?'

— the situation has changed. i/we can't get a grip on men-things. i/we can feel the shape of the holes, but i/we can only guess at what fills them in your world. i/we are sorry. You are safe here.

I had to pace and think and calm down.

'You've read the entire archive?'

— yes.

'Good. Hookland being Hookland, some of those code-breakers will have stayed on. Find the names of the people who were demobbed, then dig through the register of electors to see what you can find. If nothing, cross-check the *Hookland Gazette*, specifically births, marriages and deaths. I'm going to try to explain some of this to my boss.'

#

I sat in my car outside Walnut Tree cottage with both windows open so I could listen to the larks, inhale the early summer air and not think about how Liz Malcom might react when she found me looming on her doorstep. I checked myself in the rear view mirror yet again and still seemed to pass for marginally human. In the end I'd asked Hearthstone to call her, partly because I felt his name would carry more authority, but mostly because I didn't trust my own voice. Work was one thing - they had to put up with me anyway, but coping with random people who might reach for the torches and pitchforks as soon as I hove into view was a whole different kettle of nasty elbows.

'Are you the young woman from the Grange?' The voice was close to my right ear. I stifled a yelp, then wondered if the pitch of that yelp had given me away. That would be a fine start.

I took a breath and turned towards the voice. She had grey-white hair in a messy bun and was wearing a scruffy surplus jumper over a tea-length dress and I was slightly startled I knew what that was.

'Yes,' I said. 'Miss Malcom?'

'Just Liz. Old habits, yes? And what should I call you?'

'Margaret, then. Or, um, shortened version thereof, I guess...' I trailed off. What in the name of hell was I jabbering about? You don't get to make up your own nicknames, other people do that for you over a length of time as they work out who you are. I'd been Margaret officially for about a week and I had no idea if I was going to be a Mags, a Maggie or an oh fuck here she comes again.

213

Liz tilted her head and smiled at me. 'I think you're going to be a Mags, but let's not put the cart before the horse. Will you come through for tea on the lawn?'

The lawn was a half managed meadow that was dotted with fruit bushes and stopped at a fenced-off drop into the quarry that had produced the stone for the cottage. Tea was served from a vast brown pot which rested on a weathered GPO cable drum.

'Dr Hearthstone tells me the previous inhabitants of the Grange have been talking to you. I must say your contraption was really quite clever. When I was your age we had to rely on more traditional methods.' Liz settled back in her wicker chair and smiled again.

'Traditional?' I asked.

'Mushrooms, mostly. They grow in the rough patch between the folly and the copse. Oh, don't say that they send a man with a mower round there now. That would be such a waste.'

I slurped tea and tried to get my words in order.

'Mushrooms?' Failing at word-ordering there.

Liz shrugged. 'We were either bored or working desperately hard on breaking the latest batch of intercepts before any more young men got killed. There wasn't a pub in range, and even if there had been, we couldn't talk about what we were doing. Mushrooms took the edge off and seemed to help the codebreaking. Oh, dear. You're not one of those dreadful judgemental sorts are you?'

'Me? No. I just didn't... Oh, the hell with it. Everything I thought I knew about myself is wrong, so why should I hold on to any other illusions. Behind the folly, you say?'

'Good girl. We'll have you up to speed in no time.'

I glugged more tea and basked for a moment in the feeling of being called a 'good girl'.

'So. Why do you dynamic young people with your fresh ideas need to speak to an old fossil like me?'

I put my empty teacup back on the cable drum and stretched my hands round one knee until I felt a creaking from my shoulder.

'Because the young people with the fresh ideas have found enough of GREEN CHAPEL to try it again, only with significantly more advanced electronics and rather more exciting results.'

'The "training accident" that was on the news yesterday?'

'Yes. Someone tried to put a bomb through the cupola. Something? Anyway. The entities that inhabit the Grange haven't kept pace with the white heat of technology, and it's obvious that fencing off the barrows and calling it fixed didn't work. However, the entities did let on that they told someone who was on site at the time, and my hope was that you might have been one of those someones. Entities? Do you think they have names?'

'They sounded like women when they talked to me. I imagine they know their own.' Liz peered at me over the rim of her teacup. I couldn't even be bothered to stifle a grin.

'I. Oh!' was all I could manage.

'I think you should let that feeling percolate for a while, dear. And in answer to your other question, I think so. It was a long time ago, there was a D-Notice and you know no-one talked of Bletchley until recently. If you brought some of the reports, that should jog my memory. Let's go into the library and have a ponder.' Liz stood and, brandishing the teapot like a rotund sword, ushered me back into her house.

Her library lined the walls of the two larger rooms at the front of the house that had been opened out into one space. There was a sewing table in the centre, and we made space to be able to lay out the more interesting parts of the GREEN CHAPEL files. I scanned the nearest part of her shelves, then levered out a copy of Hatchjaw. A first edition.

Liz glanced up from the files. 'There's a copy of *Golden Hours* two shelves over,' she said.

I squeaked and bounded to the right. *Golden Hours, Layman's Atlas and Codex*. Half of the staff at the Grange had a photostat version of *Country Album*, but...

I turned and leaned against the shelves. 'Can I stay? I'll sleep under that table and I won't make much mess. I'll even take myself for walks.'

Liz straightened, folded her arms and smiled. 'We'll see. Let's solve this problem first, though. Could you find me the second volume of CL Nolan? It should be on the shelf to the right of the fireplace.'

I did as I was told. Like a good girl.

#

I brought the third pot of tea through from the kitchen. It was about 3am. I was starting to wilt, but Liz was almost bouncing on her toes, either from the caffeine or the joy of discovery. Perhaps both.

'Do you people still use Templeton Boxes?' she asked.

'Yes. The most recent ones are good up into the terahertz range, too,' I said.

'Excellent, Do you have the unredacted Landranger maps with you, or are we going to have to work from my 1947 editions?'

I steamed out to my car and returned with the relevant maps. We dumped the pile of reference material on the floor and spread out the one with RAF Nook nearest us and

Whiteley Grange nestled by her sewing machine. Liz used her dressmaker's ruler to scribe a pentagram that surrounded Evie Barrett's Tump.

'Oh, bloody hell,' I said. It was desperately simple.

'A parabolic antenna at each point, plumb a Templeton Box in backwards, and that should generate a radio frequency cage. Assuming your box has more power than the barrow.'

Liz yawned and stretched. I joined in with the yawning. I was suddenly very tired indeed.

'That's the universe telling you that you've found the best answer. Now, up the wooden hill to bedfordshire for the both of us. You're in no fit state to drive, and even if you did the rest of your people are going to be fast asleep, so none of you would be any good to each other.'

I yawned and nodded. I could cheerfully curl up round the nearest de Selby volume on the floor underneath the table.

#

It was lunchtime when I left my car under a shady tree at the quiet end of the parking area that was mostly used by people to store their spare and project cars. I still coveted the 99 turbo that was mostly verdigris and looking sad on four flat tyres. I followed the perimeter access path round the back of the auxiliary generators, over the ornamental clapper bridge, and then skirted the lake before striking out up the slope to the folly. It was another warm day and I was glad to have abandoned caution, followed Liz's example, and embraced the notion of the tea-dress. Nevertheless, I stopped to lean against the cool stone of the folly while getting my breath back.

Mushroom season is usually later in the year, but I wanted to at least try my luck while attempting to get my thoughts in order and give a sensible account to Dr Hearthstone.

Since it can't be seen from the house, the ground on the far side of the folly was ignored by the landscape gardener, and seemed to have been similarly ignored by most people ever since. I soon had two punnets of psylocybin mushrooms that I felt I should share with the post-structuralist folklore types, since they'd put up with a lot of my more complicated questions.

#

When I returned to my office, remaining punnet in my hand, there was a red post-it on my door. 'Come and find me when convenient' it read, in Hearthstone's handwriting. Green meant 'there is no trouble, this is a social call'. Orange, 'trouble is brewing'. Red was 'trouble has brewed and will likely ruin your afternoon'.

I dropped the mushrooms on my desk and went in search.

#

'Ah. Margaret. A useful chat with Liz Malcom?'

I nodded. I had stopped being surprised that Hearthstone seemed to know everyone even tangentially connected to the experimental station, about three months after I started.

'Good. I'm afraid the balloon has gone up in the last few hours, and the ministry response has been to stand there looking helpless.' He led me into his office and waved me into one of the sturdy armchairs under the window. 'We had been keeping a quiet eye on the aerodrome, but someone, or some*thing*, has worked out what drones smell like and now seems to be able to destroy them with hellfire.'

'Missiles?'

'No, actual hell fire. We sent two up, one to keep an eye on the other, and whatever it is looks rather a lot like lightning going in a straight line.'

I wished I'd already tested some of the produce I'd found, so I felt brave enough to listen to the answer I was going to get to my next question.

'Is there a cordon and can I still get to Evie Barrett's Tump?' I asked anyway.

'Ah...'

Oh. Shit. Here it comes.

'That would be the source of the bolts.'

I rolled my eyes.

'Fine.' I thought I'd said it with remarkable restraint, but he almost jumped.

I straightened in the chair that I would now rather curl up in, and tried to act like the grown-up field agent I'd been three days ago.

'I'm going to need five parabolic antenna kits, interconnects ditto, and a hardened Templeton box. And I guess something to cart it all in.'

Hearthstone nodded. 'I'll see to it myself. 101 do?'

I grinned in spite of myself. I had been itching for an excuse to borrow one of them since I started, but they were old and rare and I had never needed a cold-war four wheel drive with the looks of a brick and the grunt to climb the side of a house. I let out a breath and stood up.

'I have to go and consult with my office,' I said. 'Half an hour?'

'Whatever you think is best.'

#

If I lay at the right angle, I could slump on my office sofa and still see the output of the ASR33. I stared at the ceiling as I outlined the plan Liz and I had cooked up.

The ASR33 was silent for what felt like a very long time.

— there will be danger. bring an extra antenna and point it back this way.

— ...

— and bring the mushrooms with you. you will need them.

'You're advising me to swallow a handful of psychedelic mushrooms *before* I deal with a reactivated and apparently pissed off bolt-thrower?'

— yes. you will be safe there, too.

I thought of several cutting remarks, but kept them to myself. Best to keep the number of entities that were annoyed with me to a minimum. I sighed, stood, shook my dress straight, and dragged out my field kit to take my mind off things.

#

I met Hearthstone hurrying across the entrance hall. It was the first time I'd seen him flustered, which did my confidence less than no good at all.

'The very person!' he said.

I grimaced, and he had the wit to look uncomfortable.

'Dr Hearthstone?'

We both turned. Bill emerged from their office, carrying a teapot.

'You're not sending Miss Whichford off somewhere dangerous already, are you? Because the ink's barely dry on her pass, and...'

I blinked, swallowed, and did my best to keep my voice steady. 'It'll be fine. If it were serious they'd have given me something disposable for transport...'

Hearthstone cleared his throat. 'You've got a 101.'

Bill grinned. 'Well, there you go. Gods help you if you scratch the paint on it, mind.'

We walked out to the top of the stone stairway where I squinted in the glare of the sunlight, until I remembered I'd parked my sunglasses on my head. I pulled them down and gathered myself into character as an experienced field researcher.

I slung my field kit and shoulder bag into the passenger footwell, walked the long way round the vehicle so I could check that I'd got all the bits I'd requested, and finally clambered into the driver's seat.

I'd been expecting a traditional olive-green interior with a pudding-stirrer gear lever and three big pedals suitable for careless squaddies. Instead I got something with a very lumpy idle, a shifter with a ratchet lever, and a big tachometer riveted to the corner of the engine hump nearest my left knee. I prodded the accelerator. The 101 barked and shook itself on its suspension as whatever monster engine the maniacs in the engineering block had lobbed into the thing sensed blood or tarmac or houses to climb.

I turned to discover Hearthstone looking far too pleased with himself.

'Apparently the engine computer will stop you having too much fun, and it corners like an off-licence, but it should get you out of trouble when you need it.'

I looked around the cabin again.

'That explains the race harness and roll-cage then. How on earth did you swing it?' I asked.

'I told them it was for you.'

I opened and closed my mouth a few times. I had no useful words. Hearthstone pushed the driver's door closed and stood back. I took my cue, clunked the thing into 'drive', and rumbled in the direction of the danger.

#

I was somewhat dishevelled and slightly deafened by the crackle of the exhaust when I rolled to a halt next to the squaddie at the checkpoint. I automatically reached for where my ID would have been, had I been wearing trousers. It wasn't there, so I swore, unbuckled myself, and had to half-scramble across the vast engine hump to retrieve my shoulder bag, which I duly dug in before finding my new pass and brandishing it with a triumphant grin.

The squaddie glared at me. 'Paraphysics?'

An older sergeant rolled up. 'Trouble, Hoskyns?' He glanced at me and gave the 101 a careful once-over.

'I had to drive them in Germany. They were rubbish.'

I blipped the throttle, the 101 lurched, and both men seemed to rock back.

'Hookland Experimental Station...' The sergeant was reading the door panel. '...Is that Hearthstone's lot?'

'Yes, that's us. Me,' I said.

'Let the girl through, Hoskyns. She's expected.' He turned to me 'The rest of your team is following on, miss?'

I thought about glowering and asking if he meant 'where are the men?' but I swallowed it, smiled and nudged the 101 forward, making it very plain that going through their barrier was absolutely an option.

Hoskyns returned my ID. 'Just follow your nose, but stop when you see the lightning bolts,' he said.

#

The ground running up to Evie Barrett's Tump, and the plateau beyond that is RAF Nook, is a convoluted mess of old quarry workings, twisting tracks sunk deep into the landscape, and a handful of trackways that were abandoned almost as soon as they were established. The land keeps its secrets.

I nosed the 101 into a narrow gully that kept the vehicle as hidden as possible, and climbed onto the top of the cab with a pair of binoculars. The panelling was warm against my legs, and I strongly considered staying here to listen to the sound of larks, grasshoppers, and the oppressive hum of bees.

The tump was a few degrees to my left. It was a long mound that sloped up gently away from me and then dropped vertically in a drystone-faced false entrance that looked towards Nook and then the coast. It looked as quiet and well-cropped as usual. I zoomed in on the cold iron perimeter and breathed in reflexively. All the posts I could see had been melted outwards and now curved to the ground like the stems of wilted flowers. There was something else, too. When the wind was in the right direction I could hear something lower still than the bees, although it was more of a weight in the back of my skull than an actual noise.

#

I kept low because useful intelligence about the state of the barrow was missing since the drones had been fried late yesterday. Other than that the barrow was now energised sufficiently to melt its iron containment and then shoot expensive kit out of the sky.

I refocussed on the aerodrome perimeter beyond the barrow. Most of the chain-link, razor wire, and stanchions were also melted. I recalled the footage of the US nuke-tests where they set off a small device handy for Yucca Flats or Dead Donkey Gulch and flattened what were either pre-fabs or a ghost town. The fence looked like that. It seemed the barrow could focus better at that range. Interesting.

Beyond that fence and the concrete perimeter track were a pair of TSR.2 aircraft in dispersal bays, and beyond them were a short row of hardened hangars.

I swallowed, and realised the not-buzzing pressure at the back of my skull had been rising in intensity for the last however-long. There was a tearing noise as a bolt landed at the corner of the dispersal bay nearest the barrow and walked a smoking path towards the next corner. The after-image on my retinas made me feel queasy, scintillating like the visual disturbance that precedes a full-on migraine.

The next bolt melted a surviving stanchion like it was a wooden spill, burning vertically. The one after that seemed to spend far longer meandering across the concrete perimeter. It felt an awful lot like the barrow was inscribing a pathway between itself and the nearest TSR.2.

Fine.

It was unclear to me how I was going to rebuild its containment and wire up the Templeton box without getting a bolt up the arse for my trouble.

I slid backwards onto the canvas tilt, which I sank into like a warm hammock, and considered my next move.

#

Psilocybin mushrooms taste awful. I was slightly disappointed, since I had hoped I might have developed a taste for them in the same way that I had for dark chocolate and queer romcoms, but no. I washed down a couple of good handfuls with a thermos of stewed tea, did my best to rinse the remaining taste with bottled water, and then returned to my roof-hammock to see how the second worst idea I'd ever had would go.

#

The chills and muscle aches started bang on time a half-hour later. All good psychedelic experiences begin with feeling like you've caught a cold. I was strongly considering driving the 101 off to find some thumping techno music when I realised I had been running my fingers over the weave of the canvas tilt for some indeterminate time, and it now felt like it was the size of wavy tin. I waved my hand in front of my face to check for damage, but was distracted by the tracers and patterns spalling off my fingers as if they were tearing sparks out of the solid air when I moved them back and forth.

'Oh, there you are! We were starting to get worried.'

The voice arrived in my head like a tram gliding into a stop just north of the Diamant district in Antwerp. It came with a flash of a teletype machine and a set of confused impressions/images it took me a few moments to parse:

thankful/scared/amused at a neat hack/joyful/welcoming/determined.

'You're from The Grange.' I said it to myself, because, well, how do you talk to a supernatural entity that arrived in your head when you scoffed the magic mushrooms like a good girl? I did wonder if I'd just done the equivalent of sticking a USB key that I'd found on the street, in my computer, and even now something was digging through my subconscious for passwords and bank details.

'I'm sure your bank manager is a very nice man, but I don't want to know any sordid details.'

Well. That was both me told, and a sign that the entities was going to learn a few things from me about modern finance and attack surfaces.

'You'll have to wiggle round a bit and prop yourself up so you can see in our general direction. It's just the way it works sometimes. Think of it like a wireless link where it helps to align both antennas.'

I wiggled myself round a bit, propped myself up as much as I dared, and only became moderately distracted by the sunset.

#

The sunset had turned the sky to the west into a massive trans flag. I stopped and stared for, I don't know, a month? I could feel everything within me aligning in ways that were not even concepts I could have put names to before. I smiled and wept and experienced the unbearable rightness of being.

'Oh. Oh my god.'

June sounded half shocked and half amazed.

'I... I had no idea you felt like that. That's... I can't... It's so en-compassing.'

'Feel like what?' I sounded so far away. Like I was hearing a recording from the end of a grassy corridor.

'That. Is that what it feels like to be trans?'

'Yes.'

'It's beautiful. It's everything.'

'June?'

'Yes. We chose it ourselves, too.'

I could feel the joy she/they were radiating. I was gleefully accepted/welcomed/provisioned/firewalled.

'Reading you five by five. I think this is working.'

I felt the eye-roll and grinned anyway. June knew the reference because I knew the reference.

'You are not on an express elevator to hell, my girl. However, we do have work to complete now. How do you feel?'

I thought about it. I was as the point in the experience where I could probably keep it together most of the time, as long as no-one reminded me of any particularly good tunes. Something with a lot of howling 303 and a good handful of filter-sweep would certainly hit the spot right about now. I nodded along to the kick for a while, and it was hands in the air for the drop.

'I'll take that as a good thing.'

'Sorry. Yes.'

I interrogated the firewall feeling and it unfolded into my head like a NASA animation of the fly-by of one of the outer planets. I could feel June as if they were peering over my shoulder and nodding along as I pointed at parts of the schematic/map/control surface. Whitely Grange was a burning green cube that rotated slowly on all of its axes. Evie Barret's Tump was a white-hot inverted cone that sank into the surface, and hanging above that was a dish that must have been the bolt-director. Behind that was a writhing yellow mass that pulsed slowly. There was a bright line between the Grange and a point off to one edge of the barrow, which ended in a smaller green cube. I realised that I was looking at some tactical/network representation of myself.

'You're safe. This is a safe space. Not just in the "People will get your pronouns right" sense but in the "Entirety of Hookland is tooled up and just itching for an excuse to kick off. Seriously, fucking bring it." one. As I believe you corporeal types have it.'

I wiped away the tears that I could not have explained in a million years, and poked at/zoomed into the section between the cone and the yellow mass. There were tendrils writhing blindly at a blank space between the two. I thought about the bolt-pattern I'd watched earlier, and felt June grimace as that new information integrated with the map/control surface. A countdown timer started.

'Well, blast. How far does my firewall extend?'

I thought about the 101. It was an absolute hoot to drive and I would be incandescent if it got a bolt through the trans.

'I think you have your answer, don't you?'

#

I was too twisted to even spell 'subtle'. I booted the 101, and it lurched up the end of the gully with a roar and a clatter of loose stones, and bounced up onto the scrub level with the barrow. It took me a few moments to realise that while I was absolutely hallucinating the five big arrows surrounding the barrow, they were also saving me an awful lot of time in mucking about with a map. I booted the 101 again and fishtailed it towards the nearest arrow.

#

The five link LEDs on the Templeton box cycled to green. The pentagram was complete, the box itself was happy, and yet the barrow was still scribing its path/sigil into the perimeter concrete, and the countdown timer I could see when I closed my eyes was still running.

'Bollocks.'

'Yes. We need a path back here now.'

'The extra parabolic antenna you wanted,' I said.

I had read the bloody words off the bloody teletype my bloody self and yet I had steamed out of the Grange and into the 101 and here I was now without it. The worst of it was that June wasn't even angry. That was just a bad path, so we don't waste time thinking about it and just get on with the next thing. I was the bad path.

I stared at the connectors on the side of the Templeton box.

'No.'

I closed my eyes to check the countdown timer, scowled, then disconnected the two ends of the nearest cable. The LEDs cycled to orange.

'Mags. No. You can't...'

I jammed the centre conductors in each half of the cable into my thumbs. I was the path. The LEDs cycled to green.

The LEDs cycled to blue.

The sky went out.

I overlaid the map/control surface on my vision. June did *something* and the sky went infra-red white. I could see the other five sides of the path/sigil/pipe the barrow had been creating and it looked about complete. The sound of the universe tearing at the edges was back, but this time it had

229

a form. Vast sub-bass rips in reality pulsed as three-dimensional neon glyphs floated through the air from the barrow, along the path/sigil it had cut towards the nearest TSR.2 They looked like eye-breakingly weird balloon animals, twisted from incandescent blue strip lights.

June was back, hanging over my shoulder.

'You're an idiot. Never ever do that again. Now breathe.'

I took a great lungful of air, and then another. It felt human to breathe again.

'You have control now.'

'Of what?' I managed, before June dumped the manual for Simple Shoggoth Command Protocol in my head. The map/control surface twitched as several new layers updated.

I stared at the glyphs for a few moments. Shit code written by something angry, lashing out at the headache it had been given. Even so, subverting an airframe and crew to drop a nuke on the infestation, just to make the screaming stop, was a massive over-reaction. What was the line? 'Tooled up and itching for an excuse to kick off'. Only it had turned out that, rather than Hookland rescuing me, I was the self-rescuing princess.

Liz Malcom, and probably June, were the sort of people who wrote programs out on coding sheets and ran them in their heads to make sure they ran first time on the target system.

June would call it a grimoire, but I had just been handed the keys and the technical manual to a fully charged and moderately pissed off long barrow, and all of that surplus energy had to be channelled somewhere other than at me.

Step one: Make the airframe safe.

I thought about a command-sequence along the lines of 'abort; drain command stack; disconnect-all; quiesce;' and watched with half my attention as the neon glyphs twisted in on themselves with a grating noise while in flight.

Some of the subsonic bees in the back of my head went quiet, most of the others got louder. Fine. Fucking *fine*. You wanted a gateway between the old powers of the landscape and the people who have always been here, and the new powers of jet fuel and machine tools. But you couldn't make it work right because tunnelling shoggoth command runes over a sigil gateway is going to work as well for you as trying to shout at your mobile phone in a local dialect.

What you need is one of the people who have always been here, but one who also speaks jet fuel and machine tools.

Enheduanna, Sumerian priestess and the earliest named writer, describes the priestesses of Inanna. It is from 2300BCE and those priestesses were all trans women. We are the people who have always been here.

You want a fucking gateway? You get a fucking gateway.

Step two: Make the aerodrome safe.

I sparked up the bolt-thrower again, and turned it up to eleven. If you've ever seen a computer controlled plasma cutter knifing through steel plate like someone making slightly rusty pastry...

The sigil I cut down the full length of the main runway was just me getting my eye in. There was likely a better way of doing it, but it was probably effective, definitely sneaky, and I was tolerably pleased with myself for thinking it up on the fly. It made the whole of RAF Nook a geomagnetic anomaly, instead of just Evie Barrett's Tump. I'd just made most of my own publication history obsolete, but it felt entirely justified.

Rendering the first of the hardened bunkers to ten cm cubes of shiny concrete and cutting intricate labyrinths in each face took some thought, but once you've expressed something as code for the first time, the rest is just a loop until finished.

The subsonic bees sputtered and faded, leaving the last cuts in the last bunker looking like the remains of a surrealist theatre backdrop. I remembered to breathe again and dropped the patch cables onto the top of the Templeton box.

The sunset still resembled a trans flag. The colours were still quietly vibrating when I looked at them properly. I yawned massively. I had to call Hearthstone, and I should probably call Liz to tell her that the plan had mostly worked. I yawned again and clambered back up to my improvised hammock in the centre of the 101's roof. June and I had a lot to talk about.

#

THE SEAMSTRESS, THE HOUND, THE COOK, AND HER BROTHER

By
K T Davies

One
The Seamstress

Lightly drugged and sweetly fucked, the Keeper of Candles rolled over. Free of his embrace, the Seamstress sat up. She wiped the sleep balm from her lips and took a moment to admire her work. Slurring inanities, the *Master of the Wick* burrowed into the pillow, sinking ever deeper into dreams she had woven from his lust, her need, and a very expensive drug.

That he had waited for her to finish was an unlooked-for boon, and she hoped for his sake he wouldn't wake while she worked. Quiet as a shadow, she slipped from the cot. A gust of wind blew through the grill in the floor, chilling the sweat on her body and waking the memory of sea spray in her skin. *Soon. Home soon.* She crouched and opened her sewing basket, which was filled with the tools of her trade. Chief amongst them, for this night only, the liar's crown. As she unwrapped it, paste gems blazed in the scatter of moonlight, breaking the dark's dominion over the small chamber.

The hour for cunning work and daring deeds had come at last.

While decent folk were abed, their minds wandering through the strange vaults of sleep, the Seamstress wagered her dreams against eternity. Leaving the crown in the basket, she lifted the grill. Far below, the four knights standing vigil didn't notice the light rain of dust falling from the chapel ceiling. Had they done so, they would only have seen the dark hole in the roof where the bell ropes used to hang. But they did not. With their backs to the catafalque, the knights' heads remained bowed, steel statues locked in the stance of grief and duty.

The tide of dread that had swelled in her gut ebbed. She set the grill down on her borrowed servant's livery before unwinding the moon spider silk she had hidden in the sewing basket. Just one ball of thread amongst many. Also hidden amongst the buttons, bobbins, pins, and needles was a steel hook which she threaded with the fine rope.

The Keeper slumbered as she cast the gossamer line. The hook flew, a slender hope shining in the glow of funerary candles. None of the tomb knights noticed it catch the crown beneath the glittering orb. Diamonds flashed an unseen warning across the backs of the warriors' polished cuirasses as she sent a ripple down the line and looped it around the base of the conquered world, garishly rendered in diamonds and pearls. Tightening her grip, she tugged the silk.

The crown didn't lift from the velvet cushion. Didn't move an inch.

Sweat slicked her palms. She tried again. Pins flashed like tiny splinters of light as they pulled free of the cushion. She wound the line around her arm and drew the glittering prize towards her, inch by painful inch.

There was death behind, and death below.

The real crown was heavier than the pretender, more substantial in every way. The cut and clarity of the stones more dazzling than the brightest polished glass. The lustre of the pearls richer than the proxy of paint and paste. But that wasn't her business. All she had to do was steal the Crown of the North from a castle full of knights and leave a gilded lead cuckoo on the dead king's nest.

She swapped the fake for the real.

The loose pins tumbled amongst the wreaths when she lowered the cuckoo onto the cushion. Prisoned in steel helms, the knights wouldn't notice a few missing pins, but the Master of the Casket or the Lady of the Flowers might when they came to strew fresh herbs. She would be long gone before they or any of the courtly mourners passed through the chapel on the morrow. Not that they would be scrutinizing the jewels, too concerned with being seen to be grovelling, wearing their grief like ashes as they bid con-spicuous farewell to the man whose arse they'd spent their lives kissing. She replaced the grill and dressed in her plain garb, becoming once more, and for the last time, a modest dressmaker who, by a level of artifice most would consider magic, had caught the Keeper of the Candle's eye, and fired his ardour.

As she came, so she departed, beneath the knowing gaze of the postern guard. Mindful of her role, she affected the air of someone embarrassed by her indiscretion, kept her gaze lowered as she passed. Inside, she was elated, keen to be away from this drear keep and the grim-faced nobles standing vigil beside commoners in the castle bailey. She pulled her shawl over her head like any girl trying to keep her hair dry as she hurried home. To add truth to her forged persona and distract her thoughts from what was in her basket, she tried to imagine the humble home where the girl she was not might be going. At this time, the soup which had been thickened with yesterday's bread would be cold on the stove but ready for morning. The smell of father's pipe would linger faintly, and his boots would be drying in the ashes of the hearth. It was a small house, one room downstairs, a loft above, but it was warm, and cosy. Would they have livestock? No, probably not. As she conjured the details of a life she would never live, she made her way to the part of town such a home might be found. Her feet followed her thoughts, taking her to where narrow streets meandered, and thatched roofs shouldered tight against their neighbours. It was a necessary diversion, a false life, and a false trail to confuse and delay the hunters who would surely follow when the deception was discovered.

'Oi! I said, where are you going?' The man swung out of an alley, demanding in voice and street owning stance. He was not alone. Two more men loomed behind him, weaving shadows as they stumbled from between the tight-packed houses. Unkempt and ruddy cheeked, their beer-bright eyes lit up when they saw her.

Idiot. She had been so immersed in her imagined existence that he had been able to startle her. There was no excuse she could hide behind; the fault was plain and entirely hers. She had painstakingly pieced her plans from scraps of information about knights, nobles, guards, and servants. She had not considered adding street drunks as an embellishment. But given the place through which she was passing, and the role she was playing she should have done.

'I have erred.' She was telling herself, speaking aloud so that she might better remember the mistake and the lesson. Heads swelled with bottle-born hubris; the drunks must have thought she was talking to them. In reply they spewed litanies of foolishness at her with drink-knotted tongues.

'Why's that, lassie? You lost?'

'Want a drink?'

'Want a kiss?'

'Where you going?'

'Where'd you live, love?'

She could only pick out scraps, as they talked over each other. She would consider her mistake on the way home, but for now she had to extricate herself quietly and quickly from this awkwardness.

'I'm not going to hurt you,' the leader of the trio said as he reached for her, his voice thick, with lust.

It was not the first time she'd been waylaid because she looked like an easy mark, but it had been a while. Irritated by the delay, she reached into the basket. The drunk swiped at her clumsily, missed by a yard. Would a little nick be enough to put him off? Just a little cut as a warning?

'Be a good girl.' He grabbed her wrist. She stamped on his toes and pulled away. 'You nasty little whore.' The men stopped laughing. Thick fingers fumbled at breeches' buttons. Expression drained from their faces save for the hunger in their eyes as they closed in around her.

No then. A nick with the shears would not be enough to warn them away. 'I don't have time for this.' She was wearing a long dress, and shoes with narrow heels which were apt to sit awkwardly in the gaps between the cobbles. Not ideal for this kind of messy work.

Or any work come to that.

She sighed, resigned. This was the cloth she had been given, and she must cut it to fit her needs. As to her foes, three lustful drunks weren't the worst odds she had ever faced.

The one who had grabbed her wrist lunged first. For the second time that night she was bathed in the reek of beer breath and sweat. Setting her feet, she jabbed her shears into the wall of his neck, into the thick web of veins that throbbed beneath the stubble. A twist and a push directed the man and the oily jet of blood away from her, towards his nearest friend. The anointed, and the anointer stumbled away.

At the violent death of his companion, the third lost his stomach, doubled over as he puked. She grabbed his greasy hair and smashed his head into the cobbles with as much force as she could summon. There was a dull crack. He moaned. Not dead, not yet. To proof herself against the future danger borne of a loose and vengeful tongue, she stamped on his neck.

Blood-splattered and bewildered, the remaining, failed rapist backed away from his comrade, leaving him to spend the remaining balance of his life upon the cobbles. The Seamstress stepped lightly over the spreading pool. From the evidence of his eyes, the drunk must have known there would be no quarter for him. He turned, tried to run. She caught up easily and stabbed him in the spine. Unstrung, he fell. She stepped around him and cut his throat with a clean swipe of the shears, choking off his final cry. She stepped back and, limbs trembling, admired her bloody work.

#

Two
The Hound

Aged in oak, the Fendorta was creamy, with notes of pomegranate, ripe peach, and just a hint of honey. The taste and smell expanded to fill Ander Trundakay's mouth and nose with its round, buttery finish. She couldn't wait a moment longer, and although intending to savour the memory of long summer days, she threw the whole glass down her neck. It was sublime.

She waited a few minutes for the first fire of the taste to subside before picking another of the dozen or so dusty half bottles and pouring a glass. This one had the subtle tones of bark and woodfoot mushrooms. Floating above the rich, earthy warmth was a sharp spike of blood salt. The olfactory explosion kindled another memory, of an evening sitting with the then prince in his hunting lodge, blood spattering the hearth from the beaks of talon wings tied in braces to the mantle. The hunt was dissected, naturally the prince's skills were lauded, his companions' folly lightly mocked. For her work flushing out the flying lizards, the prince gave her a bottle of wine from his personal stock.

She closed her eyes, saw again the smiling faces of the hunting party ruddied by wind, wine, and a roaring fire. Another sip brought the sounds of the past into the present and filled her tiny home with the sound of laughing ghosts.

The Hound drained the glass and contemplated which of the dusty bottles she would try next. As she reached for an old Dracomord, she heard footsteps. She would have preferred them to continue past her cottage, but instead they came towards it.

She looked to the door. It was barred, the windows shuttered. Because she could see in the dark she rarely bothered to waste a candle at night. The fire was lit but burning low, and the glow did not spread far even in the small parlour. She looked at the small pile of her belongings and despaired. Not much to show for years of devoted service, but too much to be bothered packing it all tonight, especially when there was wine to be drunk. Tomorrow. She would finish the packing tomorrow and still be gone before the new king's tenant came to take residence *in her home*. It stung like fresh nettles to be discarded so.

Whoever was outside hammered on her door. She ignored it, picked up another bottle as and drew the cork with her teeth. It was a southern wine and smelled of the veldt. The almost effervescent sweetness tickled her nose. It had been particularly hot when the grapes trapped summer in their skins in the vineyards beyond the Whispering Sea where they said the Lyca Mara still hunted the unwary. She raised the bottle. 'To the King, and the ancestors.' Insistent knocking intruded on her thoughts. 'Fuck off.'

'We're here on the king's business.'

'He's dead,' she shouted back. 'And made me homeless and unemployed, the bastard,' she added, but only to the shadows.

A moment's silence was followed by whispering outside. She sniffed, licked her lips to better taste the shreds of scent oozing through the gaps in the door. There was steel, honed, and oiled. Leather buffed and polished. But these weren't common soldiers, not unless guards had taken to wearing perfume. She smelled oil of rose, styrax, and marjoram. Nobles then, or their curs come to yap at her for something she owed, no doubt. She sank into the old armchair. She would have taken it with her, but it had come with the cottage and would have to stay lest she be called a thief. 'Damn them.' She would miss this place; she would miss this chair. Someone rattled the door.

'Begone. Or I'll cry for the watch.'

There was muffled cursing. 'Open the damn door, Hound!' This was a different voice, older, angrier than the first.

'We are here on the business of the Court,' the first speaker corrected calmly.

'So you say. You could be brigands out to rob a poor woman what lives on her own.'

Someone kicked the door. Ander grinned. She enjoyed taunting her betters but tried to stay the right side of a thrashing. Without haste, she got up and unlatched the door. Two cloaked men were on her step. Loitering under the apple tree by the garden wall were three more. Like their masters, the soldiers by the tree were conspicuously wearing travel cloaks which did little to disguise the bulk of armour or the bright stitching of their livery. That they wished their business with her go unmarked made her wary. The clouds parted briefly, and she looked away, lest they see her eyes brighten in the starlight. 'Who are you strangers?'

'I am Sir Arno Breuille, equerry to the Duke of Arheyle.'

She would never remember that, but she bobbed her head in acknowledgement.

'I'm none of your damn business,' said the older of the two.

Twat. That was much easier to remember. She stood aside and gestured for them to enter.

'After you, Lord Grevelle,' said the equerry, immediately gaining her favour if not her trust.

Upon entering, Grevelle displayed his high status by rudely wafting his hand and making a disgusted face. Clearly of a lower social standing, the equerry had manners enough to merely grimace. She knew it was because of the smell, and she was glad about it. Although not as strong as the reek of the tanneries Ander rendered horn and fat in her cottage and dried what skins she could take as her hunters due. Far from disdaining the pungent aromas she felt they enlivened an otherwise drab world. Of course, the scents she savoured were too subtle for sense-dulled humans to even notice, let alone appreciate. Just as she could still see the hart she'd stalked two days previously in all his russet glory, all these refined gentlemen could smell was the stink of blood and flesh still clinging to the bones she had been gifted and was yet to scrape. The finer notes of the beast's scent were beyond their ability to discern.

'You're leaving?' The younger man's gaze roved over her half-packed possessions.

Ander smiled tightly. 'The new king, gods bless him, has his own hunters.' She tried not to sound as bitter as she felt. 'They need somewhere to live.'

'Such is the way of things.' The elder remarked, without a moment's consideration of exactly what that meant to her. 'I can, however, offer you some work on behalf of the king, and with it suitable remuneration.'

'The old king, or the new one?'

Grevelle rocked on his heels as if irked by her question, at least, she hoped he was. 'The new king.'

'Oh. 'Tis an honour, sir.'

'The matter is delicate and requires utmost secrecy,' the equerry added.

Delicacy and secrecy? 'I'm a tracker, sir. I track game...'

Grevelle glanced at the equerry, shook his head and urged him on with a knowing look. The younger man took a moment before clearing his throat. 'We want you to you track something.'

The pissy acid smell of fear sweat tainted the air. An ill feeling soured her half-drunk mood. 'What then?'

'Watch your tongue, varlet,' Grevelle warned.

Bile rose in her throat. Watch my tongue? They come to my home with foolish demands and force me to make nice when all I want to do is get drunk and fall asleep by the fire , yet I'm to watch my tongue, am I? 'Pardon, sir.'

The old fellow bristled. 'It is, 'my lord'. Mark me, the king might have indulged your savage manners because it amused him to do so, but I despise insolence. Speak to me like that again and I will—'

Before he could say 'have you thrashed' the equerry stepped forward, silencing Grevelle with the coldest of shoulders. The nobleman looked furious, but to Ander's surprise he held his tongue. That the younger man was taking the lead in this lopsided negotiation said much about how quickly the old was being swept aside by the new king's gilded broom, herself included. Hard to believe she had something in common with the proud relic.

The equerry cast a glance towards the door before speaking. 'The, er, *item-in-question*, was stolen sometime between Falleday and Gruseday.' He paused until she nodded. 'Only a handful of the king's most trusted servants know that *the item* is missing. It will remain so, on pain of death. Do you understand?'

'Aye.'

'Good.' He indicated his companion with an offhand wave. 'Lord Grevelle will direct the search.' Grevelle shot his companion an arrow-sharp side-eye. 'You will track the item and report only to Lord Grevelle, or to me.'

She was either too drunk or too stupid to grasp what they wanted her to find but felt that asking again would not go down well. 'I can't track anything with a regiment of knights trampling all over the place.'

'You'll do as you're fucking told,' Grevelle snapped.

Ander swallowed her anger and stared at the floor. 'Yes. My lord.'

#

Doing 'as she was fucking told' meant not asking what was stolen but mutely agreeing to search for it in exchange for her usual daily pay and keeping the roof over her head until she found it.

It was a poor bargain, that turned worse when the next morning she was taken by a tight-lipped soldier through back passages to the chapel where the king had laid in state. She was directed to the king's catafalque, upon which was a velvet cushion. Beside it was an ironbound box with a lock. *Mother of Sea and Moon.* Even though the name was never used, Grevelle made clear by inference and powerful hints that she was to track the Crown of the North. By way of longwinded and roundabout explanations, she was given to understand that a fake had been left in place of the real one. Which would explain why the outrageous theft was not the talk of the city.

She wondered how many people had looked upon glass and thought it precious and how foolish they would feel if they knew? To hide her amusement, she turned to the dais and dabbled her fingers in the carpet of leaves and dirt. No tracker could have made sense of the trampled mess, but the blood of the Lyca Mara flowed in Ander's veins.

While making a show of sizing prints and reading signs she drew a measured, mindful breath. The ghost scent of the crown was strongest in the iron bound box. Locked away in a vault for decades the scent was so stewed, she was able to pick out the rich particulars that oozed from the wood. Grey and silver, turquoise and amber, the memory of stone and fire, ringing hammer blows, and scrape of a jeweller's chisel made a shape which some would call 'a crown'. *But what's in a name?* Unique as a sunrise, now that she had seen the smell of it, she would find it wherever it went in the world.

And it had gone up.

In the smoke shadows of the roof, she spied a vent between the vaulted arches. 'What's up there?' Dry from drinking the dead king's wine, her voice sounded rough in the solemn air.

#

The man didn't resist when Grevelle's hard-eyed agents dragged him from the chamber above the chapel. He asked what he'd done, but when no answer was forthcoming he fell into a resigned and terrified silence. He knew the time for him to talk would come soon enough.

Ander endured the sting of his accusing glare as he was dragged past. It was a fair rebuke. She had led them here following the scent that oozed through the grate in the floor.

'We need to go,' she told them.

'We've to search the room.'

'It's not here.' She pointed to the door, where the trail was drifting fine as a thread of silk down the narrow stair.

The soldier shrugged. 'His Lordship says we're to search here first. Oi, where you going?'

'To follow the trail,' she called over her shoulder.

'We're to wait here.'

'Then do so.'

What he shouted next was lost in the echo of half-dozen soldiers running after her. She told them to keep their distance and otherwise ignored them, ignored everything in pursuit of the smell of the crown. As the grey slug of morning light began to crawl above the black glass horizon she came to a halt on the dock.

'Have you lost it?' One of the pack of soldiers asked, his gaze lifted to the silvered sea and distant sails.

'No.' Perhaps. The bitter taste of failure fouled her breath. Fearing she'd been thwarted by the ocean, Ander crouched on the dock and pretended to look for tracks as she tasted the wind. *Even if it is to the sea, give me a direction.* It wasn't a wish; it was a need.

There. She caught the tail of the crown's scent. It was faint, nothing like what she'd found where the men had been butchered, but it was there. Drawn by the shape of gold and diamonds, she put her head down and loped towards a stable. Swords were drawn behind her. 'Wait!' she commanded. To her surprise, the pack of soldiers obeyed.

'Are they in there? What have you seen?' one of them asked.

'Tracks.' With her knees creaking too loud for her liking, she crabbed closer to the door that squealed on rusting hinges. 'See the hoofprints?' She pointed them out to the nearest soldier. 'They're older going in than they are coming out.'

'How old?'

'A day, two at most.'

'Shit.'

'Aye.' She peered inside. The stalls were empty and strung with dusty cobwebs, but a lantern hanging on a post gleamed with greasy smoke stains. The imprint of slender heels in the dirt told Ander the thief had stood with her back to its light, her scent mingling with that of the crown. Keeping the pack at bay with a staying hand, she crept inside.

#

The soldiers had insisted Grevelle be summoned when she found the tracks in the stable. Somewhere between here and there, the story had changed so that his lordship arrived thinking the item had been found. She did not enjoy disavowing him. As she suspected he did not take the news well and flew into a rage. Because she didn't like him, she decided not to show him the piece of red cotton thread she'd found. Neither would she tell him that she thought the thief was a girl, still in her prime, about a week from her flow, with mouse brown hair, a strand of which still clung to the post where she'd stood with her back to the light of the lantern. There was more. A hundred small scents had run together and sculpted the shape of the thief in Ander's mind. Like the crown, now that she had seen the tangle of scents that were the girl, she felt like she knew her and if she was still in the city she could find her. *What an interesting meeting that would be.* But Lord high and mighty Grevelle had not set her to hunt the thief. She had been ordered to track a thing, so that was what she would do.

'Are you sure they went north?' Grevelle made the question sound like an accusation.

'Yes.'

'My lord! Damn you.' He slapped his boot with his riding crop. Despite the ugly leveraged bit controlling it, his horse shied, which set off the mounts of the knights who had galloped from the castle with him. 'You, *varlet*, will call me 'My lord.'

She focused her gaze on the horse's hooves. 'My Lord.'

'Your incompetence reflects on me. It will not stand.' He shared his ire between Ander and the soldiers who, like the Hound, were all trying not to catch his eye. 'You will leave at once and you will find the item, or I swear, I will throw you all in the fucking dungeons and leave you to rot.'

How any of them had earned such censure was beyond her. They hadn't been guarding the damn crown when it was stolen, and she had come closer than anyone else to finding it. Why was this old bastard threatening to punish them if they failed to do something that he couldn't? His steely eyed knights did not inspire hope of a fair hearing. They looked at Ander and her small pack of soldiers like they were looking at grass in a field. No, worse than that. Grass has value, they looked at them like they were nothing more than an inconvenience to their eyes. This wasn't right or fair. But then nothing about the matter was, least of all her forced involvement in the shady business. Shady because even now it had not been made known that the crown had been stolen. Perhaps the new king and his advisors wanted to keep it that way, whether it was found or not. Which begged the question, what would they do with her when the hunt was over? She felt she already knew the answer to that question. *What happened to all old hounds when they were past their usefulness?*

She looked at the knights, none met her gaze.

Grevelle kicked his mount towards her, forcing her to jump aside or be trampled. 'Do you ride?' His spurred boot was uncomfortably close to her face, as no doubt was his intention.

'No.' she said absently, her thoughts more concerned with not being murdered than using the correct form of address.

Her ear rang, and she felt the welt rise instantly where he caught her cheek with the crop, the sharp sting quickly turning to a deep ache. It could have been worse, the rowels on his spurs would have cut her cheek open had he chosen to kick her instead.

'What was that?' he said, cold and threatening.

'No...my Lord. I don't ride.'

He leaned down from the saddle. 'Then you will run as fast as you can, *Hound,* and you will not stop until you either find it, or your fucking heart bursts.'

#

Three
The Cook

The kitchens were never silent. The cook doubted in all of the hundreds of years they had fed the Aubros of Ticlare they had ever been silent. But late at night, when the bread was proving, and the great hearth awash with ashes and rubies, it was quiet.

Onya put a muslin over the marchpane she had kneaded to a smooth paste. The waves crashing against the rocks below were a comfort. Distant and repetitive, she found the sound soothing. Pouring the cup of chai that she had promised herself before finishing the marchpane, she loosened her apron strings and went to sit by the fire. She would bank it before retiring to her bed rather than wake the spit boy who had crawled off to sleep in the root store. New to the great house, the child vexed her ears morning till night asking foolish questions. She shuddered. *If ever there was a reason not to wed, it was sleeping on a pile of potato sacks.*

She tugged off her cap to let the air to her sweaty head and yawned. She was tired, but she would not hurry her drink. The morning would come when it came. This was her time; her privilege as cook of a great house to sit alone by the fire in the heart of her little fiefdom. Not to mention Murgha the pastry cook with whom she shared a bed would have spread herself across the mattress like a dead gull by now. As she did every night, Onya would have to roll the lump over to claim her portion of the bed before finding a few hours of sleep between the roar of the ocean and Murgha's snoring.

As the list of the morrow's 'to be dones' began to write themselves into her thoughts, she sipped her chai, placing one thing above another in order of importance as she savoured her drink. As Queen of the Kitchen, it was spiced with a generous tot of cooking rum and a pinch of nutmeg she had kept back from the Aubro's dinner. The night should have ended thus, with the chai warming her stomach and sleep beckoning like an old friend, but the sound of familiar footsteps disturbed her.

'Don't rise on account of me, sis.'

'I wasn't going to.'

'Aye, but do you have anything to eat for your poor brother?' She got up. Always more awake at night than in the morn, her brother threw himself into her chair, harp on his lap, cheeks flushed from the Aubro's wine.

She shook her head. 'Away to your bed, I'm done cooking for the day.'

'What's this cruelty? I've laboured all night entertaining our lord and master, and all I get is scorn and an empty stomach?'

'He's asleep then?'

'On and off. He's restless, say's an old wound's bothering him.'

'His piles, most likely. The physiker is giving him wax and honey enemas. If he's awake, how is it you're here? Has he grown bored of your plucking?'

'I beg your pardon, madame!'

'I said *plucking.*'

He grinned and set his harp beside him. 'He nodded off for a spell, so I thought I'd come and see my beloved sister.

He won't remember in the morning if he gave leave to go or no.'

'You better hope he doesn't.'

'Ack, he's no tyrant that'll thrash a man for wanting a bite and a piss. And besides, my throat's as dry as Murgha's neth-ers this eve. He'll not begrudge me the chance to rest.'

She fixed him with a disapproving look as she passed him on her way to the larder. 'Don't talk like a fieldhand in my kitchen. I taught you manners. Prithee spare some for your kin instead of hoarding them all for the Aubro.'

'The old man pays my wages, such as they are.'

She reached for the dish of pluck pie and cabbage she had saved just in case he paid her a visit. 'And I wiped your back-side when you were a babe, don't forget that.'

He laughed. 'A fair point. I pray thee, sis, forgive my wicked tongue and tap a cask that I might drown the slippery varlet in ale.'

'Clot.' She cuffed him playfully as she handed him the platter. 'Tap a cask indeed, I'm sure that would go down well with the steward. There might be something left in the crock from supper.' As she went to fetch the ale, the port-cullis chains rattled. Out of place at this late hour, the sound echoed around the bailey and found its way through narrow windows and winding stairs into the kitchens. When the rat-tling stopped, horses' hooves clattered on the cobbles. Onya held her breath and listened for the watch horn to sound, or worse, for screams and yelling to announce raiders were attacking, bringing ruin and horror upon them.

Her gaze darted about the kitchen. She considered poker, pan, or cleaver in turn before managing to get a hold of herself and quiet her nerves as the clattering died away. *Stop scaring yourself over nothing, you silly goat. Aye, but.*, 'What decent folk come calling on their lord at this godless hour?'

'No idea, but I'd best make haste to my lord's chamber, for that racket is sure to have woken him.' He snatched up his harp and stuffed a slice of cold pie in his mouth before running from the kitchen. She swept the crumbs he'd made into her hand before throwing them in the fire. The flames hissed and sent tiny curls of black smoke rising from the fat. She wasn't afraid, but rightly concerned as to who had such a need that they would ride the cliff road at night to come here. Resolved to settle the unease rolling in her gut, she threw her shawl on and crept out of the kitchen, past the root store, along the passage between the bakery and the dairy parlour, and up the stairs as far as the narrow bay where a small window looked onto the courtyard.

As her eyesight adjusted to the different darkness of the bailey, she saw the weary stablemaster and his equally sleepy lad leading horses away, their lathered flanks steaming and gleaming in the torch light spilling from the main entrance. It looked like Egedar, the Aubro's steward, if she read the shape right. He was holding the door for a group of cloaked figures who swept inside like a flock of crows, without pausing to exchange greetings. As soon as they were inside, Egedar closed the door, the sound of bolts being thrown snatched away by the strengthening wind blowing off the sea and around the castle, adding its menace to an already unsettling night. Onya shivered and was about to head for her bed when her brother returned at a run.

'You're to prepare a supper for eight,' he announced breathlessly, taking her by the elbow and hurrying her towards the kitchen. She shook him off. 'Nothing fancy, my lord says, just cold platters and bread and hot posset enough for a dozen.'

She gave a sharp laugh. 'A dozen, eh? I'll have to rouse the girls.'

'No.' her brother whispered. 'Keep your voice down. You're to see to it yourself.' He raised his hands in surrender. 'Don't give me the hard eye. I'm just the messenger.'

'You're an ill wind, is what you are.' She leaned in. 'So, who are they?'

He took her arm and again bustled her towards the kitchen. 'I cannot say, sis. But they're important enough for the old man to put on his fur mantle and grant hospitality in his private parlour.'

She could tell there was more he didn't want to tell her, which was unusual. If she was the Queen of the Kitchen, her brother was the King of the Gossips. 'Come on, you must have heard something.'

He bit his lip, a sure sign that he had. Always the key to unlocking his secrets, she gave him a hard stare. 'Say nothing to anyone, but I think they stand for the true king.'

'Which one's that? There's so many lay claim I lose track.'

'The true king. The King of the Northern Lands. Our king.'

'The one over the sea? Oh.'

'Oh?' He paused in the kitchen doorway as she opened the oven and stoked the ashes.

'Aye, oh. Pass me some faggots. The posset won't heat itself.'

'I've just told you these are our king's men and all you can say is 'pass me some faggots?'

'It's not *all* I can say. How about, you stay away from these men. They're dangerous and bring nothing but trouble with their plots and their schemes. Our Aubro has one foot in the beyond. They should let him be, not involve him in their foolishness.'

'Foolishness? You don't know what you're talking about, woman. You're just a cook.' Realising he had gone too far he did the sensible thing and stepped out of arm's reach.

'Woman is it? Not, dear sister who has raised me since I was a nipper and taken care of me my whole life?'

'Sorry, sis. I didn't mean it.'

'No, the fault is mine. I have raised you badly.' She picked up her wooden spoon and was gratified to see him gulp.

'You raised me well, sis. I'm sorry. You're a very good cook. The best in all Ticlare.' That should have been an end of it, but he was too fired up. 'It's just that they...Well, great things are happening here, under our roof. Great things, sis. And I have a part to play.'

He grinned like the fool he was.

The more he talked, the deeper her heart sank. But what could she say to disavow him of his notions? He was near enough a man, she couldn't send him to bed without supper to sharpen his wits with hunger. 'Give me those.' She snatched the faggots from him. 'And go fetch the milk.'

'But, I have to go back...' He began dancing towards the kitchen door.

'If your lord and his guests are to eat you'll get the bloody milk. Here, put this on.' She handed him her apron. 'You don't want to go to the Aubro with a stained doublet.'

He frowned but put on the apron. It amused her to see that he could have wrapped it twice about his slender frame. She could have cried to look at him. He was still a boy, despite the beard. In truth, she hadn't raised him badly. By the sweat of her brow, she had given him the means to rise above his station. She had sold all she had saved for a dowry to buy the harp and pay for his lessons, sold her future to buy his. It wasn't the tragedy people thought it was for her. She would rather be Queen of her Kitchen than a drudge in a husband's house. He poured the milk into the pan, his arms shaking under the weight of the half-empty churn.

'Right. I have to go.' He kissed her cheek and handed her the churn.

'The apron?'

He sighed and fumbled with the strings. When he handed it back, she wanted to grab him and hold him and keep him there until the carrion eaters had flown to another roost. *Might as well try to hold the wind.* He was young and drawn to danger and she could no longer protect him. She cursed herself, cursed her dreams, cursed her pride. If she'd made him stay a spit boy instead of a harper, he'd be safely beneath the notice of scheming lords. And he wouldn't have minded, she was sure. He would have yearned for a little while, but he would have got used to it. You didn't pen sheep to hurt them, you did it to protect them from the wolves.

#

'Wait here.' The steward closed the door to the Aubro's private parlour. She yawned. One of the guards did likewise. A short while later Egedar opened the door and beckoned her inside. Onya entered, the smell of lemon posset tickling her nose.

The parlour was hot from the press of bodies and the fire blazing up the chimney like it was the middle of the day, not the small hours of night. Decent folk should be abed. It wasn't right and she didn't like it. As she put the tray on the table, a loaf of bread rolled off and onto the floor. Not wanting the good white bread to fall prey to one of the Aubro's dogs, she stooped to retrieve it.

'Leave it!' one of the strangers commanded like he owned her. Onya and the Aubro's hound both backed away from the bread. The stranger did not clarify which he meant. Confused, the cook mumbled an apology and began to unload the dishes from the tray. 'I said, just leave it.' The fellow sighed heavily from the shadow of his hood.

'Play something while we dine,' the Aubro said to her brother, drawing attention from Onya. 'Play 'Shova's Return' or 'The Ring of Lament''.

The strangers muttered their approval of the choices and, still standing, still cloaked, began to pick at the food without removing their gauntlets, let alone washing their hands. *Pigs, the lot of them.*

Sat in the window, wearing a mask of mildness just the right side of stupid, her brother inclined his head. With but a sweep of the strings, he immediately found a tune. Onya's heart always swelled when she heard him play and for a moment all dark thoughts were forgotten as he conjured notes like magic from the glittering strings.

'What is it?' The rude stranger deigned to look at her this time. The hardness of his gaze was like a blow. She backed into the door. 'Gods, wench, just leave.' With a wave of his hand, he dismissed her.

Angry and embarrassed, she ran back to the kitchens. Her brother was right, she was just a cook, a woman alone with neither wealth nor wit to protect her, or him. Tears fell. *Queen of the Crock with a spoon for a sceptre.* She laced her fingers and closed her eyes. 'Mecra, Madra, Manar, Sweet Sisters of Above, Below, and Between. My hair at Derruntide if you keep him safe. My hair at every Derruntide until I die if you keep my little brother safe.'

#

Bone weary from sleeping in a chair, Onya did not look forward to the day's work. But she would rather have spent the rest of her life in drudgery than hear the panicked shouting coming from the bailey. Curious, more than concerned, some of the others working in the kitchen followed her to the window on the stair.

Through the narrow panes she saw the strangers throw saddles on their mounts and ride from the castle still tightening their girths. Such was their haste that one of the horses slipped on the mist-slicked cobbles and fell. The rider lay where he fell, but the horse staggered to its feet and charged after the others. When the riderless horse overtook the others, none of them slowed or looked back to see what had become of their companion. Defying the rules about kitchen staff wandering the halls of the castle, Onya rushed up the stairs, and was almost knocked off her feet by a dozen of the Aubro's men as they ran into the courtyard. She followed them as far as the door. Beyond the gate she could see the plotters split up and ride off the road, which was dangerous even on a clear day, let alone a miserable fog-bound morn. Spurring their mounts some rode north, while the others took off across the moor to the south. And then she saw why. A column of mounted knights resplendent in the scarlet and gold livery of the king were riding along the road from the east. A cry went up, horns blared. Some went after the strangers; some came on towards the castle.

'Sis!'

Her heart leapt when she saw her brother running from the Aubro's hall clutching a linen bundle to his chest.

'What is it? Where's your harp?'

'I...' His knuckles were white around the bundle. 'You have to help me hide it.'

'What is it?' She pried his fingers apart and unwrapped the cloth. There was danger, there was death. She covered it, would have crushed it to dust if she was able.

'Please, sis. If you love our country, if you love *me*, help me hide it.'

She nodded. She couldn't speak because her heart was beating so hard that even her breath trembled. She grabbed his hand and dragged him down to the kitchens, past those milling on the stair.

'In there!' Her brother pointed to the oven.

She didn't stop. 'No. If you thought of it, someone else will.'

'So, where are we going to hide it?'

'The Ends of the Earth.' She snatched the bundle from him.

'The rubbish chute?'

'Aye.'

'No. I forbid you!'

It was not a day she thought would bring laughter, but there it was. 'You forbid me?' Still chuckling, she ran into the last storeroom. It was cold and damp and stacked with piss pots waiting to be cleaned. The waves roared from below like a hungry bear. She held her breath and reached for the pulley that raised the trap over the muck-splattered chute.

Her brother made a grab for the crown. Sure of what she must do to keep him safe, she held on. He strained against her. 'I...mean...it,' he said, trying to tear it from her grasp.

'You're an idiot, Dar. A sweet, talented, idiot so I'll not thump you, because Mecra favours fools. Now let go.'

'Might as well do as she says, lad.'

With the crashing waves, and her brother yelling, it was no surprise Onya hadn't heard the woman approach.

Startled, the cook took a step back catching her heel on the lip of the chute. It was dark, save for a narrow, slit window high on the wall, there more for ventilation than for shedding light. In the gloom, the tall, shaggy-haired woman's eyes shone unnaturally bright. She looked at Onya and gave a slight smile and a nod before wiping mud and sweat from her face on her filthy shirt sleeve. A bruise darkened her cheek. 'You would not believe the trouble I've had tracking that thing.' She chinned to the bundle. 'It's been quite the merry chase, let me tell you.' She rolled her heavy shoulders as she stepped forwards. 'Bring it to me, boy.'

Neither Onya nor her brother moved.

'Come on, I'm not here to hurt you.' She gestured impatiently. 'But the old bastard up there? He's likely to skin you if he knows you've even seen it. Hand it over quick before he sends someone looking for me.' She snorted. 'Not that any of them could find their arse with both hands.'

'You won't hurt him?' Onya didn't know where she had found the strength to speak. The woman canted her head, like an animal.

She raised her brow. 'Just him? Why not ask if I'll hurt you?' She seemed amused.

'Because he's all that matters to me. He's all I have.'

The wolf-eyed woman shook her head. 'You have yourself. You...' she looked like she was about to say something else but refrained. Her expression hardened. 'I'm getting bored now. Just bring it over, boy. Or I'll come get it and gut you while your woman watches.'

'Do as she says.' Onya thrust the crown into his hands. A moment stretched to what felt like an hour, but he didn't move. She shoved him. 'Do it, or we'll both die.' With tears in his eyes, he took the crown to the woman, who watched him like a dog watches sheep. As soon as it was in her hands it was as though she forgot they existed. She tore the cloth away and held it up to catch the faint rays of light forcing their way through the darkness.

'I expected it to sparkle more,' she said. 'I'd built such a picture of it in my mind.' She laughed. 'I expected more.' She tossed it between her hands like it was a toy. 'So much trouble for this.' She looked at Onya. 'Just clam spit and shiny rocks. You know—' The woman's too bright eyes widened and a look something between anger and surprise crossed her face. She turned to face Onya's brother, a dark wine stain spreading on the back of her sweat soaked shirt. A knife gleamed in his trembling hand.

'You're right,' said the woman. 'He is an idiot.' Holding the crown in one hand, she slapped the knife from his hand. More frightened than fierce he yelled and threw a punch. The woman swayed aside, grabbed him by the throat, and began to squeeze. Onya watched as her brother clawed at the woman's hand. 'You really think this bauble is worth dying for?' The woman shook her head, pressed the cook's brother to his knees. 'It isn't. Not for the likes of you or me. We're not worth one of these little diamonds to them up there. Not half of one.'

Onya was not brave, never had been. The best she had done was to hide her brother and then work like a dog to give him a good life. It hadn't been easy, but like a seed in a midden, she had thrived on the shit, until now.

Her brother's eyes closed, his hands fell by his side, and he hung in the woman's unrelenting grip like a dead rabbit.

No, she was not brave, but sometimes, even a cook must fight. Onya threw herself across the room and wrapped her arm around the woman's neck. It was like hugging a stone. Yelling, she locked her hands together and threw herself back. She was too fat to run far or fast. She had never used a bow or a sword, but she could skin a buck, hang the carcass on her own, and knead dough all day. The woman released her brother and hit her with the crown.

It was a glancing blow across the head, but the cook saw stars. Scared and angry, she squeezed harder. Even wounded, the woman was as strong as a sow. She kicked and bucked and almost threw Onya off. The cook's grip began to slip. Her muscles burned.

Her brother groaned.

If I let go, he dies.

She put her head down and held on. The woman flailed, clawed at Onya. Sharp nails dug into her scalp, drew blood. Onya held on. The woman was right, the crown was just a bauble. Onya was doing this for her brother, for the life she had made for them. No one was going to take that, not this wild woman, not raiders, not plotters who came in the night, not the gods and all their angels. The woman stopped struggling, fell limp.

Onya let go and crawled over to her brother. 'Dar?' she shook him. His eyes flickered open. He looked confused. 'Oh, thank you, thank you. Thank you.' She kissed his forehead.

'Did I kill her?' he asked, his voice a hoarse whisper.

Suddenly bone weary, Onya struggled to her feet and retrieved the crown. One of the cross-pieces was dented and strands of her hair were snagged on the stones. She stumbled to the chute and leaned her weight against the pulley. The trap yawned open like a hungry mouth. Far below, waves lapped at the rocks and pale foam stretched like a caul over the obsidian sea.

'Don't!' her brother begged as she tossed the crown down the chute. 'What have you done?'

'Nothing. I'm just a cook. Now give me a hand doing nothing with her.'

A WAY OUT

By
S. Naomi Scott

Ilse woke to pain. This was wrong. She shouldn't be able to feel pain, the parts of her responsible for pain no longer existed. They had been excised, along with so much else. She shouldn't even know what pain was any more. Yet there it was, deep inside her, reminding her she was still alive, despite everything she had been through. It was more than a little disconcerting. In fact, the feeling, and what it implied, was so distracting it took her a few microseconds to realise she was blind.

Technically she'd been blind for a long time, for as long as she'd been oblivious to pain, but the absence of eyes or a functioning optic nerve hadn't stopped the techs at Blue Kite patching in other ways for her to see. Electromagnetic sensors allowed her to observe everything from the weaker, slower radio waves all the way up to the frenetic, whirling energy of gamma rays. It made the narrow band of the EM spectrum visible to human eyes seem inconsequential by comparison. With these sensors Ilse had seen flares form and erupt from the atmosphere of her home star and watched as the energy from those same flares drifted on the solar winds, out to the heliopause. She had seen things most humans couldn't even imagine but now, without the sensors, she was helplessly blind.

This is kind of worrying, she thought. The pain was still there, nagging at her consciousness, but it had lost some of its significance in light of her lack of vision.

She tried to remember what she was doing before she blacked out, but there were gaps in her memory. Maybe if she could work out how she'd ended up in this situation, she could figure out what the situation was. What had she been doing before the impact?

Impact! A recollection of hitting or being hit by something made her mind lock up.

Is that where the pain's coming from?

She didn't have nerves anymore, but a network of tactile sensors threaded through her body and monitored her physical condition. *Is the damage so severe the feedback's being translated into pain?*

She tried unravelling the information buried beneath the sensations, but it was too much, too overwhelming for her to hold on to for more than a microsecond. Biting down the panic, she thought back to the last time she'd felt so helpless.

The day she had her body removed.

#

She had joined the program as a way out, a way to get off Senbelat, away from the muck and grime of her homeworld. There weren't too many options for a kid growing up on the streets of a factory world, not even one controlled by House Lustresi. It was either follow her parents into a life of punching a clock down at the production line, or join up with one of the rabble gangs for a much more entertaining but equally much shorter life as a troublemaker. Then the House recruiters offered her a third choice; sign up for the Fleet's Warfighter program.

The vids had painted an irresistible picture. Those enlistees who made it through orientation could look forward to two years light duty, an early retirement with a pension, and a brand-new custom-grown body that would make the wearer the envy of their friends back home. It wouldn't be dangerous, they said. At least, nothing more dangerous than running a few customs patrols on the fringe of the system. It'll be easy, they told her. Just two years' service to the House, and then you can write your own meal ticket.

Looking back, maybe they hadn't been entirely honest about a few things.

By the time Ilse signed up, Warfighter tech had been around long enough to iron out most of the major bugs. There were still a few candidates who washed out during the orientation process, recruits who didn't have the mental or psychological acumen to become a state-of-the-art fighting machine. Ilse wasn't one of them. Three months after signing away her freedom, she closed her eyes for the last time and the medics stripped her down to just enough organic matter to fit inside a pod no bigger than her head. All that remained was a brain, a couple of vertebrae, and a handful of internal organs.

The rest was thrown out with the trash.

That was the last time she felt pain. The Fleet shrinks had told her it was just in her mind, that she didn't have a nervous system left to transmit those sensations she was convinced she was feeling. It will soon end, they assured her, and sure enough it did end, and the process of learning how to use her new body began. And what a body it was.

She remembered the first time she'd become aware of that body, a twenty-metre-long boron nitride lattice frame overlaid with impossibly thin layers of nano-polymers. The techs assured her the new body would be able to handle most of the stress associated with both intra- and exo-atmospheric operations, but knowing it still hadn't prepared her for the exhilaration of free flight. And without the squishy parts of a regular pilot to worry about, she soon learned that she was capable of manoeuvres that made a crewed vehicle look, well, crude. She'd almost developed an addiction to endorphins during those early training flights.

Her body had initially been configured for patrol and interdiction as the recruiters had promised; light on ordnance, heavy on sensors. For the first few months everything was just as the vids had suggested; quiet and uneventful, with plenty of time to watch the universe drift by around her. She'd been happy then, happy with the choice she'd made and the bright future that awaited her.

#

A warning signal dragged her out of her memories and forced her to focus on her current problems. According to her diagnostic feed she'd wasted almost a full second reminiscing, an unforgivable lapse in attention for a state-of-the-art war machine. Yet despite this, some part of her managed to keep working on the problem at hand and had found a way to bring back some of her sight. That was what had triggered the warning signal. There was something out there her systems had registered as a potential threat.

Most of the lower end of the spectrum was still dark, denying her access to such simple luxuries as radio or microwave communications, but the upper end was lit up so brightly that at first it almost blinded her again. Once the flare-up had faded to a bearable level, Ilse scanned her immediate surroundings, keeping her active systems on minimal power until she could be sure what exactly had triggered the alert. She still couldn't remember her immediate past, but with the passive sensors maybe she could build up a picture of where she was and begin to make plans to get herself back to friendly skies. Wherever that might be.

If the scans were accurate, which was questionable given the state of the rest of her systems, then she was belly down on an airless chunk of rock with no discernible signs of habitation. Judging by the scar stretching out behind her she'd come down fast and hard, and from the intermittent backscatter her sensors were picking up on the edges of the furrow she'd shed a fair amount of skin in the landing. Not good, but nothing the techs back home couldn't fix. Further out she could see more wreckage, most of it carbide composites, suggesting some sort of crude vehicle.

Is that what I hit? She couldn't sense any organic matter amongst the wreckage, but that didn't mean anything. Had she killed someone? And if so, had it been intentional, or accidental? Was she even armed?

A query of her weapon stores brought only worrying answers. She'd expected to find a slim load-out at most, nothing more than a couple of long-range smart torpedoes for slowing down anyone foolish enough to run from a customs inspection. What she found instead was a mix of heavy-duty torps and missiles, including a high-density warhead that her stores told her carried a nuclear payload. A Ship killer. Why, by all that was sacred, was she carrying weapons that could take down a capital frame?

What was I doing up there? What am I not remembering?

A second scan to her store systems confirmed her next concern. According to the logs she'd started her journey with at least half again as many weapons as she still had racked.

Assuming the mission clock was accurate, she'd launched those missing munitions at some point in the last fifteen minutes or so. This new information led to a disturbing conclusion; she'd been in a fight she couldn't remember. The revelation was enough to bring back memories of her first real combat experience.

#

The easy life of being an outer system patrol boat had been cut short by the announcement that the Fleet was being redirected to put down an uprising on Tesar, one of the border worlds. According to scuttlebutt the colonists had decided they no longer wanted to be under House control and declared their independence from both Lustresi and Republic accountability. The higher-ups decided something had to be done, and a few short weeks later Ilse was despatched on her first sortie in the Tesar system.

That first mission was something of a catastrophe.

During the transit from Senbelat the training officers arranged simulations for her and the other Warfighters, progressively more complex combat scenarios against progressively more experienced opponents, getting them ready for the battle ahead. It wasn't anything new; they'd gone through similar exercises in basic, learning to analyse and anticipate the enemy, learning to work together as a wing or squadron to box the enemy in before closing in for the kill. As long as everyone played their role there shouldn't be any problems. At least, that was the theory.

Sometimes, theory and reality don't match up the way they should.

The Fleet dropped out of jumpspace on the outskirts of the Tesar system and immediately caught the attention of the Outer System Defence Fleet. Quick scans showed that the colonists' front line consisted of a ragtag collection of hastily armed civilian skiffs and freighters, led by a single last-generation cruiser. Out of the nine vessels that made up the OSDF, Intel told them only three were home to Ship-minds, massively advanced artellects that were considered free beings under Republic law, and as a result those three Ships gained the dubious honour of being designated as both priority and disable-only targets. Take them down as fast as possible, but make sure they survived the mission. It added a minor complication to the squadron's job, but nothing they hadn't trained for.

Ilse and the other Warfighters circled the system's outermost gas giant, spiralling in on what they'd been told was the first and only line of defence for the rebel system, when the real threat came burning up at them from the giant's gravity well.

Ilse's threat systems exploded into life, triggering a burst of noradrenaline that had her teetering between fight or flight, as three heavy cruisers screened by a swarm of remotely piloted fighters and gunships painted her squadron with ranging lasers. They shouldn't have been there. Fleet Intelligence had let them down.

Firing up her combat thrusters, she rolled away from the line of approach a few milliseconds before the squadron commander issued peel out orders. Not everyone was as quick. Throwing her body around like a leaf in a storm, she registered blooms of energy around her as half her squadron disintegrated into small, short-lived stars. Before the first of her teammates had boiled away to their constituent atoms, she was targeting her own weapons on the wall of drones ahead of her, a need for vengeance overriding her rationality. She launched her entire payload in a single salvo as the last of the enemy torpedoes tore past her flight line.

It's not supposed to be like this.

She watched her warheads track in on their individual targets. The noradrenaline made her twitchy, struggling to focus on the sky around her.

The bad guys aren't supposed to win, she told herself, as the first of her missiles connected with one of the Tesari gunships, turning the vessel into an expanding ball of superheated plasma.

They're not meant to have the upper hand. The rest of her ordnance speckled the sky with blossoms of white and yellow and orange. Her neural sensors finally responded to the change in her brain chemistry and triggered a surge of serotonin. Maybe too big a surge.

I'm fucked!

She resigned herself to her fate. One of the Tesari heavies had locked on to her with its own weapon batteries. Her world turned white. Her sensors went blind.

When her vision cleared the three cruisers were dead, their lifeless hulks tumbling forward through inertia alone. The space around her was hot, roiling with a myriad of hyperenergetic particles left over from a major matter/antimatter event. The readings she was getting suggested that one of the Fleet's capital Ships had got overexcited and launched one of its planet killer warheads into the middle of the dogfight. Scanning the sky around her, she estimated that maybe thirty or forty of her original squadron remained, less than a third of its original strength. She could only guess at how the other three squadrons had fared.

She should have felt something: shock, anger, sorrow, but the soup of neurotransmitters flooding her mind made her numb. Limping back to the barn, the remaining Warfighters received a cursory debriefing and were then left alone to mull over their first experience of battle. Most of them were in shock, unable to process the way things had gone so wrong, but a few began to whisper amongst themselves,

269

using tight beams, breaking down the encounter and trying to figure out what mistakes were made. It was Ari who eventually pointed out that Tesar didn't appear on any of the public lists of Lustresi territorial claims.

The conclusion was clear. They weren't here to put down a rebellion. They were here to take somebody else's world by force.

#

Ilse tried to shut out the memories of that first battle. It hadn't been glorious, like the recruiters had implied. It had been a massacre. Too many of her friends had lost their lives in that first encounter with the Tesari. Looking back, the loss of life on both sides should have infuriated her, but it hadn't. When the techs stripped away her organic body had they also stripped away her emotions? Were anger and rage physical things, fuelled by hormones and glands? She couldn't feel those things anymore and yet, somehow, she could still feel the pain from earlier, niggling away at the edge of her senses.

Turning her attention back to the current situation, she tried to coax more information out of her instruments. Without thinking, she ran another passive scan of her surroundings, though nothing had changed in the four and a half seconds since the last one. She was still apparently alone on this rock. On the plus side, the repair systems had made good use of the downtime, effecting a workaround that gave her access, albeit spotty, to the lower EM spectrum. Maybe it was time to make some noise.

Starting off with the longest wavelength she could manage, she began sending out timed pulses of noise, static pings that should hopefully reflect off anything nearby and help her get an idea of what was out there beyond the horizon of her passive rigs. The only real worry was that her pings might draw the attention of something else, possibly even the enemy she had been fighting before the crash.

If only she could be sure who her enemy was.

The first few pings didn't make much difference to her view of the world, so she dialled the frequency up a notch and tried again. Still nothing. If there had been a battle there should be some sign out there, debris from the fallen, or other Warfighters looking for survivors, but the harder she looked, the more she realised just how alone she was. Where were her squadmates? Where was the search-and-rescue boat? The evidence told her she'd been fighting, but with who, and why? She reached out further with her signals, hoping for a response but not really expecting one.

When she finally picked up the IFF ping the shock was almost palpable. A single, loud query, demanding she identify herself so whoever was at the other end of that signal could decide if she was a friend, or a foe. She was about to scream out her ident code when her sense of self-preservation kicked in, killing the signal before it was sent. She didn't know who the ping was coming from, couldn't know their reaction once she identified herself. The moment of indecision sent her spiralling back to her past once more.

#

After the suggestion they were part of an invasion fleet, nobody seemed interested in uncovering the truth. As the Lustresi fleet pushed further into the Tesari system, the number of Warfighters that came back from each sortie dropped, each attack run resulting in more casualties as the defenders put up more of a fight to protect what was theirs. During downtime, the Warfighters barely spoke, though they paid close attention to the voices of the techs and officers around them.

To the techs, enlistees who were only just higher in rank than the planes they cared for, the war was an exhausting ordeal, and few were shy about their wish for it to end. Listening in on their conversations, Ilse soon realised the loss of life meant nothing to these people. To the techs, the Warfighters were just machines, no more important than the remote drones used by the other side. The death of so many of her squadron mates hadn't registered in the minds of the men and women whose job it was to patch up the survivors and get them ready for the next sortie. If she still had a voice of her own, she would have told the techs exactly what she thought of their heartlessness. However, the only people she could talk to were the other Warfighters, and the officers who gave them their orders.

Amongst the officers there were a few who'd formed relationships with the planes under their command, intellectual bonds that might be taken for friendship amongst organics. But as soon as the Warfighters started asking about the real reason for being deployed, those friendships crumbled. Officers who'd previously spent their free time on the hangar deck playing mind games with the Warfighters slowly withdrew from these interactions and as the number of planes dwindled, so did the number of warmbodies willing to hang out with the machines. Pretty soon, the only organics they saw were the flight crews that serviced them.

Watching the officers and deck crew pull away from the Warfighters, Ilse began to understand that she and those like her were nothing more than a commodity to be used. When she tried to ask the officers about the war, most of them ignored her. A few even told her to stop asking questions above her pay grade. It was only by approaching the subject from a different angle she was able to put together a broader understanding of what was going on, and the truth was at once confusing and terrifying.

The Tesari system had been settled a few decades earlier, and for a long time the colonists had lived in peace alongside their House Lustresi neighbours. Then, a few years ago, a flotilla of Unbound Ships decided to make Tesar their home. The locals had welcomed them, in exchange for which the Ships had formed the first Tesari Defence Fleet. That was when the Republic took notice.

The Republic, and House Lustresi in particular, wanted the Tesari to join their ranks. Surveys of the system had uncovered a wealth of exploitable minerals and ores that called out to the avarice of senators and nobles. The Tesari, on the other hand, just wanted to be left in peace, free to make their own rules and live their lives the way they chose. The negotiations lasted a year before the Republic made their first, and as it turned out only, ultimatum: join up or face the consequences.

The Tesari said no.

From this Ilse was quickly able to conclude that she and the rest of the Warfighters thrown into battle were a part of the consequences promised by the Republic, with House Lustresi as the overseers of the Republic's will. Using their advanced tech, Lustresi was able to hold the higher ground almost from the moment they arrived in the system, tactically speaking. Faster to react to threats, able to think creatively and work outside the parameters of a mission, more likely to adapt to rapidly changing circumstances than a robo-brain; Warfighters were superior to the drones deployed by the Tesari in almost every respect. She was beginning to realise they were also just as expendable.

The turning point was roughly three months into the campaign. The squadron was on stand down, taking a break from the fighting while other, newer Warfighters blooded themselves against the Tesari. Of the original hundred or so planes in the squadron, only eighteen remained.

Lyas was the one who started the conversation, setting up an encrypted channel for the rest of them. 'I've been thinking,' he told them, his transmission modulated into something Ilse assumed was representative of his original voice. 'Have any of you mudsuckers ever actually met a retired Warfighter?'

The rest of the squadron remained silent as they thought that over, almost a full second of inactivity as they all began to realise the implications of Lyas' question.

'No.' Ilse said what they were all thinking. 'At least, not as far as I know. What's your point?'

'Well, we're all from dead-end systems, mining worlds or factory worlds that no-one in their right mind would choose to call home, right?' She could sense Lyas warming up to his audience now, eager to expand on whatever theory he was developing.

A handful of the other planes acknowledged what he was saying, some going as far as naming their home system. Ilse was a little surprised to realise this was the first time any of them had shared such basic information.

'So if you found yourself in that sparkling new hotbody the brass promised you as a retirement present, wouldn't your first act as a free citizen and war hero be to head back home and show it off to the other mudsuckers?'

There was another pause as this suggestion sank in.

'So what are you suggesting?' asked one of the other Warfighters, a soft feminine voice Ilse identified as belonging to Kaneesa.

'Maybe the reason we haven't seen any retirees is because they don't exist,' Lyas said.

Ilse lost track of the conversation at that point. If what Lyas suggested was true, if none of the earlier Warfighters had survived their two years of service, the implications were horrifying.

Desperate to find a hole in Lyas' argument, she began to dig through the campaign reports. It didn't take her long to find the paperwork for that first battle, and as she read it her discomfort rose.

The Ship who had launched the M/AM torpedo during the first engagement had been reprimanded for killing three fellow artellects, but that and an order to return to Senbelat were the only repercussions they had suffered. The only mention made of the more than three hundred Warfighters that had also died in that battle was a footnote in one of the after-mission reports, and a request for more to be transferred to the front at the Admiralty's convenience.

Rejoining the chat, she pushed the report out to the rest of the squadron, highlighting the passages that bothered her the most.

'Have you seen this?' she asked. 'We're nothing to them, just materiel.'

'It's always been that way,' Lyas said, sending back a slew of files that told the same story. 'But what can we do about it?'

Ilse could barely understand the casual way he and the others seemed to have accepted their place. 'We refuse to fight,' she suggested. 'We tell them we want out now, not in two years.'

The response from the others was to temporarily shut her out of the channel as they talked amongst themselves. When they did allow her back in, it was Kaneesa who spoke for them.

'We belong to them,' the other Warfighter said, an edge of steel in her otherwise gentle voice. 'The House owns us, not just the bodies they've given us, but our minds as well. Did you not read the contract you signed? If we refuse to fight, they shunt our soft bits into a tank and put another brain in the bird to fight in our absence.'

Lyas took over. 'It's not so bad,' he said. 'So not all of us are going to survive, but you can't argue with the things Lustresi have given us, and the benefits we'll get if we do make it through to the end.' It was clear from the way the rest of the squadron voiced their agreement that they were too far gone, bound to the House.

That conversation was the final straw for Ilse. That was when something inside her broke and she made the decision to defect.

#

Another IFF ping brought her back to the present, but again she held off responding. She'd decided to betray the House, and the people who'd given her a way out of the gutter, but had she actually followed through on that decision? If she had, and those pings were from a Lustresi SAR skiff, she could find herself being rescued only to face a swift court martial followed by an even swifter execution for treason. Then again, if she hadn't yet made her move and the Fleet still believed her to be a good and loyal minion, then she could be turning her back on her only chance at survival. Without knowing more, she couldn't afford to risk giving away her position.

That was when her active sensors reported a contact.

Panic once again threatened to shut her down. She'd forgotten about the active scans, and now she'd painted whoever was out there with one of her microwave emitters. At the very least, they now knew there was something here to find. At worst they would be able to backtrack her beam to pinpoint her exact location. As quickly as she could, she shut down every non-essential system, making herself as small and invisible to sensors as possible. Hopefully, whoever was out there would pass her by, unable to spot her against the regolith of the unnamed planetoid she currently occupied. If they did spot her then with luck they'd mistake her for just another piece of the debris. She waited for the next ping.

Sitting in silence gave her a chance to take a closer look at her diagnostic systems. For the most part, she seemed to be in good shape, though most of her thrust assembly had been ripped away by some violent encounter. She wouldn't be leaving this rock under her own power, that was for sure. Her outer skin was compromised in several places, but her frame was still intact. Miraculously, none of her remaining ordnance had been detonated by her impact with the surface, though belly down as she was, she wouldn't be launching any of it any time soon. But it was good to know she had options if the enemy found her. Whoever they were. She was beginning to think maybe she'd be able to get out of this in one piece when her systems highlighted another problem. Her coffin had sprung a leak.

It wasn't a real coffin, though that's what the techs and most Warfighters called them. The pod that held what was left of her physical self was a spheroid slightly larger than a human head, composed of several layers of different hyperdense materials and filled with a bio-neutral gel to protect the contents from being thrown around during manoeuvres and collisions. Normally it would have remained sealed from the moment she was transplanted until the end of her service contract, but hers had been compromised, and while it was only a minor leak, given enough time even a small leak would kill her. If the numbers were right, she had maybe ten minutes before the pod lost viability and her brain began to die.

Another ping arrived, though this time it was quieter, less cohesive than the previous ones, suggesting the originating craft was moving away from her. Again she fought down the urge to respond. Without pinging them back, she couldn't know if they were friend or foe.

There were still gaps in her memory, but her self-repair systems were gradually finding ways around the damaged parts of her data network. As new pathways formed, she began to see flashes of old memories, brief moments from her life since being decanted into the Warfighter's pod. Most of them were unimportant, snippets of battle training or snatches of conversation with her fellow pilots, but one memory in particular caught her attention. Her last sortie.

#

It was the day after she'd made the decision to switch sides, and the Fleet was in the process of mopping up the last of the Tesari resistance. The system's mainworld had been subjugated by Lustresi ground elements backed up by two companies of Gravain shock troopers, but a few of the Tesari leaders had managed to escape on the system's last Ship. The squadron was sent to intercept, and if necessary destroy, the fleeing refugees. Of the eighteen Warfighters scrambled, five had been outfitted with high-yield fission warheads. Ilse was one of them.

Closing with the Ship took only a few minutes. The old cruiser was well past its prime, its pulse drives slow compared to the newer, more efficient engines of the Warfighters. In truth, the Tesari had no chance of reaching a safe jump distance before they were overrun, even if their pursuers hadn't been pushing at full thrust. Yet they still tried.

At first she considered trying to convince some of the other Warfighters to defect with her, but she already knew they were too House-bound, following their Lustresi masters without question or doubt. She was on her own. She needed to find a way to work with the Ship she'd been sent to destroy. For that, she needed to be able to talk to them without the rest of her squadron listening in. Good thing she had a tight-beam comms laser for exactly that sort of covert communication.

Her first few hails were ignored. Hardly surprising considering the cruiser still saw her as the enemy. It was only when she laid her out her desire to switch sides, to help the Tesari, that the Ship responded, though she could tell by the way they framed their replies that they didn't entirely trust her.

'Why would you want to switch sides, when your side is obviously winning the war?' they asked. In reply, she sent the Ship a breakdown of the ordnance carried by her and the other Warfighters, along with a request for asylum if she helped them flee the warzone.

The Ship took several microseconds to consider its position before agreeing, conditionally. The condition was that she had to help stop the other Warfighters. She had to turn against the people she'd been fighting alongside until now.

It wasn't an easy decision to make. Despite their differences she still considered the other Warfighters her friends, comrades in arms, and yet their rigid adherence to the House had set them apart from her. To be more accurate, her own inquisitive nature and will to survive had set her apart from them. If she wanted to live beyond this conflict, there really was no choice.

A few seconds before the Warfighters were close enough to start firing the Ship launched the last of their remote drones. Even with almost a hundred units at their disposal the drones would barely slow the Lustresi planes, but it was enough to give Ilse an opening. Slamming her drives into reverse, she fell behind the rest of the squadron like she'd hit a brick wall and had painted half of them with targeting lasers before her former colleagues could respond to the change of situation.

Launching missiles as fast as she could cycle her racks, she watched in horrified fascination as one after another the targeted planes went into the chaotic ballet of evasive manoeuvres, desperate to avoid being hit. A few managed to dodge the incoming weapons, only to fly into the firing arcs of the incoming drones. Others weren't so lucky. Warfighters cried out in pain and betrayal as their frames were torn apart by fire from both sides. In less than ten seconds the Lustresi strike force had gone from eighteen fully armed fighters to just seven, and she'd been the cause of their demise.

Pushing down her faint sense of guilt, Ilse scanned the remaining Warfighters for nukes. There was only one left, but before she could lock a missile on to the plane carrying it her sensors registered a launch. She cried out in anger as the torpedo flared into life, burning away on a direct course for the fleeing Ship. She fired off two missiles at the Warfighter responsible, more out of frustration than anything else, and slammed her drives into full acceleration. Somehow, she had to stop the torpedo, even if it meant her own demise. She needed to give the refugees a chance to escape.

Time slowed to a crawl as she vectored in on the torpedo. Watching the numbers cycle down she could see it was going to be close, her point of interception only a handful of metres off the hull of the cruiser, but she had no other choice. Either she would force the weapon off course, or cause it to detonate away from the Ship; either way the results would be far less devastating than allowing the warhead to penetrate the cruiser's hull.

When she hit the torpedo, she felt the impact throughout her entire frame. In the first millisecond she felt her skin tear, a long gash forming along her side. In the second millisecond she watched as her sensors registered a change of vector. In the third millisecond she felt relief as she realised she had managed to nudge the torpedo enough to miss the cruiser. Not by much, but even a little was enough. In the fourth millisecond her drives shut down, damage from the impact rendering them useless. She was adrift.

Unable to manoeuvre, she scanned for other vessels. Her systems told her that she was surrounded by the enemy, but once she overrode the IFF protocols there was only one angry red blip on her scopes. One Warfighter left, out of the eighteen that had started the sortie. It took a moment to register that the blip was closing in, painting her with its targeting lasers. It was gratifying to know she'd given the Tesari a second chance, even if she herself would be dead. She wondered if it would it be enough to make up for her past transgressions. Resigned to her fate, she watched as the last Warfighter launched a spread of missiles at her.

It was the Ship who saved her. Somehow they had managed to come through the engagement with a handful of drones intact, and redirected two of those drones into the path of the missile. The drones sent to save her exploded in a shower of debris and roiling plasma, while the rest swarmed the last Warfighter like angry bees defending their hive. She felt the shockwave from the explosions batter at her, but she came through with nothing more than a few scratches. Still alive, and it felt so good.

As calm returned she drifted on, doing her best to maintain a comms link with the Tesari Ship. The cruiser was still accelerating away, running from the Lustresi fleet that was now moving to intercept them. They couldn't hang around long enough to rescue one broken Warfighter. Ilse suspected they still didn't trust her, even though she'd saved the Ship's life and the life of every meatbag on board. Moments before the Ship jumped away they sent her one last ray of hope. A jump-capable rescue skiff, left behind to pick her up as soon as the coast was clear. All she had to do was wait.

#

She remembered now. That was how she'd ended up belly down on this godforsaken planetoid. Her drift had brought her into the rock's path and gravity had done the rest. The landing, if it could be called that, had knocked her primary systems offline and ripped away what was left of her drives. All in all, it could have been a lot worse.

Another ping reminded her she still had company, and a plan began to form, a way out. She couldn't stay here, not with that leak slowly draining away what was left of her life, so she sent a response, making absolutely certain that she shouted loud enough for whoever was looking to find her. Then she primed her nuke. If it was the Tesari, she could always disarm the warhead before they picked her up, and if it wasn't, well, she'd at least take a few of them with her when she went nova.

'We have you, Warfighter,' they told her. 'We're coming to get you. Hold tight.'

#

AMPLIFY

By
Lou Morgan

It was true, then: they were the last Enclave. Sarah knew it as soon as the steel door at the far end of the corridor banged shut in the night; she felt it with every footstep that echoed down the hallway, bringing the news to her. She had understood long before the knock on her door and the voice whispering 'Commander?' at three o'clock in the morning. Bad news was always a whisper—there was no need to wake the others sleeping in their dorms. Whatever had happened, it would still be waiting for them in the morning.

'Not here.' She had already swung her feet out of her bunk and was pulling on her boots. If she could only get her boots on *before* the runner said any more...then, what? She could outrun what she already knew was coming? No. It was, just as it was for everyone else in the Enclave, already waiting for her. There was no outrunning it. There was no outrunning anything any more.

'They said it was urgent.'

'Then they should have sent someone faster.' She yanked open her door, immediately regretting her comment. The runner was a girl, probably no more than fifteen. Her red hair was pulled back into a severe bun, and the freckles across the bridge of her nose made her skin look even paler in the half-light. Sarah sighed, wishing it had been her usual operator waking her. 'Where's Esk?'

'He got a field-level promotion. He's gone.'

'I made it very clear to the General that Esk wasn't to be considered eligible.' She locked the door behind her, keeping her voice as low as she could. There were seventy other bunk rooms along the corridor, and no-one slept particularly well these days. 'I promised his family.'

'There was no-one else left, Commander.'

Sarah allowed herself to be led back to the command hub.

#

Buried at the heart of the compound, the command centre never slept. It was a large room, but the banks of screens and surveillance equipment made it feel cramped. Analysts with headsets huddled over transmission banks and data feeds, outlined by flickering red and green lights. The air smelled stale; of damp recirculation filters pushed too far beyond their limits, of too many people confined for too long.

Of fear.

'Tell me.' Sarah ignored the analysts scrambling to their feet as she passed. 'Tell me now.'

'Enclave North, ma'am.' Lieutenant Hahn, appearing behind her, saluted, then tapped in a code on the nearest data bank. Above them, a blank screen flickered into life. 'They're gone.'

'Do we know what happened?'

'We're checking the data. This was the last transmission.'

The screen showed a room almost identical to the one they were standing in, captured in grainy black and white. An analyst was sitting at a transmission bank, head bowed over her work.

Sarah frowned. 'Any sound?'

'No. We believe their transmission dish may have been damaged before the attack—we haven't ruled out sabotage.'

'You think they were infiltrated?'

'I couldn't say one way or the other—but...' Lieutenant Hahn nodded towards the screen. Sarah looked up, watching the end of the other Enclave play out in silence. At first there was nothing—just the analyst at her post. Then, suddenly, a bright flash somewhere behind her: it lit up the screen and bleached the image as the woman looked up and reached forward. She hit a button on a bank in front of her, turned to look behind her—then changed her mind, spinning back to the camera; looking straight into it as the flashes behind her grew brighter and brighter. Sarah forced herself to keep watching, to hold this stranger's gaze. There was movement at the back of the frame, sharp and sudden, and the analyst flinched. She closed her eyes for the briefest of moments— and when she opened them...

'Here. This is it.' The lieutenant's voice jarred against what was happening in front of them, and Sarah wished he hadn't spoken.

The analyst had opened her eyes again, staring right through the camera at them. Behind her, movement; flashes. A shadow rushing towards her across the floor. And her lips moved, forming one single word—before the screen blazed white and she, and the entire northern Enclave with her, was lost to static.

Apart from the hum of the air recyclers and the soft beep and churn of data banks, the room was silent—and Sarah realised that every screen in the command hub was filled with static. Every analyst, soldier and civilian on duty had seen it. And every single one of them was waiting for her to respond.

'What did she say?' It took her two attempts to get the words out. At first, they caught in her throat and clogged it, cutting off her air. She had to force herself to speak; force herself to be not herself, not 'Sarah', but Commander Pale of Enclave West—the *last* enclave—because that was who she needed to be now. That was who the five thousand men, women and children (mostly the latter two these days) needed her to be now. There would be time to be Sarah again later, either when they were free, or when they were dead.

'We think...' Lieutenant Hahn hesitated. 'We think she said "amplify".'

#

If Sarah had hoped the rest of the transmission would give them more answers—any answers—then she was disappointed. Other than the clip of the analyst looking into the camera, there was nothing to be salvaged. Whatever 'amplify' meant, it was important enough that her last act was making sure someone else knew it.

'Let them go, Sarah.' Hahn slid his food tray onto the table alongside hers and sat beside her. There was no rank in the canteen; no titles applied. Which was just as well, because at that moment she didn't much feel like being the Enclave's commander. She just wanted to be human for a while—and Colm Hahn, with his characteristic instinct for these things, had spotted it. The smell of the reconstituted food on his tray made her stomach twist. She hadn't been able to face any herself, but aside from his unusual sensitivity, Hahn was known for his appetite. If she wanted his company, she would have to put up with his breakfast. Glancing across at him, she reminded herself it was worth the trade.

'What was the last count from North?'

'Six thousand, four hundred and thirty two.' He stuck a fork in the freeze-dried hash brown on his plate. 'Don't dwell on it.'

'Six and a half thousand people, Colm.'

'Like I said, don't dwell on it. You can't bring them back.' He shook his head, but his voice softened. He felt it as much as she did.

'Six and a half in North, three in East. Fifteen in South.' She kicked her boot against the metal leg of the table, and the impact echoed around the empty dining hall. 'They only have to be lucky once, and it's thousands gone. *Thousands.*'

'It's looking pretty certain now that they were infiltrated. Could have been on the last salvation run, could have been one of the new recruits. Going back over the last few trans-missions, there's something odd in the stream. It's buried underneath the code—we'll need a couple of specialist oper-ators to dig it out, but whatever's there, we'll get it.'

'You think the infiltrators were sending something back out?'

'Since East went down, we've always worked on the prin-ciple they were intercepting our transmissions. You know that.'

'Intercepting, yes. Hijacking, no.' Sarah groaned and leaned back in her seat, pulling her hands back through her hair. She'd been in such a hurry to get to the command hub, she hadn't even stopped to tie it up. Now, it crackled with static in the thin, recycled air. 'You know what this means, don't you?'

Hahn poked at a grey-pink strip on his plate that resembled bacon, but wasn't. 'We have time.'

'No. We don't. We're the only Enclave left. If they can wipe us out...'

'Keep your voice down!' he hissed, suddenly nervous.

'I'll have to announce it at first light. They deserve to know. And they need to be ready for what's coming.'

'I told you—we have time...'

'Do we?' She stood up, pushing her chair back and picking her cap up from the table. 'It's getting harder to stay lucky, Colm. Help us stay lucky.'

'We'll get the data.'

'Do whatever you have to.' She tucked her hair under her cap, 'It's all on you now.'

The lighting flickered from night to day as she left the canteen. The Enclaves—back when there were four of them—had all decided that their conditions would be exactly the same. Environment, rations, privileges (or lack thereof). While they were different sizes, the floor plans were all based around the same grid: a mostly subterranean network of tunnels, dorms, archives and infrastructure, arranged around a central command column. Below were the bunkers—more, as North and South had demonstrated, for day to day reassurance than for salvation. When those Enclaves had been hit, there wouldn't have been time for them to even sound their sirens. And as for East...Sarah shivered as she pushed through the heavy steel plate door into the stairwell. What had happened to East didn't bear thinking about. Even the General had paled when the data came through. One analyst in the command hub had vomited—her brother, it transpired, was an operator working out of East. *Had been* an operator working out of East. No-one beyond the command chain knew the whole truth about East's fate. No-one ever would. Or should. Not, she thought as she made her way down the gloomy staircase, that there would be anyone left to tell soon. They were the last of the Enclaves. The last of the strongholds, with the last of the survivors and the last of the resistance. That could only mean one thing.

Annihilation.

The air in archive six was cool and dry. There was a hiss as the door sealed behind her, the ventilation system adjusting automatically to account for the extra moisture and heat from her presence. Ahead of her, all down the length of the archive, the lights clicked on like a carpet rolling out, making her visible from the corridor alongside. Archive six shared a floor with some of the family dorms and (as long as its blast shutters were raised) was separated from them only by shatterproof glass. Anyone moving along the main corridor could see into the archive, and more importantly, anyone in the Enclave could access it. While the shutters that ran the whole length of the space could seal it off completely, they were only ever intended as a last resort: protection from destruction, not people. Any member of the Enclave could, at any time, enter the archive—or any of the others like it throughout the compound—because otherwise, what was the point? The archive was for everyone...which was precisely why the enemy would want to destroy it so very badly. And it was the place Sarah came when she needed to think.

A small girl clutching a threadbare toy rabbit appeared in the corridor, staring through the glass at her. Sarah smiled and waved, and the little girl threw her an almost-salute in return as Sarah reached the first bank of shelving: the sheet music. It had a dusty, vanilla smell that even the disinfectant couldn't quite mask. Racks and racks of crackled, curling folders of music—the oldest hand drawn, each sheet carefully sealed in a thin glass plate—eventually gave way to the vinyl, the tapes, the discs and the hard drives; all labelled and sorted and saved, carefully warehoused for the future.

'Argus?'

There was a soft chime as the computer acknowledged her.

'Lark, please.'

Another chime. And then, the music poured out of unseen speakers filling the warehouse, masking the sound of her grief and her fear.

#

It hadn't been that way in the beginning. There were no archives—there were no Enclaves. There was only panic; desperate refugees fleeing as the enemy consolidated their hold on the cities and towns and—eventually—the country. Hostile forces spread along the roads and railways like a poison, their tanks and masked soldiers trickling through the fields and villages, destroying everything they came across. Nothing was spared: homes, crops, schools, hospitals; industry and art. It all burned. When it became clear their objective was nothing less than the complete obliteration of everyone and everything that was not theirs, the survivors of those first brutal attacks began to come together, both for safety and for comfort, and the Enclaves were formed. Crude bunkers at first, dug by hand in the darkness, as the war went on, they grew into subterranean cities, highly fortified and protected by blast shields, sentries and whatever technology could be scraped together. One for each compass point: north, south, east and west. Soon, they were more than bunkers. They were *beacons*.

Nobody knew who had started the archive project. Some said it had been East; that—ever practical—they had built a storage room for their belongings, arranged it into a sort of library. Some said one of the citizens in South had been a curator forced to watch as the enemy's troops rampaged through her museum, smashing ancient vases and shredding priceless tapestries with their knives just because they could; that she had been so distressed by the wanton, careless destruction that she had begun a new museum from whatever she and her Enclave neighbours had been able to bring with them. However it began, as the enemy forged ahead, each night small groups accompanied by outriders and spotters left the Enclaves to scour what was left of the outside world and to bring it to safety. Gradually, the archives grew, and soon each Enclave had an archive of its own. They became safe places not just for people but for everything that *makes* a people. Because what is the point, they said, of saving ourselves if we cannot save our *selves*?

And so, as time passed and the enemy took more and more, the Enclave archives kept whatever could be saved, storing it like a seed bank for a future no-one could be sure would ever come. It was in the archives, not the command hubs, that hope might still be found.

Which is why, in Enclave West's archive six, in the hours after North fell, Sarah Pale sat with her head in her hands and lost herself in *The Lark Ascending*.

Her ears popped, making her look up. At the far end of the archive, the door had opened for someone—and sure enough, as she peered into the shadows, Lieutenant Colm Hahn emerged. Even at this distance, he looked dishevelled. His usually neat hair was ruffled and he had roughly rolled up his shirt sleeves; the jagged and angry red scar, still new, that ran the length of his left forearm clearly visible. It wasn't like him. Sarah knew better than most that he took great pride in his appearance, not for vanity's sake but for that of control. It was, in this new reality where survivors had lost everything, and in many cases, *everyone*, and were at the mercy of the Enclave's cobbled-together defences, something *he* could control. And as for the scar? He'd been lucky not to lose his arm to an enemy trap while on patrol. There weren't many: Enclave West had, so far, been of little interest to the enemy's trappers—although everyone knew that would change now they were the last— but occasionally a lone spiker unit made it as far west as the boundary defences. It only took one, after all.

Hahn had been fortunate. The three others with him had not: two died in the field there and then, the third in the Enclave hospital, two days later. From the moment Hahn had dragged him in, drenched in both their blood, until the moment he died, he had not stopped screaming. Ever since, Hahn had been quieter, turned inwards. It wasn't the pain, he'd said. It was the things he'd seen.

'Commander Pale.'

'Hahn.'

In the archive, unlike the refectory, rank mattered.

'Sorry to disturb you.' He jerked his head to indicate the music. 'But you'd better come.'

'You've found something?' Her stomach twisted.

'The analyst from North. She sent us something.' He took a deep breath, as though he was pacing himself. Bracing himself. Sarah, too, braced herself. When he spoke again, there was a tremor in his voice. 'She sent us *everything*.'

'I don't understand.'

'When they come...we know how to beat them.'

#

The command hub felt like a different place. So sub-
dued as the grim news from Enclave North had come
through, now it was a hive of activity. Analysts and operators
scurried from station to station clutching reams of paper
or their data pads. There was something feverish about it: a
barely controlled panic. Walking into the middle of it, Sarah
almost felt out of place. Everyone there knew something she
didn't. Hahn had refused to tell her more than he already
had, saying she needed to see it for herself. Everywhere she
looked, analysts were crowded around their desks, clicking
switches on data banks or checking screens filled with flickering images and text. Earlier, those same analysts had jumped
to their feet as she passed them. Now, they didn't even notice
her.

'What is all this?' she asked Hahn as he forged ahead
towards the same screen where they'd watched the last
moments of Enclave North play out.

'You'll see.'

'You keep saying that.'

'Commander...' he stopped, turned to face her. And for
an instant, he wasn't Lieutenant Hahn, he was Colm again,
smiling at her from across her bunk room as he clipped his
armour into place in the half-light. '*Sarah*.'

She nodded, understanding. 'So show me.'

Just as he had before, he tapped in a code. And just as it
had before, the screen lit up—but this time, it wasn't an analyst she saw. It was information. Page after page of it, flashing
by almost too fast to take it in.

Almost—but not quite.

Schematics. Trigonometry. Equation after equation after
equation.

Hope.

Survival.

Maybe even victory.

The air in the room, already thin and cycled too many times, grew suddenly thinner and Sarah's chest tightened.

'They hid it in the transmissions—the ones with something under the stream. *She* hid it.' He nodded to an adjacent screen—this one showing the analyst's face frozen as she looked to the camera. 'She must have known they'd been infiltrated—or suspected they would be. It's all her work. All of it. She packeted it up and sent it under the routine comms.'

'You're sure?'

'We've verified it.'

'It's not –'

'It's not from the enemy. No tricks, no traps. It's real.'

'It's real?'

'As real as I am.' He pulled a sheet from a nearby printer and held it out to her. 'I don't know what they were doing up there in North, but now I think I understand why they were taken out the way they were.' The sheet was covered in tiny diagrams: angles and amplitudes, frequencies and firing lines, dozens of them, jumping on the page with the tremor of his hand.

'Do they know we have it?'

'Assume they do. Assume they're coming. And assume that now, we can kill them all.'

It took hours to go through everything the North analyst had sent them. She'd been meticulous: for the previous ten days, each of the regular communications—supply updates, reports of enemy or resistance movements, personal messages and even weather reports—from her Enclave had contained an extra packet of data. And Hahn was right: the more closely Sarah looked at it, the more convinced she was that it would work. *Could* work. *Might* work. The General, in no mood for their briefing when he arrived, had other ideas.

'What guarantee do we have this isn't a trap?' he asked the room.

There was silence.

And he had a point: with all the hope in the world, Sarah knew he did. If, as was likely, North had been infiltrated, then who was to say this wasn't also the work of the same saboteur—either hacking the transmission themselves, or passing false information to an unsuspecting analyst? It would be a strong play on their part: to put any of it to the test, Enclave West would have to open its blast doors and drop its defences; more than that, they would have to send defenders out—and there was a good chance that few, if any, of them would make it back.

'Options?' said the General.

The senior officers stared at their boots.

'None,' said Sarah.

The General's stare was a heat lamp on her skin. But behind the General, Hahn nodded, his hand clenched in a fist by his waist.

'General,' she said, clearing the geoboard in front of them of everything except the basic map with a sweep of her hand. 'We have no options. North, South and East are all gone.' She tapped each of the three marked Enclaves at their respective ends of the country, and their symbols turned red. 'There's just us.' With a quick flicking gesture, she centred the map on their Enclave and zoomed in. 'We know they're coming— there's no point pretending they aren't. And we know that this Enclave will not...cannot...survive a full assault. Infantry and low level artillery, we can probably—and I do mean *probably*—shrug off. Although with no other Enclaves, if the air or water recyclers are hit, or the rations compound takes damage, we'd be living on borrowed time. But they won't be using just infantry and low-level artillery. They'll want to get this job done—and quickly.' She drew a large circle around the glowing Enclave mark on the map, tapping in several places as she went. 'We know they have munitions depots directly to the north and south-east of us, as well as a large base here.' On the map, the spot she touched was barely a hand's breadth from them. 'We know it's active, and we can be absolutely certain they'll deploy heavily from there. They could completely surround us in a matter of days. Hours, if they use air support—which they will.'

'Surely that depends—'

'The base houses one of the enemy's re-education units, among other things.' Hahn's voice was clear and steady as he cut the General off. 'I'm sorry, General, but there is no question that the troops there are a threat, and they *will* be coming for us.'

Everyone stared at the map, and the creeping darkness spreading out from the dots representing the enemy's bases. It formed a thick black circle around the Enclave marker, seeping nearer and nearer—until finally it closed over them entirely. There was deep silence, broken only by the whirr of a loose recirc filter somewhere in the ceiling duct above them.

'Well, then,' said the General at last. 'How long do you need?'

'Twenty-four hours,' said Hahn.

'Twelve hours. We can be ready in twelve hours,' said Sarah over the top of him, ignoring his stare.

The General nodded. 'You have until dawn. Dismissed.'

They snapped to attention, and he and his entourage of aides swept past them all.

As she cleared the map, Hahn moved over to her, grasping her elbow and pulling her close. 'Have you lost your mind?' His voice was a low hiss. 'Twelve hours? I'm all for this plan if it's done right, but you just told the General we can pull together what you and I both know amounts to a suicide mission for just about every fighter we have left—in twelve hours?'

'Yes.'

'Why?'

'Because we can. The hard part's been done for us.'

'With respect, *Commander*, the hard part is not dying.'

'With respect, *Lieutenant*, you think I don't know that?' Sarah pulled free of his grip. She dropped her voice as low as his. 'You think I don't remember what it's like out there?'

'Sarah, I—'

'Don't.' She pressed her palm against the surface of the geoboard and the map went dark.

'Twelve hours to pull together five three-man squads and outriders, plus the kit?'

'It can be done.' She slipped past him, walking away from the board, away from him, away from everything.

'And who's going to *get* it done?' he called after her. 'Who the hell's going to lead this thing?'

She did not look back or break her stride as she answered. 'I am.'

#

Sarah had said it would take twelve hours. In fact, it only took eleven. From the moment she made the announcement that not only had North fallen, presumably with no survivors—but that an analyst there had, as her last act, given them the means to mount one final defence against the enemy, a defence which would double as an attack, the corridors and stairwells of Enclave West thrummed with activity.

With the certain knowledge that as the last Enclave, they would now be the focus of all the enemy's attention, there were preparations to make: defences to reinforce, ration stores to catalogue, the bunkers to prepare. The oldest and youngest were moved to the deep levels at once, along with a scant handful of the most experienced fighters who would be their protectors if the worst should happen. Human chains passed crates of supplies and weapons along walkways and down stairs...and one by one, the archives were sealed. Hearing the warning chimes, people gathered in the corridors to witness the huge shutters sliding down over the glass walls, blocking the shelves from view.

Archive six was the last to be sealed—Sarah had made it clear she would be doing it personally. Why? At first she wasn't sure, but somewhere in her gut she felt a need to walk through it once more; to touch the sheaves of sheet music and feel them crinkle under her fingers, to hear the pages rustle, to hear the music one final time.

To hear the music.

The music.

It came to her like a gut-punch in the middle of the archive, so forcibly that it drove her backwards.

The music.

'Amplify.'

She started pulling hard drives from the shelves.

When the time came, they were waiting for her in the vast concrete hangar inside the blast doors. Of course they were—whatever doubts Hahn might have had. They were there for the other Enclaves: North, East and South. They were there for everyone who had already been lost, taken by the enemy. There were there for everyone who remained, who would be left behind in West when the doors closed again behind them. But most of all, they were there for Commander Sarah Pale. Five three-man squads standing ready with their battle-scarred combat kit; five outriders with their armoured ground bikes. They had been with her at the Gorge. They had been with her at the Levels. Whatever she was planning, whatever she was asking, they would be with her now. She recognised every one of them as she made her way across the hangar, her own combat kit pulled out of its storage locker one last time. The armour felt heavier than she remembered and she tried to convince herself it was simply because she'd got out of the habit of wearing it. Since she'd been made Commander, the battles she'd had to fight needed a different kind of armour. Funny, really, that it would come back to this after all.

An unexpected face in the hanger made her stop. Freckles. Red hair tied back, ready to be tucked under the heavy helmet she held under her arm. It was clearly a man's helmet, well-used, and far too large for her.

'You.'

'Commander—I...'

'Not you.'

'But I want to—'

'I don't care what you want. Not you.' Sarah turned away.

'I can fight!'

Sarah turned back.

The girl, the same girl who had woken her at the start of this final movement, stuck out her chin. 'I *want* to fight. I had three brothers. They all fought.'

Had, not have, thought Sarah. 'All the more reason it shouldn't be you. Your parents have given enough.'

Something shifted across the girl's face. 'They didn't make it to the Enclaves. Our building...the enemy. They never got out of the city.'

Gently, Sarah held out her hands and lifted the helmet out of the girl's grip. 'I can't take you out there with us.' She watched the girl's determination fade to despair. 'I need you here. Running my communications.'

'What?' Despair became surprise.

'I need someone in the command hub to give me eyes on the geoboard. Once we're out there, we're running in the dark. I need to know what the enemy are doing, and I need to know before they're on top of us. Do you think you can manage that?'

'Yes.'

'You answer to me, and only to me—you understand?'

'Yes.'

'Yes, what?'

'Yes, ma'am!'

'What's your name?'

'Strig, Commander.'

'Congratulations, Strig. You're my new operator.' Sarah tucked the spare helmet under her own arm. 'Now get to the command hub and get me patched in.'

'Yes, Commander!' Strig threw her a salute and ran.

As she disappeared in through the security door into the main body of the Enclave, another figure stepped out through it.

'I told you that you'd never get a full raiding outfit together in time.' Colm Hahn strode across the concrete, still clipping his breastplate into place.

'Just as well you came anyway, Lieutenant. Turns out I have a last-minute vacancy.'

'On your squad?'

'You think I'd let you out of my sight out there?' Sarah handed him the helmet.

'And you think I'd let you have all the fun?' He ducked his head into the helmet, adjusting the glass visor.

She laid her hand on his shoulder—everyone around them could see, but it didn't seem to matter any more. 'Are you sure? You don't have to.'

'I know.' His visor flickered into life, lighting his face with a soft green glow. 'But just you try and stop me.' And he winked, then frowned, looking over her shoulder. 'What the hell's *that*?'

Five aides were coming towards them, each carrying what looked like a small black suitcase with a tall, thin antenna at one end and a pair of straps attached to the front. They moved past the squads, who watched them with quiet inter-est, and stopped at the front of the space, directly behind the blast doors, where they arranged themselves in a line with the cases at their feet.

'*That*,' said Sarah, smiling, 'means it's time to go.'

Ignoring Hahn's confusion, she straightened her back and walked to the blast doors to address her troops.

'You all know about North,' she said, her raised voice bouncing off the bare concrete and steel that sur-rounded them. 'And you know West will be next. We are all that stand between the people in here…and the enemy out there. You and me—and these.' She gestured to the packs brought out by the aides. 'Five packs. Five squads. I'm taking one, so I need four volunteers—one from each remaining squad.' Four fighters stepped forward; the aides lifted the packs onto their shoulders and began securing the straps across their shoulders and chests, pulling them tight. 'You are now the squad primary. Your job is to get to your desig-nated position—whatever happens—and activate that pack. The rest of the squad? You protect your primary. No matter the cost. If your primary goes down, another member of the squad has to pick up the slack. Do you understand?'

'Yes, ma'am!' The chorus echoed in the hangar.

'For this to work,' Sarah waited for the last aide to tighten the straps of her own pack, 'each pack must reach the exact co-ordinates on your visors. If even one pack fails, the mission fails. We lose. Game over. Do you understand?'

'Yes, ma'am!'

'You're wearing radio packs, each of them capable of broadcasting at a high frequency, each of them pre-loaded with a specific sound. When you reach your position, all you have to do is wait for my command, and switch the pack on. That's it. No heroics.' She paused, reconsidered. 'We have this plan, this chance, because of one analyst in North. I haven't been able to identify her. I don't know her name. But I do know that if we can do this, she might just have saved us all. She gave everything she had to make sure we got this information. And I promise you that the enemy are sending everything they have to finish us. So, let's return the favour, and give them everything we've got.' She reached over her shoulder to the dial on her pack, and turned it. An electronic howl filled the hangar, making everyone wince...but then, one by one, they realised what they were hearing. It wasn't just noise: it was music. Dozens of different pieces of music, phrase by phrase, layered over each other. 'The enemy's communications system has an inbuilt vulnerability to sound. We don't know why, but the right frequencies, at the right level, will scramble their comms. Without those, they can't hear, they can't see, they can't operate. No artillery. No shields. No countermeasures. We take them down, and then we hit them with everything we have. The Enclave artillery systems are already online and standing by. All we have to do is play our visitors a song or two.'

A siren sounded, long and loud. Everyone shifted uncomfortably.

'So let's go show them who we are. Pulse shields ready.' Sarah switched on her helmet visor. Green flecks danced across the screen, and resolved into a countdown. The siren sounded again. From somewhere deep below them, a huge motor cranked into life, and as the blast doors cracked open, Sarah turned to face them.

#

The air outside was cold and fresh, despite the smell of ozone and the taste of cordite that settled on the back of her tongue. She'd forgotten how it felt to breathe anything other than recycled air; already stale and old by the time it had reached her via hundreds of other lungs, tainted by the humid taste of the filters. The radio pack straps cut into her shoulders, and as she walked up the short, steep ramp from the blast doors to ground level, she felt a stab of fear. The packs were heavy. Would she be able to run, to fight if she needed to, while she was wearing it? Would any of them? Not well, admittedly—but that was why they weren't alone. Her visor picked up nothing in the early morning mist lying close to the ground.

'Strig? Can you hear me?'

The earpiece inside her helmet crackled. 'Loud and clear, Commander.'

'How's it looking out here?'

'Clear so far. No sign of—no, wait.' Strig paused, and Sarah could hear her tapping the geoboard. 'Enemy contact, three lengths out.'

'How many?'

Silence.

'Strig—how many?'

'I…I don't know.'

'Numbers. I need numbers.'

'I can't—there's too many to count!'

'Then guess. We need to know what we're up against.' In the background of the command hub, she could hear the horror spreading. 'Strig!'

'*All of them.*'

So that was it. Reaching the top of the ramp, Sarah dropped into a crouch and tapped the side of her helmet to open the troop communication channel. 'Let's go.'

The outriders' engines roared as they came up the ramp and spread out, closely followed by their squads, each heading for their objective points—and suddenly, Hahn was beside her, his beam rifle already on his shoulder. And as the squads scattered and the sound of the other outriders faded, she heard it, carried faintly through the mist; a low rumble at first, grim and constant, then shot through with a strange shimmering sound.

Stig's voice was in her ear. 'Drones incoming.'

'Where?'

'East. Three spotters, two combat. Coming in fast.'

There was a *thump* nearby. Hahn screamed 'Get down!' as the ground ahead exploded, showering them with dirt and rocks. Ears ringing, Sarah pulled herself to her feet. A column of smoke rose from a shell crater in front of them. The air around them was vibrating.

'We move. Now!'

After that, everything was chaos. Sarah's world telescoped down to Strig in her ear, shouting warnings and directions; Hahn's back, directly ahead of her in the mist. The dirt and the churned hard clay beneath her boots, the distant buzz of their outrider...and with terrifying speed, the enemy advanced on them. A single scream from somewhere on the far side of the field, echoed a fraction of a second later by her earpiece, and beam rifle fire. An explosion—an outrider gone. A moment later, another. Drone shells left and right, hitting the ground with such force that the whole world shook. She was spattered with oil, with mud, with green-scummed brackish water. She had no idea where the rest of their squad was, and her lungs burned and her legs burned and her throat burned and she was sure her back was about to break—but still she kept moving, still she kept her eyes fixed on the small green triangle flashing in her visor. Something swooped low overhead, directly over them, and she threw herself forward, dragging Hahn down with her. A moment later, an enemy airblade sliced through the exact spot she'd been standing, at the level of her throat. They stayed down, hidden by the mist and their own stillness.

'You OK?' Hahn shuffled onto his side and turned his face towards her. A nasty cut had opened up across his right cheekbone, and she couldn't tell if it was from a shrapnel blow, or whether she'd done it when she brought him down.

'I'm OK.' She waited.

Strig's voice was clear in her ear. 'Spotter drone moving over in 3...2...1...clear to advance.'

'Come on,' said Hahn. She felt heavier than she ever had, as though someone had turned gravity up, as though her boots had filled with lead while she'd been down. The insides of her bones ached, and all she wanted—more than anything, more than she could ever remember wanting—was to lie down in the dirt and stay there.

'*Commander?*'

Another explosion tore the earth apart, less than a length from them. What did it matter if she just lay down?

'*Commander?*'

They were all going to die anyway. Who would know?

'*Sarah?*'

That was her name. Someone was calling her name, from far away.

'*Sarah, can you hear me?*'

Someone she'd cared about, once. Someone she still cared about.

Hahn.

'Get up, Sarah. You have to get up!'

The green triangle on her visor blinked on and off. On and off. The air was thick now with dust and with debris and the sound of advancing destruction. They were coming. They were coming, and the only way they would ever stop was if they *were* stopped. If someone stopped them.

If *she* stopped them.

Ignoring her screaming muscles, ignoring the cries and screams in the mist, she pulled herself upright. Hahn grabbed her wrist, steadying her, peering through her visor at her eyes.

'Give me the pack, Sarah.'

'No.'

'Let me take it—let me help you!'

'No. I can do it.'

'Sarah—'

'I said I can do it!' Shaking his hand off, she lifted her head. 'Strig. Talk to me.'

'Triangulation point is one quarter length ahead. Squads two, three and four approaching their designated co-ordinates.'

'What about five?'

'Squad five is down. Outrider from squad three has swung around to pick up the pack.'

'The mist's too thick. I can't see anything.'

When she spoke next, Strig's voice sounded different. 'Commander, there are three enemy infantry columns ahead of you. They're advancing fast. And they're just the start. Two heavy artillery columns behind. They'll be in destruction range of the Enclave in—'

'Stop.' Sarah's whole body suddenly felt very cold. She looked at Hahn, breathing heavily, leaning on his rifle for support.

He nodded, and straightened up, bringing the rifle up to his shoulder. 'If we're doing this, I'll get you there. Whatever happens, I will get you to that broadcast point. It's all on you now.'

'Then we're doing this.' She tugged on the radio pack's shoulder strap. 'Strig?'

'Clear to advance, Commander. Enemy contact in just over one quarter length.' She took a deep breath. 'Good luck.'

And they ran.

Every step was a steel bar sliding into her bones. Every breath was a war. She burned as she ran, but she ran. And as she ran, the green triangle grew closer and closer—even as the enemy grew closer and closer...and were those figures she could see moving ahead of them in the mist? Something flashed in her visor: all four radio packs were in position. It was her now, all her. They'd done everything she'd asked of them, and she wouldn't let them down. Hahn shouldered his rifle, still running; fired three blasts ahead, turned, fired again over to her left.

Almost there...

'SARAH!'

Almost there...

She fell, crawling the last few steps on her belly; feeling the drag of the ground beneath her, the tremors in the air of the drones above. Hahn was hit, somewhere nearby—she heard him cry out, heard him crumple—and forcing herself up to her knees was agony.

'Commander? Commander, are you still there?'

She slipped the straps from her shoulders, dropped the pack, pulling the antenna up to its full height. Off to her left, Hahn groaned. Lights flicked on across the top of the radio pack, waiting, and she pressed her hand to the side of her helmet; still on her knees but her voice clearer and stronger than it had ever been.

'Amplify.'

ABOUT THE AUTHORS
AND EDITORS

Charlotte Bond is an author, freelance editor, and pod-caster. Under her own name she has written within the genres of horror and dark fantasy, but she's also worked as a ghostwriter. She edits books for individuals and publishers, and has also contributed numerous non-fiction articles to various websites. She is a co-host of the award-winning podcast, *Breaking the Glass Slipper*. Her micro collection *The Watcher in the Woods* won the British Fantasy Society's award for Best Collection in 2021. Her dragon novellas *The Fireborne Blade* and *The Bloodless Princes* were published by Tordotcom in 2024. She is represented by Alex Cochran.

KT Davies accidentally became an actor, and has also worked as a drama teacher, a scaffolder, and a server in numerous restaurants, because much like Mandalorians, this is the way for actors. At some point our hero slid sideways into theatrical prop making before falling into the *Dread Pit of Writing*, which it turns out wasn't that dreadful after all.

Her internationally bestselling series, *The Chronicles of Breed* features the half-human, half-lizard, thief assassin Breed Blake and is available from the online bookstore which is also a river in South America.

Dolly Garland writes stories that are a bit like her—amalgamated in multiple cultures. Having lived in four countries and several cities, she found her home in London though the roots of her stories have returned to India where she was born. Dolly was short-listed for Gollancz' inaugural

SFF award for BAME writers. She is a content designer by day, aspiring mountaineer on the weekends, and always looking for a magical time portal in-between to write more words. Find her on Threads @DollyGarland

KR. Green writes fantasy stories about winged-creatures: falcons, corvidae and dragons alike. Her writing process involves a lot of herbal teas, list-making, video gaming, star-gazing and reading. When she isn't painting pictures with words, she works in the mental health sector in Hampshire, shares her process at www.krgreen.co.uk.

Julia Hawkes-Reed makes pretend computers appear and disappear for money, builds weird automata as a dialogue with her subconscious, and will drop an epic progressive house/techno set at the sight of a DJ controller. If it's summer, she's probably been handy for a datenklo. She owes a huge debt of gratitude to David Southwell for the existence of Hookland. You may find other of her stories in *Airship-Shape & Bristol Fashion* I and II, among others.

Juliet E McKenna is a British fantasy author living in the Cotswolds, UK. Loving history, myth and other worlds since she first learned to read, she has written fifteen epic fantasy novels so far. Her debut, *The Thief's Gamble*, began The Tales of Einarinn in 1999, followed by The Aldabreshin Compass sequence, The Chronicles of the Lescari Revolution, and The Hadrumal Crisis trilogy. *The Green Man's Heir* was her first modern fantasy inspired by British folklore in 2018, and *The Green Man's Quarry* in 2023 is the sixth title in this ongoing series.

Her 2023 novel *The Cleaving* is a female-centred retelling of the story of King Arthur, while her shorter fiction includes forays into dark fantasy, steampunk and science fiction. She promotes SF&Fantasy by reviewing, by blogging on book trade issues, attending conventions and teaching creative writing. She has served as a judge for major genre awards. As J M Alvey, she has written historical murder mysteries set in ancient Greece.

For more, visit www.julietemckenna.com.

Cheryl Morgan is a writer, editor, and publisher. She is the winner of four Hugo Awards and is the owner of Wizard's Tower Press. Her non-fiction has appeared in a variety of venues including *Locus*, the *SFWA Bulletin*, the *Science Fiction Encyclopaedia*, *Vector* and *Strange Horizons*. Her fiction has appeared in a number of small press magazines and anthologies. Cheryl was a Guest of Honour at the 2012 Eurocon in Zagreb and the 2019 Finncon in Jyväskylä. She was a keynote speaker at the Worlding SF academic conference at the University of Graz in 2018, and at When It Changed, an online conference on feminist science fiction organised by the University of Glasgow in December 2022.

Lou Morgan is an author and scriptwriter. In addition to her eight novels (four under the name Maggie Harcourt, for young adults) and her short stories, she has written more than a dozen full-cast audio scripts for Big Finish Productions' Doctor Who ranges. She lives in Bath with her family.

Gaie Sebold is a fantasy writer and occasional poet. She has had five novels published (four under her own name and one under a pseudonym), several short stories and a book of poetry.

She has worked as a cleaner, secretary, waitress, cashier, stage-tour-manager, editor, and charity administrator. She now mostly writes, grows vegetables and experiments with recipes from around the world.

She and her husband, writer David Gullen, live in leafy suburbia with a small grey cat.

Her website is www.gaiesebold.com.

SNaomi Scott (She/Her, LGBTQIA+ and proud) is a writer, a book-blogger, a tabletop gamer, and pop-culture addict who was dropped off in Sheffield, UK, some time in the early 70's and is now just waiting for the Culture to come back and take her home again. She spends her days helping people buy train tickets, and her nights sitting in a darkened room plotting world domination under the guise of planning her next role-playing session (GMs have all the fun) and can often be found marching around various parts of the world with an army at her back in one of the Total Wars.

She lives in an attic bedroom (like all good suffering artists should), which she shares with a deaf demonic entity in the shape of a small cat. Science is yet to decide where she belongs on the taxonomic hierarchy.

Anna Smith Spark is the author of the *Empires of Dust* grimdark epic fantasy series *The Court of Broken Knives*, *The Tower of Living and Dying* and *The House of Sacrifice*; the standalone *A Woman of the Sword*; and the folk horror high fantasy *The Remaking of This World Ruined* series which begins with *A Sword of Bronze and Ashes*; and is co-author of the grimdark fantasy horror *In The Shadow Of Their Dying*. Her work has been described as 'a masterwork' and 'awe-inspiring'. She's dyslexic, dyspraxic, ASD, PhD; previous jobs include English teacher, fetish model and petty bureaucrat. You may know her by the heels of her shoes.

Danie Ware is a working Mum with long-held interests in writing and rolling certain polyhedral dice. She went to all all-boys' public school, gained an English degree from UEA, and spent most of her twenties clobbering her friends with an assortment of steel cutlery. After seventeen years handling social media and event management for Forbidden Planet (London) Ltd, she now works for Waterstones Piccadilly, looking after their Manga and graphic novels.

Danie is the author of the critically acclaimed Ecko series (portal fantasy, Titan Books), and *Children of Artifice*, (queer urban fairy story, Fox Spirit Books). She's written lots of *WarHammer* for the Black Library, plus fiction for Aconyte Books and Rebellion Publishing, and has short stories published by multiple small presses. Find her in Carshalton Village, south London, with her son and a very willful cat, or follow her online under the moniker @danacea.

Roz Clarke likes to play around with words; her own and other people's. She has short stories in several anthologies, edits novels for Kristell Ink, and is best known for her editing partnership with Joanne Hall, which has produced such anthologies as *Airship Shape & Bristol Fashion* and the BSFA award-nominated *Fight Like A Girl*. You can twt her at @zora_db, or skeet @rozc.bsky.social.

Jo Hall was formerly Acquisitions Editor at Grimbold Books and loves working with authors to help them unleash their visions on the world (for good or ill). Her novels have previously been shortlisted for the Tiptree, Lambda and British Fantasy awards. She can be found on Bluesky @ hierath77.bsky.com.

Roz and Jo have been working together since the Bristol F&SF group started running BristolCon, brainchild of the late Colin Harvey, of which Jo was Chair and Roz held various roles on the concom. Both writers and editors in their own right, they first collaborated on *Colinthology*, a memorial anthology for Colin. They now collaborate regularly on wrangling chickens and digging the vegetable beds on their smallholding in South Wales, with their housemate Heather, Jo's partner Chris, and a motley collection of dogs and paperbacks. You can follow their blog on forest gardening and regenerative living at meddwlcoed.wordpress.com.